THE
CRISPIN
AFFAIR

By
JACK SHARKEY

I0541512

ARMCHAIR FICTION
PO Box 4369, Medford, Oregon 97504

*For more information about Armchair Books and products, visit our
website at…*

www.armchairfiction.com

Or email us at…

armchairfiction@yahoo.com

A RACE THROUGH OUTER SPACE!

When Morgan Blane first heard Lora Merrick's tale of woe he didn't believe it. Stolen maps and stolen mines on a distant planet? It sounded like the stuff right out of an old B-western movie plot! "Please, Mister. Help a poor damsel in distress won't you?" Right.

But when a shady attorney showed up (a notoriously shady attorney who had his "pals" with him) an interplanetary land grab was in the making.

Now the race was on and Morgan was throwing in with the beautiful Miss Merrick. Who would be the first to lay claim to the fabled wealth on planet Crispin?

FOR A SECOND COMPLETE NOVEL, TURN TO PAGE 129

CAST OF CHARACTERS

MORGAN BLANE
This playboy millionaire had money to burn, time on his hands and a woman in need…what's a guy to do?

LORA MERRICK
She needed a rocketship and needed it fast—even if it meant putting up with an arrogant, spoiled rich guy.

FLAX DEMPSTER
She was many a man's ruin and every woman's nightmare—a crooked flaming-hot redhead with the body and attitude to match.

MAX BARTON
This shyster lawyer was determined to secure the pot of gold at the end of the rainbow—and he didn't care how he did it.

BINKY SEERS
Sure…he was willing to pilot the millionaire's rocket on a dangerous trip through space, but he wanted his money up front.

FRASER
He could fix any mechanical problem you threw at him—a pretty valuable asset when stranded on a hostile planet.

ANSEL
Hired to pilot Flax Dempster's ride to Crispin. It was discovered too late that his pilot skills weren't all they were cracked up to be.

CHAPTER ONE

ON SEPTEMBER the 18th, 1983, I had never even heard of the planet Crispin. As far as I was concerned, there was the sun, the moon, Venus and Mars, and a few other celestial bodies which inhabited the universe, and that was enough for me. After all, it wasn't my place to know about such things; that's what we paid astronomers for. Any time I really had the urge to learn more about the cosmic roll call, I could always go to the lending library and get a book on it.

My place, I felt, was in New York, where all the plays, nightclubs and luxury liner berths were. When you're born into the world with sixteen million dollars waiting in a trust fund for your twenty-first birthday, you don't really worry too much about anything, let alone the names of far-off planets. The grimmest thing you can imagine befalling you is forgetting the tickets for an opening night.

On this date, September the 18th, 1983, my twenty-first birthday was seven years behind me, and a lot of carefree years ahead. I was sitting in my bedroom in the Barbizon-Plaza, with the window blinds drawn against the glaring afternoon sunlight, sipping black coffee and whiling away the few remaining hours till nightfall by boning up on my favorite subject, show business. I was thumbing idly through *Variety*, noting casually which celebrities were staying at which hotels, which plays were opening, which closing, and being mildly amused that Hollywood had once again made "the greatest motion picture ever filmed," when the door buzzer sounded.

I was a little curious about the buzzer. None of my suits were at the hotel cleaner's, nor had I ordered anything more than the coffee I already had from Room Service. My social circle kept the same hours I did, which meant that they, like myself, were undoubtedly just pulling themselves out of the sack, so it couldn't be any of them. If it turned out to be someone selling something, I determined to take him downstairs by the scruff of the neck and use him to brain the desk clerk, who had orders about such people violating my privacy.

I thought all these things in the brief time it took me to toss aside the paper onto the unmade bed, tighten the waistcord of my robe, and cross over to the door, leaving coffee cup and saucer teetering precariously on the back of the couch as I passed by.

I twisted the bolt open, and widened the door a crack. Then I swung it completely open. "Well!" I said, softly. "Well, well."

The girl stood just outside, timidly, staring into my unshaven face with a tiny line of puzzlement appearing like an exclamation point between her brows.

"Mr. Blane?" she said. *"Morgan* Blane?"

"Yes," I said. "Somewhat obscured by black stubble, I admit, but it's me, all right."

"Oh." The tiny line vanished. She licked her lips, uncertain as to how to proceed. I made the plunge.

"If you're not afraid of being compromised, come in Miss...?" I stepped back and held the door for her.

"Merrick. Lora Merrick," she said, with a quick little smile that flicked on and off faster than subliminal advertising. She hesitated, looked at me once more, then took three short quick steps into the room, with the same enthusiasm I imagine would be evinced by a first-time fire-walker in India.

I shut the door, before she could panic and rush right out of my life, and gestured her to a chair. She took it, perching carefully on the very edge of the cushion, ready to leap for safety at the first provocation.

"Well, here we are," I said, standing facing her, my hands in the pockets of my robe. She nodded, but didn't say anything. I tried prodding a little. "Do I have to play Twenty Questions to find out why you're here, or am I supposed to know?"

She looked up at me, her dark brown eyes woeful, and a kind of helpless look came over her features. For a hopeful moment, I thought she was going to say something to clarify things, but all that came out was a miserable, "Oh—Oh dear!" She gazed at the carpet, trembling just a bit, and giving the faintest of shuddery signs.

I studied her a moment, then said, "All right, let me guess... You came here to see me about something. Whatever it was, it's taken you a long time to work yourself up to actually gaining entrance here, and now that you have, you suddenly have lost your nerve. Is that it?"

Those dark brown eyes swept up from the carpet and locked on mine, and then her lips formed themselves into a brilliant smile of almost abject gratitude. "Oh, thank you, Mr. Blane," she murmured. "I didn't know how to get it out. I've been standing in that hall for twenty minutes, working up courage to ring your bell. And then, when I did ring it, I almost ran away."

"I'm glad you didn't," I said sincerely. "I'd have gone crazy trying to figure out who it was. I'd call all my friends, curse at the desk clerk downstairs, badger all the bellboys—"

She laughed, then. A soft, apologetic chuckle, in a warm contralto that perfectly complemented her mellow-toned voice. Feeling I was making progress, I settled down into a chair opposite her perch, and retrieved my coffee, with a long stretch of my arm, from the couch.

"Now, then," I said, after a fortifying sip. "What can I do for you, Miss Lora Merrick?"

Her face looked into mine, hovering small and solemn before my eyes, then she said, swiftly, "I want two million dollars."

The coffee cup didn't shatter on the carpet, but it clattered something awful in the saucer. I stared at her, thoughtfully, then said, "Who doesn't!"

"I suppose I put it rather too bluntly..."

"There—There *was* a certain lack of subtlety—" I remarked. "Would I be terribly boorish if I asked *why* you wanted this money?"

"To buy a spaceship," she said.

"Uh-huh," I nodded, as if her statement were the most reasonable request in the world. "Couldn't settle for a Cadillac? Or a Schwinn?"

"You don't understand," she said, "I—I *need* it."

I eyed her warily. "You—uh—You're not out on a sort of— scavenger hunt, or anything?"

"Oh, no. You see—I have to get to Crispin, urgently. And it's outside the regular space lanes. I can't even hire a pilot to take me there, for less than a hundred thousand dollars— Which I haven't got, by the way—"

"Look, Miss Merrick," I said, intensely curious, "the price you quoted me, as I recall, was two million. Why not simply ask for the hundred thousand? Assuming, of course, that I'm willing to give it to you..."

"Because I'd never be able to pay back a debt like that," she sighed. "I only earn ninety dollars a week. Even if I gave you my full salary, that'd take me—"

"A hell of a long time," I nodded. "But if you can't repay the hundred thousand, how did you expect to return the two million?"

"Why, I'd simply let you have the spaceship when I was through with it," she said brightly. "I don't want it forever, just for the trip to Crispin and back."

Insane as her attitude was, I found myself liking it. She was crisp, honest and businesslike about the thing, even if her request was a bit balmy.

I glanced at my watch.

"Look, Miss Merrick— Do you have to leave at any special hour, or have I time to shave and get some clothes on before blastoff?"

She sank back into the chair, hurt. "You—You're making fun of me," she said, with chagrined realization.

I stood up and glowered at her. "Miss Merrick, I am not the fun-making sort. If I had opened my door just now to anybody but a pert little brunette like yourself, that other party would now be picking himself up at the foot of the main staircase in the lobby, and—Have you had lunch?"

She jumped, caught by my sudden question. "Why—no, I haven't, but—"

I pointed to the phone. "Order some—"

"Oh, I can't—"

"Easiest thing in the world," I said. "You just pick up the phone, get Room Service, and ask for anything that comes into your head... And make it for two."

"I couldn't impose—" she began, awkwardly.

"Impose!? You come in here, a total stranger, and ask me for two million dollars, and when I offer you a free lunch, you can't *impose?"*

"Well," she laughed uncertainly, "if you put it that way—"

"I do," I grunted. "And order a bottle of beer on the side for me. Excuse me." I went into the bedroom and shut the door. I started to undo my robe, then had a thought. I pulled open the door again, and caught her just about to lift the phone. "Hey, Merrick?"

She looked up, startled. "Yes, Mr. Blane?"

"Look, I know why you came to me in one way: You need money, and I've got it. But why me in particular? There are oodles of millionaires in New York City. What made you pick on me?"

She flushed a lovely scarlet. "Your...picture was in the paper, in the society column, and—"

"And—?"

She squared her shoulders, swallowed, and said, before she could reconsider, "I said to myself, 'If you've *got* to pick a millionaire, why not get a good-looking one?'..." She caught her lower lip between her teeth, embarrassed. "Do you mind?" she said, after a moment.

I shrugged. "Hell, no. Matter of fact," I grinned at her, "that's what I just figured." I matched her dropping jaw with a friendly droop of one eyelid, then went back into the bedroom to shave and dress.

"This," I said to myself in the bathroom mirror, "looks like the start of a very interesting afternoon."

We were dawdling over our dessert, on the small roll-table on which lunch had been brought, when I suddenly asked her, "Any particular color?"

"...Color?" she said, bewildered.

"You know. The spaceship."

"Oh. Oh, yes, that." She sat back in her chair and frowned. "You know, Mr. Blane, I don't think you really believe me."

I set down my spoon carefully, thinking. "Well, now, I wouldn't say that. Lots of girls would like to meet a millionaire. I believe *that* part, all right. But as for the other— Well, let's just mark it down to a successful method of introduction. It had novelty, a certain amusement, and— Hey, where are you going?"

She'd thrown her napkin down onto the table, and was reaching for her handbag. She turned to face me. "I'm sorry I wasted any of your valuable afternoon, Mr. Blane—!"

"Which old movies have *you* been watching on TV?" I said, shaking my head. "Until now, you had a nice flare of originality! However, you forgot to wear glasses."

"...Glasses?" she said hesitating.

"You know. To take off, so I can suddenly discover that you're ravishingly beautiful. Which, by the way, you are not."

She sank back into her chair. "I'm—I'm not?"

I had to smile, then. "Well, to be utterly frank, yes, you are. But it was the easiest way I knew to get you back into that chair— Ah-ah! Stay put, now. How about we continue with a few less histrionics, hmmm?"

Mentally, I kept my fingers crossed. Then, Lora Merrick muttered something under her breath, and tossed her handbag back over on the couch. "You're right, Mr. Blane. I was being dramatic. But you have got to believe me about this spaceship! I *do* need one, desperately."

"I won't ask why, since the obvious reason is that you can't very well *walk* to whatever-it-is…"

"Crispin. It's a planet, very much like our own—in *some* ways— It's in Andromeda."

"Which is where?" I asked politely. "And if you say 'up thataway', I'll crown you with this coffeepot!"

"Well," said Lora, "Andromeda is about two million light years from here—Do you know what a light year is?"

I shrugged. "Sounds more buoyant than a *heavy* one…"

"It's the distance that light can travel in a year. And light travels a little less than two hundred thousand miles a second."

I started to do some mathematics in my head, then gave it up. "I repeat, you can't very well walk there."

"But the new Lectralifts can make the trip in under two weeks," she said.

"How long'd it take the old ones?" I asked.

She narrowed her eyes. "Are you amusing yourself at my expense, Mr. Blane?"

"Honey, I know less than nothing about outer space. Any queries I voice on the topic come from the heart, believe me. And what *is* a Lectralift, now we're on the subject?"

"It's a non-combustion rocket engine," she said. "Do you know what a Venturi tube is? Or an electromagnet?"

"Ah, good! A familiar word in that jungle of technical terminology. The magnet part I recognize. I used to have one as part of my Lionel train set—" I caught her look. "When I was much younger, of course. But the other part leaves me baffled as ever."

"Oh, dear," she said, then plunged onward grimly in the cause of my scientific education. "A Venturi tube is a tube, such as on a ramjet, that is wider at the intake end than at the outlet end. So a gas rushing through there, in order to get out, has to go out faster than it came in, to negotiate the lesser diameter of the tube. Is that clear?"

I nodded. "Crystally. Like tightening the nozzle on a hose, sort of. Okay, teacher. But what's a Lectralift?"

"A combination of the two," she said. "Someone found that by winding copper wire around a hollow tube—rather than the soft iron solid center of a normal electromagnet—so that the number of windings grew greater as the tube diameter grew less, you got a violent magnetic reaction, that would propel anything even slightly magnetizable through its length at a fantastic acceleration, which— Well, they eventually were able to use plain old carbon particles as fuel. You could go to the moon on a teaspoon of soot..."

"Not much seating room," I remarked. Then, as she opened her mouth, "Apology! Apology! Sorry, Merrick, I was only kidding. Okay, so these new Lectralifts can take you to Crispin in two weeks. How many teaspoons of soot are going on the current market for two million bucks?"

"Mostly," she said, "you're paying for the copper wire. The bottom two-thirds of the ship is nothing but windings of wire about the central tube."

"And the other third?" I said, interested.

"The upper third is divided into two levels, the bottom of which contains the fuel, polarized carbon particles. The top half of the upper part is the living quarters and control cabin."

"And where do I plug in my Eveready batteries?" I said. "Or is the electricity for the magnet kept in a bottle someplace?"

"Oh—Well, there's an atomic generator housed in the very bottom of the ship, near the tail fins—you know, to keep the radiation at a safe distance—and it has a closed cycle of water-into-steam-into-water, running the generators."

"Mm-hmmm," I nodded. "Sounds neat and compact. And all at once, I begin to believe you *are* serious about this cosmic excursion. Otherwise, why have all this info on hand? ...Unless you're a space technician in private life?"

She shook her head. "Just a secretary. But I've always been a bug on science. And when the new propellant method for spaceships came out, I read up on it."

"Tell me," I said, "your love for matters scientific can't be your sole motivation for this jaunt. What's the reason behind this sudden urge for another planet?"

Her teeth were working on that lower lip again. "I—I can't tell you that," she said, softly.

"Honey, look—" I said, kindly, "even if I were sap enough to drop the two million in your lap without asking questions, the Federal people might take a less tolerant view of my listing 'I can't tell you' on my income-tax report, under 'Reason for Expenditure'. Am I not pardonably entitled to *some* curiosity about why the money was spent?" I reached out a finger and touched her chin lightly. "And stop that; you'll fray your lip."

"You—You won't believe me," she said.

"After all I've believed up until now, honey, *anything* would sound reasonable! I'd even believe you if you said you were claiming Crispin as an inheritance— Did I say something wrong?"

Lora Merrick was staring at me, wide-eyed. Then she reached to the couch for her handbag, opened it up, and took out an envelope. She handed it to me, wordlessly.

I opened it, after a puzzled look at her, and slipped out the contents. It was a single sheet of paper, with very little writing on it. I read it, slowly. Then I read it again. I handed it back.

"Is this thing on the *level*, Merrick?"

She nodded, anxiously. "I'm the sole owner of the planet Crispin."

CHAPTER TWO

I LET out a slow, solemn whistle. Then I extended my hand, to shake hers. "May I be the first to—Or *am* I the first?"

"That's just it!" she said, angrily. "You're not! I made the mistake of telling—telling someone, and he—the louse!—

started legal proceedings to stake a claim on the planet. The only way I can legally enforce this deed is to *be* there, in person, and—"

"Whoa!" I hollered. She stopped. "Look, honey, have a cup of coffee, switch your gears into low, and start from the beginning, huh?"

She paused, then gave a mute nod. I poured her a fresh cup of coffee, then one for myself, then sat back to hear her story…

Her grandfather, said Miss Merrick, had taken off, ten years before, in one of the "slower" ships that would take a year or so to get to Crispin, to try and find a nice war-and-tax-free planet to set up housekeeping on. That was the last she'd heard of him until the week previous to her visit at my place, when she'd received a letter, brought in after various interplanetary shuntings, from him. He had, he wrote, discovered vast deposits of most valuable—since the invention of the Lectralift—metal of the current era, copper, there for the taking on Crispin. He sent her, along with the holographic deed, a map, indicating the location of the copper deposits. He further stated in his letter, however, that he was worried about his health, which seemed to be declining, and was going to rocket over to one of the neighboring systems for a medical checkup. The day after getting the letter, Lora said, she'd received a cosmigram from a physician on that planet, regretfully telling her of her grandfather's death, due to advanced age.

"—and so," Lora said, blinking back a few suspicious droplets from falling down her cheeks, "I went to see a lawyer, Maximilian Barton—Do you know him?"

"I've heard of him," I admitted. "But go on."

"There isn't much more to tell," she said. "I told him my story, showed him the deed, and asked his advice."

"Which was?" I asked, as per my cue.

"To forget it."

I raised an eyebrow.

"He told me it was undoubtedly the wandering mind of an old man, that Crispin had already been explored for cupric deposits and found unprofitably barren of them, and—"

"You'd be wasting your time," I finished for her.

She nodded. "So I was going to give the whole thing up, but then, he wouldn't let me have the map back."

This time I raised both eyebrows.

"Why didn't you call a cop?"

"He—He said it had been lost. You see, I sent it to him through the mail, when I first got in touch with him. He returned my letter, and the deed—it's made out to me, so it wouldn't do him any good—and said that the map had been somehow lost by an error on the part of his secretary. So—I got suspicious."

"Naturally," I said smoothly. She gave me a funny look, but I kept my face expressionless, so, after a moment, she went on.

"I decided to file the claim, anyhow. That was three days ago. Today, the government assayer's office sent it back. A prior claim, with map, had already been filed."

"By Maximilian Barton?" I asked.

"By some woman, named Flax Dempster," she said, "but it was handled through Mr. Barton's office…"

"So, let me get this straight," I said, lighting a cigarette, then remembering to offer her one, which she declined with a quick little headshake. "You think that Barton has grabbed your map, which is probably genuine, and used some girl as a 'front' for the claim?" She nodded. "Well, tell me, how would it help you to get to Crispin, in that case?" I said, slowly. "Why make the trip?"

"Because if I can get there before Barton or this Dempster woman or somebody else does, I can prove the truth of my claim by finding my grandfather's original diggings, or mines, or whatever you have when you search for copper. But if they get there first—"

"They bury the evidence," I said. "Uh-huh…And how would *you* find this planetary pinpoint without a map?"

"I—I don't know, I was going to leave that part to luck," she said sorrowfully.

I shook my head. "You've left out just one thing."

"What's that?"

"The mortgage," I said.

"...The mortgage..." she repeated, confused. Then she shook her head. "What mortgage?"

"The one on the old homestead, honey," I smiled. "Hell, you *can't* have an ancient Western without a mortgage! Does Barton have one of those sinister moustaches to twirl, by the way?"

She came violently to her feet, her face white with fury. "You haven't believed a word!" she whispered, tense with the grip of her emotions.

"Aw, let's face it, Merrick, that plot's right out of Death Valley Days! The old prospector, the granddaughter, the deed, the mine—Wow!" I threw back my head and roared with laughter, which had been building up throughout her narrative.

The next thing I knew, there was a loud smacking sound, and I was watching a myriad of dancing white lights, and sitting on the floor nursing a numb-feeling left ear. In the eerily ringing distance, I heard a door slam. I don't know what she carried in that handbag, but it packed a mean wallop. I got to my feet, still chuckling, and picked up the saltshaker, carried with me to the floor in my tumble.

Then I noticed the envelope, lying on the floor. Her bag must have come open when she slugged me with it. I picked it up, and looked at it. Then I looked again.

The postal mark on it bore the name of some planet I'd never heard of. But the cosmic designation was one I knew.

"Andromeda..." I said softly.

It didn't, of course, *have* to mean anything... She could have gotten the letter from anybody—that envelope, at any rate—and simply made up that deed. Getting a properly postmarked envelope isn't impossible… But it was a hell of a lot of trouble to go to. I sank onto the couch and tried to think.

Her story was corny, but didn't all girls have grandfathers? And weren't some grandfathers prospectors?

And wasn't Maximilian Barton one of the most notorious grafters alive, if casual gossip meant anything?

I nearly picked up the phone to have her stopped, down at the desk, then I pulled my hand back and didn't. What the hell. If her story *were* true, then she'd want the deed back, so she'd have to return to my suite, and—No, that wasn't right. The deed was worthless, with Barton's prior claim registered. So maybe she wouldn't be back…

"So what?" I said aloud. "So you never see her again, so what?"

So it bothered me, that's what.

"Sucker!" I growled at myself, but I picked the phone up, anyhow. At that moment, the doorbell sounded, the insistent buzz catching me short. Grinning, I replaced the receiver, and stepped to the door. Now maybe I could get the real facts out of her…

But it wasn't Lora there at the door. I found myself looking into the tanned, very handsome face of Maximilian Barton. And he had a woman with him.

"…Yes?" I said, but I had a not-so-small inkling of why he was there.

"I believe you have a young lady here," he said, his bright eyes burning with some kind of inner amusement, "by the name of Lora Merrick?"

I didn't move aside to admit him. "Sorry, Mr. Barton. The ship has sailed without you."

If he was surprised I knew him, he didn't show it. I guess a guy that well known gets used to being recognized.

"You're saying she's left already?" he said.

"I'm not only saying it," I said curtly, not missing his inflection, "she *has* left."

"Mind if I come in—?" he said. He didn't add, "—and have a look," but I felt the words, anyhow.

"Damned right I do," I smiled.

"I can get a warrant, if necessary," he said, less urbanely. "Miss Merrick is a dangerous woman. She is in the process of spreading slanderous lies about myself and this young lady here, Miss—"

"Flax Dempster," I supplied for him, still not budging from the doorway. Barton was taller than me, but I think I had a slight edge on weight, if not exactly muscle.

"Then she has been telling you things," he snapped.

"Family stuff," I smiled.

"Tales her grandfather told."

"Mr. Blane," Barton said stiffly, "if you attempt, in any way, to aid this young woman in her ridiculous scheme to preempt property rightfully belonging to Miss Dempster, I shall be forced to swear out an injunction against you for—"

Miss Dempster, apparently more sensitive to rising temperatures than her legal friend, laid a hand on his arm, and he stopped talking.

"Wait, Max," she said, with a sweet smile. "Let *me* talk to him."

She stepped forward, and I got a good look at her. She was tall, and slender, but by no means flat looking. Her eyes were a dull cat-green, and her hair was pulled back into a tight chignon of red hair that would have seemed severe on a less beautiful woman.

"Mr. Blane," she said. The voice was husky, but I felt it wasn't a natural tonal quality. She'd had a lot of practice using that voice, Flax Dempster had!

I didn't respond, just waited for the pitch.

"While we regret the annoyance this afternoon's interruptions must be causing you, I do feel you should do us the simple justice of hearing *our* side of the story...?"

Well, she had me, there.

Grudgingly, I stepped back and waved the two of them into my suite. They took seats on the couch, both of them noting with interest the table set for two, before they turned their gazes back to me.

"Before you contact the local scandal sheets, Max," I said, noting the satisfied glint in his eye, "the young lady and I were having *lunch* together, not breakfast!"

"I didn't say a word," said Max Barton, very blankly.

So what's to do? You can't slug a guy for what you think he's thinking. "Okay, forget it. What's your side of the Crispin story?"

"That it was Miss Dempster's grandfather, and not Miss Merrick's, who found and mapped the Crispin copper lode."

"And the proof?" I said.

"It's on file in the government claim office. I can procure you a photostat, if you so desire."

"Of the *map?*" I asked, softly.

Barton blinked. "Well, of course not the *map!* Just the statement of claim—What do you take me for?"

"I can't very well tell you that in front of Miss Dempster..." I said. Then I looked her over again. "On second thought, maybe I *can.*"

They both came to their feet. "Very well," Maximilian spat. "If you're going to indulge in childish repartee—"

"Childish?" I said, blocking his path to the door. He stopped, eyeing me cautiously. "If I'm being childish, Barton, then tell me something..."

"W-What?" he said, after a brief puzzled eye contact with Flax Dempster.

"If Miss Merrick's claim is false, what do you care if she gets to Crispin or not...? *If* there's no proof there for her to find?"

He seemed to have swallowed his tongue.

I nodded. "The door, kids, is over that way."

For the second time that afternoon, my ears echoed with the sound of slamming oak. I went to the phone.

"Desk? Grab a phone book and find me the number of Miss Lora—that's l-o-r-a—Merrick...Merrick...Yes, that's right..." While I waited, I said a silent prayer that she'd have a listing. After a moment, the switchboard operator came back on. "Lyceum 5—" I said, starting to scribble it down, then, "Wait, hold it. Better just give me the address. If I show up in person, she can't hang up on me... No, I was talking to myself."

I had a heap of apologizing to do. And also, I realized suddenly, a heap of spending, too.

It'd mean cashing in some of my securities, and—I whistled. I hoped my stockbroker wasn't standing near an open window.

CHAPTER THREE

BY NOON of September 20th, just short of forty-eight hours after my meeting with Lora Merrick, we were floating high over a green-blue orb that my mind, if not my senses, told me was the Earth, in a glittering metal needle that had cost me approximately one hundred thousand dollars per vertical yard. We were about to go into overdrive, which had been patiently explained to me before boarding by Lora, who seemed to know more electronics than any physics professor I ever met at Harvard, and I still didn't understand it. It had something to do with Einstein's theory—which also had to be outlined for me, and made things no clearer—about faster-than-light travel, and increase of mass to infinity under normal space conditions, and— Well, whatever the reasons, we were about to go into overdrive and avoid taking slightly less than forever to get to Crispin.

As per our pilot's instructions, Lora and I were self-lashed to rubberized cots which were hooked to a gyroscopic arrangement that would give us a reverse-spin as we went into sub-space (I'm *quoting* most of these terms, by the way), the purpose of the spin to prevent the ship's initial warping of the space-time barrier from flinging any of *us* into it, lest we be irretrievably lost in some odd non-extant limbo which would nevertheless be quite real to us. Or is that clear?

Let's just say we put our trust in the pilot and General Electric and God, and lashed ourselves in as bidden.

Rather than give you all the details about how my stomach reacted to space warping, let me tell you something about how I happened to wind up on the trip.

After an expected ten minutes of icy hauteur from Lora, I had managed to convince her that whatever her personal opinion about my manners and sex appeal, I was still probably her only ticket to Crispin, after which she became quite docile, and accompanied me on probably the most expensive one-day spending spree in history, if we don't count the government's expenditures. First, we had to get flight clearances. This proved unexpectedly easy, since Crispin was not one of the regular spaceports, and therefore little knowledge was had about what sort of provisions or medical preventive inoculations we would need. We got off with standard army surplus assault packs, and an armful each of just-in-case shots for everything from motion sickness to elephantiasis. The reason I was exposing my flesh to this invasion of privacy was the pilot.

See, Lora had planned on making the trip alone. She insisted she was quite capable of flying the Lectralift—called "Brunhilde," after the Valhalla agent in an opera—all by herself, if she could just have an hour or so with an instruction booklet. This, I had said, was *Out!* After all, I had a two million-dollar investment to protect. So we got a pilot, named Binky Seers. That's the name was on his license, too, which shows either a certain droll outlook of his parents, or the extreme laxity of the Intergalactic Aeronautics Authority.

Binky was about forty years old, had scraggy neutral-colored hair, eyes and skin, and bit his nails. But, even if he wasn't quite the image of the smiling uniformed gentlemen who appear to captain all luxury flights, at least in the ads, Binky had one qualification that put him foremost in our thoughts when we chose a pilot: He was available.

It was only after hiring him (the one hundred thousand dollars—a drop in the bucket after buying the ship—was payable in advance, to be banked for his would-be-widow in case he didn't return) that it occurred to me that it was unthinkable to let a young attractive girl ride for two million light years with a middle-aged male of unknown behavior. I didn't have much choice. I couldn't let her go alone, nor could I go along with her going alone with him, so—

Well, what the hell, I was paying for the trip! Might as well go along for the ride. So I did.

Preparations for boarding were exacting. Due to the nature of the Lectralift's drive, we could take along no metallic objects, unless we cared to spend our voyage magnetized to the cabin floor. Watches, eyeglasses, belt buckles, hairpins, coins, and even metal shoelace tips had to be left behind. They even sprayed the fillings on our teeth with a compound which could partially nullify the enormous "tug" of the forty yard electromagnet we'd be riding atop of.

"If you feel 'em loosening," the man with the atomizer had said, "try grittin' 'em. Sometimes it helps."

"Only sometimes?" I said, imagining myself arriving on Crispin with teeth looking like buckshot victims.

"But if they *do* start t' loosen, son, *spit!*" he went on, ignoring my comment. "Otherwise, you may end up with a nice hole right through your jaw."

"I'll remember that," I promised easily enough.

And so, smiling apparatus intact if not in evidence, we blasted off for Crispin, slid queasily into overdrive, and settled back to enjoy the trip.

"Scared, Morgan?" asked Lora, coming over to where I still lay in my reverse-spin harness. (I'd told her to call me by my first name. Two weeks of sharing a cabin as Mr. Blane would have been silly.)

"Very," I said. "This is my first time off Earth. It feels strange."

"Don't worry," she said. "If I'm not scared, why should you be?"

I caught myself short of telling her that she didn't have the brains to be scared, but decided against it. After all, I had to be living with her for the next fourteen days.

"Come on, Morgan. Unstrap yourself, and let's look at the view," she persisted.

"I thought you told me there *was* no view," I muttered, all the while unstrapping myself. "You said we'd be faster than light could catch us."

"That's only behind us, silly," she laughed. "Up ahead, we get a regular Doppler-effect of spectrum-bands—"

"Don't even tell me what that means," I groaned, swinging my legs off the cot. "My head's already cluttered with the jargon you've been spouting at me the last few days."

"Don't you ever want to know anything about electronics, or physics, or—"

"What for?" I said, following her across the cabin floor toward a metal iris on the wall. "You don't have to know Newton's third law to get a seat at the Stork Club."

"There! You *do* remember some of it," she exclaimed.

"Only the number. The law itself eludes me."

"Well," she gave a matter-of-fact shrug, "it's a start, anyways." She fiddled with a dial beside the iris.

"Toward what?" I complained, "An editor's chair at Space Comics?"

"Don't be a grouch, Morgan," Lora smiled, and spun the dial. The metal iris, like that lens gadget on a camera, opened at its center into a tiny circle, which soon widened to almost the full diameter of the port. I looked out into rainbow chaos, then clutched my stomach and turned away.

"What the hell was that?" I gasped, steadying myself on the edge of a cot. "It looked like a shower of neon signs!"

"That's what I was telling you about before, the Doppler-effect producing spectrum-bands. See, Morgan, we are approaching the light of those stars faster than the wavelengths of the light rays, and—"

"Spare me!" I moaned, holding up a hand toward her. "Bad enough to turn inside out without getting the scientific explanation of my troubles dinned at me."

"…I'll—I'll close the port, if it bothers you," said Lora, much subdued.

As usual when dealing with a woman, although I was the party being afflicted, I was suddenly placed in the position of the heartless perpetrator of *her* woes.

"Leave it!" I snarled. "Watch your damned dappledopple, or whatever it is. I'll just remember to face the other way for the next two weeks."

There was a sharp snicking sound, and I knew the port had irised shut, despite my magnanimous gesture. I turned back around. "So now I'm a louse?"

She nodded, then smiled. "But a nice louse."

The door at the end of the cabin opened, and Binky slouched in, nibbling at a nail that had somehow attained a length greater than a millimeter beyond the skin.

"All set," he said, amicably, and flopped with a yawn onto one of the bunks.

"What's all set?" I asked.

"The course. Nothing to do now but listen for the bell when it's time to come out of overdrive."

"You mean you merely aim this thing, and then relax for the next two million light years?!" I exploded.

Binky didn't seem upset by my wrath. Millionaire or not, I was pretty much at his mercy as soon as we left the spaceport behind.

"Sure," he said. "I'm just aboard for blastoffs and landings."

"If the landing takes the time the blastoff did," I observed, "you'll end up doing about twenty minutes' work between Earth and Crispin!"

Binky held up a cautioning finger. "And twenty minutes' work coming *back*," he reminded me.

"A hundred thousand bucks for forty minutes?" I said.

Binky reared up on one elbow and fixed me with a glassy eye. "Can *you* land a Lectralift?"

I withered before that cold gaze. "Well...no."

"So all right," said Binky, and lolled some more in the sack. Subject closed. I turned to Lora, disgusted.

"I'll bet he never loses at poker, either."

"Poker?" came a cheery cry. Binky came bounding over to us, flipping the lid on a well-worn deck. "What stakes?"

I decided to go easy, "Dollar ante?"

"You're kidding," said Binky. "Man, I don't even *shuffle* for less than five!"

We left Lora to make us some coffee from the powdered stuff in the assault packs, and settled down to a nice, friendly game...

By the time we reached Crispin's star, I owed Binky almost half of what I'd already paid him as salary. Whoever the man was who quoted the tremendous odds against drawing to inside straights, I'm certain of one thing about him: He never met Binky Seers.

CHAPTER FOUR

THERE it is!" Lora exclaimed, clutching my arm excitedly as we stared together out the port. We stared first at shimmering silver plateaus of cosmic dust, lighted by the alien star of Crispin. These clouds masked all but the barest shape of the whirling globe toward which Binky's steady hand was directing the nose of our ship, and then our ferocious mass lanced through that airless haze, and exposed Crispin, in its uniquely formed strangeness.

"Holy heaven!" I choked out, despite myself. "It's like a—a basketball! Look at that lacing!"

"Triple mountain ranges," Lora laughed. "North to south. But the discoverer thought their shape looked more like the lacing in a shoe. Hence the name of the planet."

"Why hence?" I asked, bewildered.

"For Saint Crispin, of course. He was a shoemaker, in the third century. The first man to sight this planet thought those three ranges, with their tangent X-shapes, looked like laces. Hence—" she gestured down at the bright blue-gold globe, *"Crispin!"*

I leaned back from the port and stared at her, hard. "Tell me—Is there anything you *don't* know?"

She turned to face me, a smile toying with the corners of her mouth, then said saucily, "Nope! I even know the real reason you came along, Morgan Blane."

I squinted, trying hard to ignore the sparkle of those dark brown eyes. *"The* reason? Young lady, I have two million reasons. All dollars."

"You may be fooling Morgan Blane, but you're not fooling Lora Merrick," she lilted, oh-so-nonchalantly.

"Okay, I'll bite: Why *did* I come along?"

She laid her hands on my forearm, close together, then gazed solemnly into my eyes and whispered, "Because of me."

"Oh, marvelous!" I chuckled, turning away from her. "Perfect! And typical! Precisely what I might expect from a woman: *Because of me!* Oh, honey, that's priceless!" I spun back to face her. "Did it ever occur to you that a man with my money and position can see any number of highly delectable young ladies, at any time he desires? Why, I know a dozen I can name right now who make you look like a reject from Lane Bryant! There's Charlene, and Patsy, and—" I'd been ticking names off on my fingers, but I stopped all at once. "Aren't you even angry at me? Why are you still smiling in that maddening way?"

Lora folded her arms, and bounced lightly on tiptoe, surveying me from head to foot with a casual flicker of her eyes. "If—uh—Charlene and Poopsy—"

"*Patsy!*"

"—if these *femmes fatales* mean so much to you, why aren't you with them right now? Hmmm?"

"Because," I growled, annoyed at her confident grin, "I have a sizeable part of my inheritance tied up in this overgrown sparkplug, and—"

"Oh, pooh!" she said.

"And what," I said, arms akimbo, "is with this 'Oh, pooh'?"

"If it was the money, Morgan, why didn't you just have the Lectralift *insured?*"

"Because the damned premiums were too high!" I snarled.

"For a millionaire?" she said, with scandalized incredulity.

I stiffened, then leaned over her until she had to bend her head back to look up into my face, which was nearly nose-to-nose with her own. "It so happens," I said maliciously, "that their rates go *up* when they know there's a *woman* on the ship!"

As my lips came together to form the final consonant, hers suddenly darted the intervening distance in a quick peck that caught my own inadvertent pucker unawares. I jumped back as if a bee had stung me, and swiped the back of my wrist across my mouth. "That'll be enough of that," I warned. I was annoyed by the sudden creak in my normally well-modulated voice.

She narrowed her eyes, raised an eyebrow into a provocative arc, and smiled like the Mona Lisa. "Oh yeah?" she whispered.

While I tried to think of a comeback, she turned casually back to the port and watched the planet growing in size beneath the descending ship. I found myself facing her back, my forehead hot and perspiring, and my hands clenching and unclenching of their own accord.

Stifling an urge to scream at her, I stepped forward, and began, in my best threatening tone: "If you don't behave yourself, I can still order Binky to turn the ship and—"

The rest of my threat was forgotten as the deck suddenly leaped beneath my feet. Lora, flung from her stance by the port, fell back into my arms, and we ended in a painful tangle on the still-heaving floor. The door to the control room was flung open violently, and I caught a brief glimpse of Binky, rocking in his seat, fighting a sparking, smoke-billowing control board. The good ship Brunhilde gave a crazy shudder, then something went *"zzzputch!"*, and—we fell.

Lora struggled in my arms as the cabin tilted wildly back and forth.

"It's all right," I declared. "I've got you!"

"That's the trouble, you idiot! Let me *go!*" she yelled, pulling free of my embrace. I sat up on the rivet-studded metal deck and watched, bewildered, as she made her staggering way toward Binky, still fighting the controls.

"What's wrong?" she yelled, over the deep hum and crackle that came from the board. At that moment, Binky's hand tugged at something, and the humming and crackling faded and died.

"The ship's gone crazy!" he gasped, staring numbly at the control board. "I had to cut the magnet out. It was ready to fuse!"

I clambered up, and made my way across the still-swaying deck to the door of his compartment. "Is that bad?" I asked, clinging to the frame to keep from sprawling.

Lora, her knuckles pale from the grip she had on the headrest of Binky's chair, turned an even paler face up to mine. "Couldn't be worse, Morgan. It means we have no power, and we came out of overdrive at less than orbital velocity. We're spiraling down toward Crispin with no way to block ourselves from crashing." She spun about. "Binky! How long do we have before we touch atmosphere?"

He drew a shaky hand across his brow before leaning forward and squinting at a dial on the panel. "Well, if the altimeter is still working—we came out of sub-space a thousand miles up… We're about eight hundred, now… That gives us— an hour, at the outside." He shook his head, dazed. "After that—" He let the words die on his lips and gave a weary shrug.

"What caused it?" Lora demanded urgently.

"Another magnetic field. Powerful. Boosted the current in the windings by induction and brought the copper above its caloric limit."

Binky couldn't look as dazed as my brain felt. I put a hand on Lora's shoulder, and she turned back to face me, startled, as if I'd interrupted her in deep thought.

"Merrick, I don't get it. What—?" I stopped. I didn't even have an intelligent question to ask. This space life was a far cry from my normal existence. I was used to being suavely in control of things at all times; here, in outer space, I felt like a slightly retarded imbecile.

Lora, however, was patient with my shortcomings. She smiled wanly, and said, "Binky means that he can't use the magnet-power. There's a magnetic field around us that boosts the power in the coils, Morgan. Ten minutes of using them in that state of stress, and the last two-thirds of the ship become a forty-yard electric *heater!* But if we *don't* use the magnet, then we're without power, and we crash. It's simple as that."

Binky turned his head to face her. "Sorry, Miss Merrick, but it's worse than that. Look over here." He jerked a thick thumb toward another dial. Lora looked, and gave a beaten sigh.

"What?" I said, the dial and its calibrations being outside my experience.

"The other field's increasing," she said dully. "The nearer we get to the planet, the stronger it gets. That means that we won't even have those ten minutes of power when we need them. Otherwise we could—"

"Could what?"

She pushed a lock of hair back from her forehead. "I was hoping we could ride the Brunhilde down to a point, then use the coils for the landing. It'd be rough, but possible. See, Morgan, once we hit the atmosphere, we're going to be in trouble. It's like belly-landing a plane on a choppy sea— We pancake the ship on the crests of the air, then eventually dive into the air and use the fins to get us down slowly."

"We can't glide?"

"Not enough surface to the fins. They can slow our descent some, though, by keeping us moving in a horizontal direction instead of an increasing curve toward the planet. And then, our gyrostabilizers could turn the ship around in the air—I hope— and we could slow our motion with a blast from the firing chamber, then swing the tail down and try to drop safely. But now— Well, we won't have the power for that last, and most important thrust."

"You mean that after two million light years' of travel, we don't have the power for the last few *feet?*" I said, slowly. "It's— It's kind of ironic, isn't it!"

She nodded, then reached out a hand and, looking at the deck, toyed with a button on my shirt. "Morgan— When it comes— Would you...Would you hold me?"

The switch from her former self-assured romantic attitude was refreshing. My hands went to her shoulders. "I'll hold you from now till then, if you like..."

Binky whistled tunelessly between his teeth. "Wonder what my wife'll do with that hundred thousand...?" he said out loud but to no one in particular.

"If only," said Lora, coming softly into my arms and nestling her head against my chest, "there were some way—"

I started to say something soothing, when she suddenly tore herself from my arms, her eyes wide and bright. "There *is* a way! Binky, where's the toolbox?"

Binky got out of his chair and opened the lid on a metal box built to the wall. The tools lay in neat racks inside, all of steel-strong nylon—because of the magnetic field in the ship—

excepting the short-handled sledge hammer, which looked like metal to me. This last item Lora grabbed up and handed to me, along with a small hand-torch, used for emergency weldings.

"Here, Morgan. Take these and come on with me. Binky, see if you can dig up an emergency meteor-hole patch— And close the sphincters on the fuel-injector!"

Binky hurried off to obey, and I followed Lora to the side of the room, where the circular hatch leading to the polarized carbon chamber lay.

Lora jammed her fingers into her hair at the temples, shut her eyes and thought, hard. Then she pointed to the hatch, on the side away from the wall. "The ladder's on *that* side. Good. Morgan, I want you to burn the head off one of those rivets in the deck beside the hatch, and knock it through with that hammer—I'll find you a metal dowel or something to punch it out with…"

"Hey, hold on," I said, in some trepidation, "didn't you tell me that there's nothing but *vacuum* under us? What happens to our *air?*"

"We'll only lose *half* of it, Morgan. The fuel chamber has the same volume as this area, and Binky's sealing off the injection system to the magnet."

"What do we do, then? Breathe with one lung?" I asked.

"Will you *please* get moving!" she pleaded. "We have less than an hour. Once we hit the atmosphere, we'll be bouncing like ping-pong balls in here, and it'll be too late to work, then!"

While she hurried off to find that dowel for me, I ignited the torch and proceeded to obediently burn the head off that rivet. It took nearly fifteen minutes, at the end of which time Lora was practically dancing with impatience at my side. But finally the head was gone, leaving only the rivet-hole and shaft showing.

"Here, I'll hold the dowel," said Lora, placing a pencil-thick rod about six inches long upright on the stub of the rivet. "Come *on,* Morgan! Smash it through!"

"I—I might hit your hand…" I said. "Why don't *I* hold it and—"

"You'll need both arms, that's why! This rivet was put in here to *stick!* Come on, now, hit it!"

Her slim white fingers held that rod rigidly vertical on the rivet-stub, and she waited. It was nerve-wracking, but I held the sledge's short handle in two hands, tapped it lightly on the top of the rod, then lifted it high, shut my eyes, and came down with a blow that lifted me off my knees.

There was a hissing shriek of escaping air, and I opened my eyes to see that rivet, and the rod itself, had vanished down that tiny hole, now thirstily drinking away our air. But Lora, who had yanked her hands swiftly away as the blow fell, now picked herself up from her sprawl on the deck, and was watching an indicator on the wall. I stood behind her and watched a needle drop from a fifteen mark to just above a seven. I felt suddenly woozy.

"Pressure's equal!" Lora sighed gratefully. Then she whipped out a handkerchief and started tying it across her nose and mouth. "Morgan," her voice came through, muffled, "undo the wheel on the hatch, will you?"

"You're not going down into the *fuel tank?*" I said, appalled.

"It's got to be done," she said simply. Binky came running over, with a strange object in his hand. It looked like an oversize thumbtack, except that the underside of the disc had a canvas patch covering it. As I watched, Lora peeled this patch away, exposing a silver-green underside.

"What the hell is that?" I said.

"Meteor-hole patch," said Lora. "If a pebble-sized rock *did* bust in here through the wall, and our air was leaking, this's what we'd use. The colored part is auto-thermite. You just poke the rod-part through the hole, the escaping air pressure slams the disc home, and the auto-thermite heats up and welds itself in place… I'm going to use it on that hole you just made."

"But why *make* the hole, then?" I said, although I was already spinning the heavy horizontal wheel that undogged the circular hatch lid.

"Later, later, for pete's sake!" she said. Then her hand shot out in a frantic point behind me. "Look out, Morgan!" she cried.

I turned my head and witnessed the damnedest thing. Oozing up into the cabin through that rivet-hole was some stuff that looked like oil slick, except that it was weaving in the air like a cobweb come to life. "What—?" I choked, jumping away.

"Carbon, polarized," Lora said. "To be used in one of these Lectralifts, they can't chance the particles adhering to one another, so they polarize them. They come about a hundred particles to a pinhead, Morgan, so they can defy gravity and flow through air."

"And you're going *in* there!" I said, incredulously. "Why, in ten seconds, your lungs'll be clogged with soot!"

"I'll hold my breath," she argued patiently, "and when that gives out, this handkerchief will keep the particles away for a while longer. Meantime, all you have to do is wait by that hole, and grab the tip of this patch when I poke it through. But *don't* pull it *tight!* I don't want the auto-thermite sealing the hole until we pump the oxygen down there—"

"Huh?" was all I could manage. Then Lora and Binky had the lid flipped back, and she started cautiously down the built-in steel ladder underneath. Carefully, I leaned over the hole and looked down. A few feet below her shoes, a weird sea of sullen carbon heaved and rolled, looking like a pool of unrefined oil, black and glittering. If she fell into that, she'd drown just as surely as in a liquid. I watched her cling to a metal rung, and lean out underneath the deck, one arm outstretched before her. Then the tip of the patch came poking up out of that rivet-hole and I snared it, being careful to simply hold it, and not pull the disc beneath the hole into contact with the metal of the deck.

I squatted there, much confused, as Binky helped Lora out of the hatch, then slammed it shut and dogged it again, with a few grunting twists of that big wheel. Lora, despite her short sojourn below, was a mess of black greasy-looking spots. Her white blouse, tan slacks and pretty face were a symposium of smudges. She sank down beside me on the deck, threw me a grateful smile as she tugged off the handkerchief from her face, then she took the tip of the patch, and bent it against the edge of the hole with a few light taps of the sledge.

"There, that ought to keep it from slipping back in," she said, satisfied. "Binky, where is that hose?!"

Binky, who had been occupied behind me, now came trotting over with a long tube of rubberized nylon mesh, which he handed to her. Without further ado, she stuffed the mouth of this tube down into the hole, then sat back with a small sigh.

"Turn it on," she said, wearily. Behind me, Binky made a movement, then the hose jumped, and I heard the hiss of a gas rushing down into the carbon chamber beneath us. Lora wiped futilely at a smudge on her nose, looking at it cross-eyed to get at it, then she gave it up, and smiled at me. "Now, Morgan, what do you want to know?"

"What's that going in there?" I asked.

"Oxygen. From our tanks."

"Why?"

"Well, it's this way: We can't use magnetic power, right?"

"Right."

"And the reason is that the nearer we get to Crispin, the less the interval between turning on our power and melting the copper windings into an electrical blast furnace, see?" I nodded. "Okay, then. If we can't *avoid* turning the last two-thirds of the ship into raw heat, we turn around and make *use* of it. See, I'm fixing it so that the carbon below is mixed up with lots of oxygen. When we reach that point where we need the final thrust, we let the carbon-oxygen mixture into the firing cylinder, flip on the power, and the coils heat the tube almost to incandescence—"

"Setting off the carbon!" I realized. "But will it work? We can't control it— Just one big *boom,* and then we're out of fuel and on our own…"

Lora licked dry lips. "It's a risk, all right. But it's our only chance…"

"But what's the patch for?" I said, suddenly recalling the part that puzzled me the most.

"Two things. It keeps the oxygen from leaking back in here when we pull out the hose, and it keeps the explosion down below from sending a fatal flare of exploding fuel up here into the cabin. Soon's the hose is pulled, the oxygen will start pushing to get out the hole, and that'll slap the patch in place. Simple?"

"Yes, all at once. You make physics sound like child's play," I said with admiration.

"Easiest subject to learn. All cause-and-effect stuff. Most of it makes you wonder why you didn't think of it on your own without having someone else discover it—Oh, here we go. Come on, Morgan, strap in!"

I looked up. Binky was twisting a valve shut on the bank of oxygen cylinders bolted against the hull. He gave Lora a nod, and she tugged the hose out of the rivet-hole.

There was a short whistle of oxygen from the tiny aperture, and then the stem on the patch leaped up as its disc slapped and fused onto the underside of the deck.

"Time!" Lora yelled to Binky, who was scurrying for the control compartment. "Hurry!"

The disc humped up against my feet without warning, and sent me about two inches into the air. Even as I came down, there was another bump, and then another. The whole place was shimmering before my eyes.

"Strap in!" Lora screamed at me, over the sudden din. I raced to my cot as she dashed for hers, and dived atop it, fastening straps furiously. I glanced toward her, but she was already lashed efficiently into hers, lying braced for the oncoming impacts with fringes of atmosphere. I wished, somehow, that there were something I could do for her that she couldn't do better than I could. My money didn't carry much weight where I was at the moment...

The bumps increased in frequency, in noisiness, and in intensity, and then the ship was bathed on all sides with a sound that resembled a sustained scream.

"Air!" Lora called over to me in explanation. "Rushing past the hull—"

"It sounds like a thousand women being burned alive!" I hollered back. The scream grew higher and louder. "A thousand *cowardly* women!" I added.

Suddenly, I noticed a peculiar phenomenon. The wall, usually a dull silver, was changing. It began to look a drab shade of white, then this evolved slowly into a smoky orange glow. "Merrick— The wall, look!"

"Friction!" she called back, a note of fear in her voice. "We've entered the atmosphere too fast. We're burning up—" My face began to prickle with the heat and perspiration was evident.

"Can't we blast?" I cried out.

"Not yet! We only have the one chance—"

"But, Merrick— If it gets any hotter— The *ship* will set the carbon off!"

"Yes," she yelled back, miserably. "I know!" Then she shut her eyes, and her face wrinkled into tense lines of concentration. Probably praying.

I shut my own eyes and, joined her. What a hell of a fix we were in. Here I was, Morgan Blane, millionaire many times over, young, happy, beloved by all my friends—about to die. And, most likely, about to die of *windburn*! It wasn't quite glorious enough to suit me...

I looked toward Binky's compartment, but the door was shut. I had no idea if he were praying or steering. Both, I hoped.

Then I had a ghastly thought.

"Lora!" I yelled. Her eyes came open, and she turned her head to look at me. "Lora, if we've only got one blast, that means we can't stop our horizontal motion and have fuel left to stop our succeeding vertical motion!"

"We're splitting the difference!" she called back. "The gyros have us coming in at an *angle* to the planet. We'll land on a slant, tail-first, and hope the impact either straightens the ship up as we stop, or that our angle is low enough to make our fall easy, see?"

"I wish I didn't!" I groaned. I closed my eyes again.

My ears were ringing with the shriek of air-abrased metal, and the glow in the room was cherry-red, now. At any moment, I expected to be slapped in the face with a gob of hot metal from where the ceiling should have been. Then my stomach and whole world turned over, sickeningly.

"The gyros—" Lora gasped, from the cot beside mine, "we're moving in tail-first— We're going to hit— Brace yourselves—"

The shriek outside grew to a roar like a stadium full of football fans going crazy over a touchdown, I looked toward the port, but only a whirling blur of colors met my eyes. I looked hastily away, and waited, my flesh hot from the shimmering crimson glow of the walls and peaked ceiling.

Then the deck heaved and tried to burst itself in the center, and my ears were numbed with the vicious brunt of the blast that came from the chamber only inches below the fuel that was only inches below us—

There was a screech of agonized metal, and I suddenly felt myself jammed against the rubberized cot as if some monster millwheel had suddenly been dropped onto my body. The air rushed from my lungs and then my consciousness exploded into fragments of sparkling red lights...

My mind cleared amidst a giddy rocking motion, as the ship, flung by the impetus of striking the ground into a nearly vertical position, teetered nauseatingly back and forth, trying to find stability. Then the huge metal needle caught its balance, gave a final shudder, and came to a halt, nicely upright.

I decided that—ten minutes or no ten minutes—Binky Seers was worth every penny of the hundred thousand bucks.

CHAPTER FIVE

THIS," I said to Lora, between automatic munches on an army-surplus wafer from an assault-pack tin, which had the golden-brown light flaky consistency of fried plaster, "is just dandy, Merrick! We're alive, which is something, but the coils are fused. And if they *weren't,* they'd only fuse again when we tried lifting *off* this nightmare place!"

Lora, seated beside Binky on the opposite side of the campfire—which burned with an eerie green blaze—looked glumly at the ground and murmured, "When my grandfather told me there was lots of copper here, he didn't tell me it was the basic ore of the whole planetary crust..."

"But we found *out* quick enough, didn't we!" I muttered, crunching the wafer between my teeth in disgust. "Look at the fire! Grass-green, thanks to copper in the wood! And the lovely deep-blue lake beyond the ship— Owes its color to copper sulfide—"

"Sul*phate!*" Lora supplied automatically.

"All right, all right! Sul*phate!* A deadly poison, yet! We have to *distill* every drop we want to drink."

"Just be glad we have the distilling apparatus, son," said Binky, softly. "Imagine eating this stuff without anything to wash it down."

"Imagine my eating it *with* water!" I exploded. "I could be out at Leone's right now, sipping Chianti, glutting myself on eggplant *parmigiana*—" I stopped, and swallowed. The mental image was too painful to bear.

"So could we," Lora said, gently. "You think *we* like the bill of fare, Morgan?"

There was no real anger in her tone, just patience, as with a beloved but willful child. I had a sudden guilty sensation that that was exactly what I was behaving like. Small wonder Lora kept taking the reins; I was no great shakes as a leader, so far…

I thought briefly of asserting my male prerogative of assuming command, and— And what? Lead a wild charge into the jungle that bordered the lake? Toward what? Where were we at? Where were we going? And what could we do when we got there? I decided the moment was hardly propitious for taking over. Well, maybe I could protect her against the wildlife, if any. We had three small, small revolvers, and a box of shells, one hundred of them. I'd learned to handle a rifle in service— the army gives not a damn about a man's bank balance or social echelon—and I was hoping that pistol-shooting was merely a refinement of technique already learned.

We'd seen no animals yet, nor any birds, but I didn't figure the local fauna had enjoyed that violent carbon-oxygen blast any more than I had. Any wildlife with good hearing was probably still running the other way.

I hadn't answered Lora's question; it was rhetorical, anyhow. But she was watching me over the dancing green flames, her dark brown eyes couldn't keep off my face. She seemed pinched with worry, anxious.

"Hey, Merrick," I grunted, avoiding that earnest gaze.

"…Yes, Morgan…?"

"Next gripe I make, you just haul off and paste me one, okay?" I brought my gaze up to see how she took my offer.

A little twitch at the sides of her mouth told me she liked what I'd said. I threw her an apologetic grin.

"Well," said Binky, after observing this silent interchange of amity, "we may as well pack up and get moving."

"Get moving where?" I asked, uncertainly.

"Miss Merrick," he said, jerking a ragged thumbnail in Lora's direction, "says she remembers some of that map. It had the mine marked off as being in the eastern angle of one of these X-shaped ranges. Now, I was pretty busy while we were coming down here, but I was able to see that we hit nearly in the western angle of such a range. That means we have one chance in three of being opposite the right spot. I say, let's go have ourselves a look."

I rose to my feet, on the opposite side of that eerie campfire, and stared at him. "You mean we take off through this nightmare jungle here, climb the mountain range beyond it, then clamber down the other side because we have one chance in three of finding a mine that won't do us a damned bit of good if we do locate it?"

Lora and Binky exchanged a look, then Binky said to her, "Looks like he wants you to paste him one!"

"Oh, now, hold on," I objected. "I'm not being uncooperative, just reasonable! What good *will* it do us to find the mine, huh?"

Lora shrugged. "We—We came two million light years looking for it… It seems foolish not to go the last few miles, Morgan…"

"And old man Merrick may have had a shack or some kind of shelter there. We can't just stick around here. So we might as well head on."

"We could live in the ship—" I said, stubbornly.

"And die in it," said Binky, emotionlessly, "when these food-packs give out. Besides, Merrick may have had a shortwave. We could signal for help. Our radio set burnt up with the propulsion coils. A fleeting smile flickered on his homely face for an instant. "Unless you *like* the idea of staying forever on Crispin?" He bent over and started packing the food-cartons into a knapsack. Lora, after a moment, followed his example.

I watched them in silence, then said, "What about the distilling apparatus?"

"Too heavy to tote," Binky said, fastening the straps on his bundle. "I filled the three canteens. They hold a quart apiece. And there's snowcaps on the mountain. We can refill them up there."

I looked at him, then turned my head and gazed at the odd blue-and-red foliage of the lush jungle that sprawled before us, a few hundred yards from the border of the lake. The trees were basically the same as Earth-trees, what with being affixed to the ground with a root structure, and having a vertical trunk with extended branches bearing foliage, but they didn't look like anything I'd ever seen on Earth, not even in a Tarzan movie. The trunks were shiny and smooth, and a dull lead-gray, and a cross-section of them would have shown a more-or-less regular triangle. The branches jutted out from the trunks in a symmetrical circle, three to a "face" of the trunk, and slightly upward, like an umbrella blown inside out and stripped of its cloth. And the leaves were the shape and color of the pips on the diamond suit of playing cards, red and rhomboid.

Lora had tried to explain to me about some mineral forms of copper called chalcocite and cuprite, which she'd said probably accounted for the color scheme and shape of the trees, but knowing the reasons for their distorted forms didn't make them any easier on the eyes.

And Binky, with undue relish, had given me the cheery news that the highly cupric nature of the planetary crust was the reason for our crash— Crispin, its magnetic poles abetted by its electrically-conductive crust, was a king-sized magnet itself.

"Lucky thing," he'd said, "that old man Merrick came here in one of the old combustion-drive ships, or he'd never have gotten off again; if, indeed, he ever got down here safe in the first place."

"Lucky thing for who?" I'd grumbled. *"Us?"*

Binky had dropped the subject in a hurry.

However, questioning Lora later about some things that still bugged me, such as the cans in the assault-packs, the metal sledge, and the guns, in view of the highly magnetic condition of the planet, she'd explained that they, in order to be usable on a Lectralift, had been coated with the same stuff we'd had sprayed on our fillings, to partially nullify the tremendous tug of the ship's drive.

"So we're very fortunate we can still pick them up off the ground," she'd told me happily.

"Makes that much more junk to carry," I'd said, grumpily, and Lora, too, had dropped the subject.

I wasn't very popular with those two, I could see, but I wasn't in the mood for popularity at the time. However, by now, three hours after the crash-landing, I began to realize that I'd either have to get along with them or be miserably alone—even when with them—for whatever length of time we remained on Crispin. So I gave in, but just a little.

"You know, Morgan," Lora said, as we were strapping on our canteens and packs, "this may do you some good..."

I was way ahead of her. "If the army couldn't do it, Crispin won't," I said, shoving my pistol into my belt at the waist.

"Won't what?" she asked, puzzled by my response.

"I can follow your mind's peregrinations a mile off, Merrick," I said. "You've got me in a slot: Spoiled young millionaire, about to meet nature in the raw, where his money can't help him! Right?"

"I...Well—" She stared at the ground. "Not as bluntly as you put it Morgan..."

"But I've been through it before. In service, my money didn't mean a damned thing. I had to rely on myself, on my physical stamina, intelligence and courage, just like I'm going to have to do it here on Crispin. And so, you think, I'm going to realize that since money can't buy everything, such as survival, that there are better things in life. Well, there aren't!"

"But, Morgan—" she said, then halted.

"All I learned in service, when I was separated from my ready cash, was that it would be just that much more enjoyable to get back to!" I growled.

"All right, Morgan," she said, and turned away.

Feeling I'd made my point, I lifted up the case of shells for the guns, slipped its web-strap over my shoulder, and moved over to where Binky was dumping a pan full of poisonous blue lake-water on the embers of the fire.

"All set, Mr. Blane?" he asked.

"If you mean am I looking forward to this trek, the answer's no. But I'm still capable of movement, if that was what you wanted to know."

Binky muttered something under his breath, then hitched his knapsack up onto his shoulders, and started trudging off toward the tangle of blue-and-red jungle ahead. Lora, with a pack just as heavy as his—her own insistence—followed after him, and I brought up the rear, my thoughts as black and seething as polarized carbon.

At the edge of the wooded area, I turned for a final look at the Brunhilde. "Two million bucks, shot to hell!" I whispered. "And for what? So I could go mountain-climbing and eat C-rations!"

"What did you say, Morgan?" Lora called, partway into a blue-grassy glade of towering trees.

"Nothing that would make your conscience any lighter," I mumbled, scuffing after her into the dappled gloom...

Crispin's rotation was a little faster than Earth's, the days being about twenty hours long from dawn to dawn, so before we got many miles into the tangled shrubbery, a tar-colored blackness blotted out all vision. Binky figured us to be near enough to the planet's equator to have ten hours of night ahead, so we made camp in a small clearing, drew straws—stiff green weedy things—for who pulled the first watch, and I came in second, Binky last. Lora won.

I was awakened in midnight gloom by a cool hand upon my cheek. I lifted my head from the tussock of ground that served me—insubordinately—as a pillow, and sat up.

"It's your turn, Morgan," Lora's voice floated to me in the shimmering green twilight that my eyes slowly became aware of. "I think we need some more wood cut for the campfire."

I shook my head to clear away the cobwebs of sleep that still clung to my consciousness, and glanced over at the pale heap of glittering emeralds that was the dying fire.

"Just my luck," I muttered, getting creakily to my feet. The dim glow of the embers showed me Binky, rolled in a blanket, snoring lightly beyond the range of their heat. His thumbnail, as during his waking hours, hovered within nibbling distance of his even white teeth.

Lora, satisfied that I wasn't going to doze off again, began to move off into the semi-darkness. I reached out and caught her arm.

"Whoa," I whispered. "What's become of the girl who was so amorous aboard the Brunhilde?" I asked.

Her brown eyes, jet black in the green light, seemed to shrink a bit at the corners, and her wrist, between my fingers, was trembling.

"Morgan, let me go," she said softly.

"Why should I?" I said. "Faithful Fido's asleep, isn't he? For all practical purposes, we're alone here, Merrick." Still, she held back. "Change your mind?" I asked.

"N-No," she said. "I *do* like you, Morgan. That's why I won't— Please let me go…"

"What are you, one of those look-but-don't-touch girls? You practically started playing Delilah just before the crash came— Now it's Little Eva all at once."

"I—I was kidding, then," she said earnestly. Then, catching my expression, "No, not in that way, Morgan. I did mean it, but I didn't, too."

"That's a pretty typical female statement," I muttered.

"Morgan…" She yanked free of my grip, and then with feminine inconsistency, took a step toward me. "I was acting like that because I like you, and you were being stand-offish.

44

Maybe it was silly. Score it as a little amorous horseplay, if you like. Maybe when we get back to Earth—" She halted.

"*If* we get back to Earth—" I said.

She didn't say anything.

"Come here," I said softly. Lora stood facing me in that pale viridian campfire gleam, then took another step forward, and put her tiny hands upon my shoulders. I could feel the tremor that passed through her, as she stood looking into my face, a foot away from her own. My hands went to her waist. I was surprised to find that they nearly encircled it, without stretching so much as a finger...

She stood there, trembling, waiting—

Then I let go, and took her by the wrists, instead. Gently, I lifted her hands from my shoulders, and brought them down to her sides. I leaned forward and pressed my lips down on hers, firm but gentle. Then I opened my fingers and stepped back.

"You better get some sack time," I grunted, flicking my index finger toward her waiting bedding beyond the campfire.

"Yes, Morgan," Lora said, obediently. She turned and went to her blanket, and in another minute, was curled up like a kitten in its folds, upon that alien sward.

My eyes stayed on her there, for a long moment, then I wrenched them away. "*Sap!*" I raged at myself, but I went out into the trees to gather some more of the green-burning branches for the fire.

The jungle, silent as a midnight graveyard when we'd first entered it, was perking with night-noises now. Whatever creatures had been scared off by our landing were back in the area again. Somewhere up in the branches ahead of me, an animal gave a peculiar ratchet-like cry, a clattering whistle that swooped from a bass quaver to a ridiculous soprano whoop before cutting itself off as if the perpetrator had been neck-wrung in mid-song. Which I hoped.

In lieu of an axe, which we didn't have among the tools back at the Brunhilde, I carried that short-handled sledge. It couldn't cut anything, but it smashed firewood loose from the trees easily enough, if you picked the smaller twigs.

My gun—loaded, just in case—was stuck in the front of my belt, against my stomach. I didn't know how big the local fauna grew, or how ferocious, but I was determined to fire at anything that didn't run the other way when it saw me. A few yards from the clearing, I found a likely looking tree with thin lower branches, and I began battering at them near the bole with the sledge, while tugging and wrenching at the leafy end with my free hand, to speed things up.

Halfway through with demolishing the butt of such a twig, I became aware, with a chilly jab of ice into my back, that there were two shining golden eyes staring down into my own, from that upper foliage. I jumped back from the trunk, and had the pistol out in an instant.

The eyes blinked a little at my sudden motion, and then their owner clambered deftly, if carefully, down the trunk, face-first, to have a curious look at the damage wrought to that half-splintered twig.

I couldn't make it out, in that arboreal gloom, but whatever its shape, it was tiny. That helped my nerves a little, but I remained cautious. Coral snakes and Gila monsters weren't very big, either, but it didn't pay to get too close to them. Then this thing chattered a little, and looked toward me once more, making little peeping noises.

Keeping the pistol ready, I moved back toward it, trying to pierce the gloom and determine its shape. On closer inspection, it proved to be monkey-like in appearance, except that it had pointed ears, like a terrier's, and a wicked-looking dark-snouted muzzle, from which two sharp canines protruded and gleamed, even in that uncertain light.

And its long tail was forked at the end, into two parts, each about a third of the tail's total length. I bent, picked up a small chunk of slatey rock, and tossed it at the beast, lightly, not to hurt it, just to scare it off.

The fork-tailed thing, instead of dodging, reached out a tiny paw and *caught* the stone, easily. Then, with another little peep, it tossed it back, not at all gently. I ducked just in time to avoid losing an eye, the sharp edge of the stone catching me a glancing cut on the forehead. I stood up muttering a curse, and then, hefting the sledge, stepped in to give that thing some *real* trouble.

Even then it didn't flee, just dangled by its forked tail from an overhead branch, and made that peeping sound some more, its golden eyes glinting brightly at me. I stopped at arm's length, feeling suddenly silly attacking such a tiny creature with a thing as dangerous as that hammer.

"Go on, shoo!" I urged it, poking at its belly with the top surface of the sledge. I kept at it.

The tiny paws darted down, and before I knew what was happening, it had torn the hammer from my grasp, and was scuttling up the tree with it.

"Hey!" I cried, making a futile leap to grab it in its agile flight. Then I recalled its propensity for hurling things, and suddenly crouched close to the hole of the tree. If it took it into his head to hurl the *sledge* at me, from the darkness—! I huddled there, my eyes shut, waiting for the blow to fall. Then the peeping came again, but from another treetop. I didn't know if it was *my* fork tailed thing, or another of its kind, but I took a step that way, anyhow, my hands ready to protect my head from that hammer if it came my way from the blackness.

"Hey, Buster!" I called softly. "Drop Morgan's hammer, huh...? Come on, dogface, *you* can't use it... Let it drop back on the ground, huh...?"

Again that unearthly peeping, only farther away, this time. I sighed and gave up, turning back toward my half-attacked tree. I'd simply have to *rip* the damned branches loose, and bear the disgusted looks of Binky and Lora in the morning.

I got back to the tree and searched for that partially severed twig, moving slowly about the triangular bulk of the trunk. I couldn't find it.

Puzzled, I went around once more. The twig had been a little better than face height, so I couldn't very well miss it— Unless I'd come back to the wrong tree, maybe... "Be the easiest thing in the world to miss a tree in this green-gray muck," I said to myself in the semi-darkness.

Irritated, I moved to another tree. That wasn't the one, either. All the stupid trees on Crispin looked alike to me, I realized. Maybe a native could tell them apart, but—I wished I hadn't thought that.

Lora had assured me that her grandfather's letter made no mention of intelligent life on Crispin, but maybe he just never *met* any.

They might be watching me from the shrubbery, even now, I thought, awaiting their chance to strike... "Don't be an idiot, Morgan!" I muttered. "Come on, get the firewood and go back to camp..."

Which was, I suddenly asked myself, *where?*

I stood stock-still in that alien jungle, trying to think. If I were at that ragged branch, then the camp would lie a few yards directly at my back... But where the hell was that branch at? I thought instantly of calling out, but then decided to hold off for a minute or so. I didn't want the double embarrassment of admitting I'd gotten lost so quickly and of awakening Binky and Lora from their needed sleep to bring me back to camp...

I tried another tree, then another and another. Not a scratch on any of them. I felt like an idiot, but I had to find the camp before I wandered any farther. Binky had been guiding us through the woods by the expedient of noting the fall of sunlight through the trees, then striking eastward toward the mountains. I could, of course, wait till daylight, and then strike out in the same direction— Only, they might go back westward, looking for me...

Well, nothing to do but call out. I cupped my hands about my mouth, took in a good lung full of air—and then froze, my skin prickling with fear.

Something was coming through the jungle, something that gave low growls; and crunched the shrubbery aside noisily with the force of its passage. And it was coming my way...

My immediate thought was to start clambering up into the branches of a tree, in the hopes that this predator—which I assumed it was; better safe than sorry—couldn't follow after me. Then I thought of our camp. I was on *watch,* wasn't I? This was the very sort of thing I was awake to look for. The campfire might scare the beast off— No, that's right, there wasn't any campfire any more; that's why I was *out* in the jungle, getting wood...I had to do something—

But if I cried out, or chanced a gunshot, the thing might hear it and come after *me*— The low rumbling growl was getting nearer to where I stood. Swiftly, I pulled the pistol from my belt and flicked off the safety catch, aiming the barrel into empty darkness. Would I *see* the thing before it attacked me, or would it spring at me in a rush that the gun wouldn't stop?

I braced my back against a tree trunk and stood waiting, too chilled with fear to even perspire. My flesh felt icy and dry as old bones. The growling paused, as if the thing had scented something. Probably me.

I squinted in the darkness, trying to catch some sign of movement. After a moment, the growl came again, and was echoed by another, close by. And another. Whatever it was, it wasn't travelling alone!

That decided me. In another instant, I had jammed the gun back into my belt and swung myself up into the tree I'd been standing against, scrabbling with my shoes against the smooth face of the trunk, and then drawing myself clumsily up until I could stand on two divergent limbs, my back once more against that hard, glossy trunk. Then the bushes parted a short distance away, and something loped into the area beneath me.

A formless gray shadow, with a forked tail swaying back and forth behind it, glided easily to the base of the tree. Bright golden eyes gleamed up at me on my precarious perch, and I caught the glint of sharp teeth in a long muzzle. The shadow was joined by another, and then more, until eight of the creatures were seated on their haunches, staring fixedly up at me. From what I could make out, they were something like wolves, except that twin bony spikes jutted up about six inches above the thick bony ridge of forehead, slightly curved, like a goat's.

"Go away," I said, my own voice startling me. "Go on, beat it or I'll blast you!"

The lead animal stood up gravely on all four feet then rose swiftly on its hind legs, its forepaws bracing on the tree trunk a few inches beneath my feet. A low, angry growl was quivering in its shaggy throat. Then it telescoped itself downward a few inches, readying its powerful hind legs for a leap that—if it were even half as good as a wolf—would carry it all the way to my throat. My balance wasn't good enough to fend off a charge like that. And I lacked two bullets toward the destruction of the pack, assuming I made the six I had, all fatal.

"Sorry, White Fang," I said, and fired the pistol right down into the spot between those bright golden eyes.

The horned wolf gave a yelp, and went sprawling back into the pack, which leaped out of the way with fantastic agility, as the woods rang metallically with the sharp crack of that shot. The double tail twitched in a violent tremor then the beast lay still on the ground. With vicious enthusiasm, the pack fell upon it and began ripping its still-warm body into shreds.

I looked away, and waited, expecting at any moment to hear Lora and Binky, aroused by the gunshot, coming through the jungle to find me. I had to be ready to pick off any of the pack that made for them when they appeared...

But aside from the greedy snarls of the pack, there was no sound in the darkness. Neither Lora nor Binky appeared.

I don't know how long I stayed there in that tree. Maybe an hour, maybe more, passed before I nerved myself enough to slip down the tree, beside the deserted remains of the horned wolf, the pack having loped away as swiftly as they'd come, once their savage feasting was over with.

"*Lora!*" I called. "*Binky!*"

There was no answer.

My emotions cracking back and forth between fury at their apparent deafness and cold fear lest they be beyond the range of my voice—or beyond hearing *anything* anymore—I started moving forward through that black jungle, calling out loudly with every third step or so.

I don't remember much more of that night, except that it was the most terrifying I'd ever spent. The pale pink glow of sunrise over the mountain told me that I'd been wandering for over six hours. I didn't know where I was, where the ship was, or where my companions were. And I was too bone-tired to care.

Finding a thick spiny bush nestled against a thick grouping of tree trunks, I crawled inside there, braced my back against the protection of the trees, and went to sleep with one hand on the grip of my pistol.

I awoke, much later, to the sound of someone weeping. I scrambled out of the prickly shrub, staring about me. The sky was a dull pink again, which meant that sunset was not far off. I held my breath and listened for that sound again.

It came from my right, just beyond a copse of those dull-gray tree trunks. I jammed the gun back into my belt, and hurried around the trees, my heart beating frantically.

Then I came to a halt, stopping as if I'd run into a wall. Seated on the ground before me, in ragged slacks and grimy blouse, her flame-colored tresses falling in tangles about her hands, which were covering her face, was a woman. And it wasn't Lora. I went to speak to her, then—

I stopped, as she turned, panic-stricken, to see who had come upon her there. "Mr. Blane!" she gasped.

I was looking into the tear-streaked face of Flax Dempster.

CHAPTER SIX

WELL, well," I said. "If it isn't the Copper Heiress!"

She let my sarcasm go by as if she hadn't heard it. Instead, she clambered to her feet and rushed over to me, taking tight hold of my hands. "You have got to help me, Mr. Blane!" she said, her green eyes desperate.

"Help?" I said. "Lady, lest we forget: It's *your* fault that *I'm* in this fix!" However, my curiosity got the better of my bitterness, and I added—"What the hell are you doing here, anyhow?"

"We had to come; when Max learned that you'd purchased a starship, he…"

"Hold it—*Max* is here with you?"

"Yes—No…" She shook her head, angry at her own confusion. "I don't know," she finished, "we came in separate Flickers, with our pilots."

"Flickers? From where? A Flicker wouldn't make the trip from Earth…"

"Radnor. It's a military base on the next planet out from Crispin's star. There weren't any regular flights to Crispin, so we had to come as near as we could, then rent the Flickers for the rest of the trip."

"But why *two* Flickers?"

"They only hold two passengers. Max and I can't fly them. So we each had a pilot."

I looked around the clearing, palely visible now in the roseate light that came from the setting sun. "And where's yours?"

"I don't know. After the crash—"

"You *crashed?!* I thought the Flickers had a combustion drive."

"These are newer models, with the new magnetic propulsion units. Only the Space Force has them yet, but— What has the drive got to do with the crash?"

"Everything, honey," I sighed. "I'm no expert, but I'm informed by reliable sources that this planet's polar magnetism gets a booster from the highly cupric nature of its soil, or something. It overloads the power units on the new ships."

"But— That's terrible! It means that Max has crashed, too, doesn't it!"

"More than likely," I grunted, nodding. "But why did you two make the trip? And where is your pilot?"

"As answer to your first question: Money. The copper ore on this planet is worth its weight in gold, what with the new drive-principle. Max says that if the map's any indication, this mine could be sold to the government for just under a billion dollars."

I whistled, softly. "No wonder he dropped everything and skedaddled out here! He must've figured that even with our head start, he was up on us because he had the map, and could get to the mine quicker to cover up. Nice move."

Her dark lashes curved down over her eyes. "Or to make certain that Miss Merrick didn't *fake* evidence that her grandfather was here…"

"Still sticking with your story, huh?" I said. "Well, go ahead. Lot of good it'll do you here in this jungle. But wait a minute— If you crashed *here*…" I did a quick mental calculation. "The mine must be just beyond *this* range! Lora was right!"

"You still believe her lies!" Flax said angrily.

"If they're lies, then when'd she see the map?" I said. "She knew at least that the mine lay west of the intersection of *one* of the three X-shaped ranges here on Crispin!"

"A wild guess!" said Flax, with hardly any conviction.

"Sure. And she pulled the name of the planet out of a hat, and the galaxy, and—"

"All right," Flax said. "I told Max it was a stupid scheme!"

"I'll bet you did!" I laughed. "Max says 'Here's a way to pick up a billion dollars' and you said 'Never! It's not the honorable way!' Sure you did, honey."

I glanced around. The jungle was turning gray in the gathering twilight, now. I took Flax's arm.

"Look, we can have our Morality Play later. Right now, we've got to find some kind of shelter for the night— You never did say what happened to the pilot. Did he survive the crash?"

"...He parachuted," she said, bitterly. "When the control board sat there whistling and smoking, he flung open the dome and dived out. I—" she buried her face against my shoulder. "I thought I was going to die."

"And what happened?"

"The ship glided in, and came down in an open area. It hit pretty hard, but my seatbelt saved me. I left it, and I've been wandering, ever since. I thought I might find Max, but—"

"But Max may be having troubles of his own, right now," I finished for her. "Yeah... Did your Flicker have any food or water aboard?"

"I don't know," she said. "I didn't think to look."

"That was intelligent," I sighed. "Look, Flaxy, I don't suppose you know the way back there from here?"

She looked around the enclosing foliage and forbidding trees, staring first here, then there, then facing me again. "I'm afraid not," she said. "As I said, I've simply been wandering..."

"Okay, okay... Say, which one of you two had the *map* on him?"

"Max," she said. "He never even let me look at it."

"In that case," I said, "I hope he *is* down. Not dead, but good and lost, anyways. Then we'll *all* have a fighting chance of locating the mine. Tell you what— It's dangerous traveling after dark around here. Let's follow the sunset west, while we still have some light, and maybe I can find *our* ship again. There may be some extra canteens there, and I *know* we didn't bring along all the food we had. So let's get moving, and find that ship as soon as possible."

"No," said Flax. "If we find the ship, I'm through with looking for the mine. Let's go back—Morgan— Let's fly back to Earth and forget this crazy idea... You don't need money. What do you want with a mine of—" She stopped, as I burst into laughter, despite the desperation of our plight.

"Flaxy, old girl, didn't you pause to wonder why *I'm* at large in this tanglewood? We had that magnetic drive, too."

"Then we're *all* trapped here?" she said, horrified.

"'Fraid so. Until the folks on Radnor start wondering when you two are bringing back their ships. And pilots."

"But Max paid them for three weeks' time!" she exclaimed.

"And the trip here took—?"

"About a day. That means that we have at least twenty days before they start—"

"—adding overtime to Max's bill," I said, interrupting. "No, honey, they won't come looking for you. In fact, if I know Max, he never even told them where you two were going! Admittedly, a Flicker wouldn't take you out of this system, but look at it this way: They won't raise a fuss for at least two months. When they do, they have a whole system of planets to investigate. And if they happen to pick Crispin, it's a pretty good-sized globe. Could *you* find eight people lost in—say—the South American jungles, for instance? The chances are good and slim."

"But what'll we *do!?*" she cried.

"Right now, we'll find ourselves food and shelter. We have maybe half an hour before total darkness. Let's move."

With Flax tagging sorrowfully at my heels, I started off through the shadowy forest, keeping the sun always at my face. After a while, though, I couldn't even detect glimpses of the disc through gaps in the foliage, so I had to set my course by the ruddy hue of the western edge of the otherwise black sky. And then, that too was gone, and the eerie green-black gloom fell upon us.

I thought of pushing onward, in hopes of coming upon the border of that lake where we'd landed the Brunhilde, but then decided that shelter was a much better idea. At least, being myself barely awake from a daylong sleep, I'd be able to take the watch all night.

I picked a likely looking tree, and gestured to Flax to climb it. "Time for bed, honey. It'll be safer up there than on the ground. I've *seen* some of what prowls the ground at night."

"But—" She held back. "What if there are animals up *there?*" She pointed a shaky white index finger into the tree.

"They only steal sledgehammers," I said. "Come on, climb."

Flax, it turned out, was no great shakes at climbing, but a cupped-hands assist under her sandals got her onto a lower limb. I was just about to follow when I heard the unmistakable crack of a gunshot. I stood still, waiting.

"What was that—" Flax began.

"Ssh!" I hissed. "It may be a signal…"

Another shot sound. This time I caught the direction. It was from the west, the way we'd been heading. Maybe Lora and Binky had retraced their steps to the ship, hoping I'd do the same, and they were trying to attract my—

This kind of conjecture ceased instantly as I heard another sound, one that made the hair prickle at the back of my neck. An infuriated growling. More than one animal doing it, too.

"Wolfpack!" I whispered up to Flax. "Someone's being attacked by wolves!"

"Well come *up*, for heaven's sake!" she said. "Hurry!"

I hesitated. Whoever it was might need help. I had only five rounds left in my pistol, but— Hell, if they were as bad as I was, they only had *four.*

"Look," I said, trying to keep the tremor out of my voice. "You stay up there. I've got to go and help. Don't make any noise, though, unless you hear me calling you for directions on getting back…"

"You can't leave me *alone* here—" she gasped.

"Believe me, I wish our positions were reversed!" I snapped. "Now stay put, and stay quiet!"

Rather than stand all night arguing, I set off at a trot through the underbrush, my pistol out, safety unsnapped, and muzzle preceding me through the gloom. I had no trouble at all following those ravening barks and howls, and as they grew louder, I had to will myself to take each additional step toward them. What if the other person weren't alive anymore? That'd mean I'd be facing the wrath of the pack on the ground, alone, with five bullets... It wasn't a pleasant line of thought, but I couldn't turn it off.

"Move, you yellow-bellied coward," I muttered. "That might be Lora out there, in trouble!"

I wasn't sure why this thought kept me moving. I made up my mind that it was solely because she was a woman, and therefore helpless, discarding memories of her damnably perfect efficiency during the crisis on the Brunhilde.

The growls were near at hand, now, and I was careful to be especially noiseless as I crept forward for a peek. A low bank of thornbushes lay between me and an open glade. I rose on tiptoe and looked over their spiny tops, into the more open area beyond.

The first thing I saw was a white billowing thing that hung like some gigantic tree-caterpillar cocoon over a wide space of branches almost above the center of the glade. From it dangled a skein of twisting cords, and heavy cloth straps from an intersection of two groups of the cords. The straps were part of the parachute harness that had held Flax's pilot. They hung open, now, and were stained and dripping with some liquid. Three guesses what.

His pistol lay on the earth below, and the fang-worried remains of a boot. There was continued growling coming from the other end of the glade. I couldn't see over there, too well, but I caught the motion of gray shadows, and once I spotted a flicker of bifurcated tail.

The only way I could figure it, he'd stunned himself coming down through the trees, and had hung there unconscious until awakened by the distressing sight and feeling of one of those horned beasts chewing on the toe of one of his boots. I didn't see anything that looked like a wolf-corpse in the area, so I assumed he was either very nervous at his predicament, or a lousy shot anyhow, or that this was the pack I'd met last night and they'd learned to dodge the White Man's Firesticks.

I'd have gone back right then, but I figured I'd need that gun. I had *two* people to protect, now. Assuming Flax wasn't being nibbled to death by those chihuahua-headed monkeys I'd met up with the night before. The wolves seemed too busy to be sniffing the air for trouble, so I stepped around the bushes, took a careful three paces into the open area, and picked up the gun. It was a .45, a good club type weapon even when empty. I stuck it into my belt, and began to back toward the bushes, keeping an eye on those flitting, feeding shapes not ten yards away.

Suddenly, one of them broke from the group, and loped toward me, coming into a patch of starlight. The black muzzle drew back from cruel fangs as it stood there, and a low growl shook the fur of its thick neck. I aimed my pistol between those golden eyes again, and waited.

The horned wolf surveyed me, silently, for a second, then apparently the sounds of its buddies' glutting revelry got to it, because some of the flame left its gaze, and it turned its head back toward the feast, hesitating. I held still, waiting. Then the wolf turned and trotted back to its hard-earned dinner.

I turned about myself, then, and pushed my way through the jungle shrubbery toward Flax's roost. This sojourn I'd noted my outgoing passage, and I was careful to move back in exactly the same bushy lane I'd taken on the way to that glade. When I was a good way from the scene of slaughter, I called her name softly.

"Morgan?" a voice came floating plaintively to my ears.

I moved toward it, and found her still perched on that branch. "Greetings," I said, stuffing the pistol in beside the .45 as I pulled myself up to where she sat. "I just met your missing pilot."

"I hope you clouted him one!" she said. "The dirty—"

"De mortuis nil nisi bonum, honey," I said. "There's a little wolf pack down the road that doesn't like deserters, either." I paused, then, "Except in a gustatory way."

She said, "Oh!" in a small voice, and shivered. "That was him you heard shooting?"

I nodded. "So that makes one less person for the Jiffy Flicker Loan Company, or whatever, to look for. I wonder how many people will be here when they do decide to nose around…"

"Morgan— What are our chances?"

"Well, if we don't starve, get cupric poisoning, get eaten by wolves, succumb to thirst, or fall out of this tree— They are still pretty lousy."

"If we could only send a message…" she sighed.

"We could," I said, "but I doubt if smoke-signals would travel to the next planet."

"You're taking this awfully lightly," she observed.

I shrugged. "A long face won't make things any cheerier."

She was silent, then. So silent that I wondered if she'd dropped off her branch. It was impossible to see in that inter-foliage gloom. Then a hand pressed lightly on my leg.

"For a young red-headed heiress, that's a man's leg, honey," I said softly.

"I know," she said, huskily.

"Oh, now look, lady, I admit you're attractive and all that, but we're balancing in a *tree* at the moment."

"Morgan," she went on, softly, "we may never get back to Earth alive. We may not—"

"Survive the night," I finished, nodding in the dark. "You sound like an old war movie. Don't you know that this sort of thing brings on hasty marriages? 'Let us not think of the future, there's only just tonight!' Bull! I'll bet more GIs came marching home to girls they couldn't stand the sight of—"

"*Oh!*" came a cry, and the next thing, both hands were on that leg as Flax slid off her branch and nearly plunged to the ground. Muttering, I grabbed her by the wrists and heaved her up beside me.

"Satisfied, Honey?" I growled, as she pillowed her hair against my chest and wound an arm around my waist.

"Mm-hmm," she murmured, hanging on, and giving little contented sighs every so often.

My neck inside my collar was getting warmer than could be blamed on the jungle climate. "You know—" I said, then cleared an annoying frog out of my throat. "You know, this won't get you any leniency when the case comes up in court…"

She stiffened, suddenly. It was easy to feel, her being so close and all. "…What case…?" she said, after a moment.

"Why, when it's proven that Max has filed a false claim to the mine here, with you as an accessory, well—I have to do *something* toward getting my lost two millions bucks back. A lawsuit might help a bit."

"But, Morgan—" she said, then paused. Even feminine-type logic couldn't out-maneuver my position. She knew I had a strong point.

"A fraud is a fraud," I went on, "and redhead or not, you could still go to jail for it. Of course, an all-male jury might be a little lenient, but—"

"You wouldn't dare!" she said. "I could say that—that Max—uh—Yes! Max *told* me it was my mine that my grandfather had found it and had left it to me. I was his unwilling dupe!"

"Really?" I said, unimpressed. "And what happens when investigation shows your folks are still extant in Cheboygan or wherever? Or have already passed away on Earth? Or—"

"Please, Morgan, don't," she said, earnestly.

"Hell, relax. They haven't even sent out the subpoenas, yet, honey. You don't have a worry till we get Earthside again. Then, of course, watch out!"

Silence. Her arm, still about my waist, was just there for support, now. Her head had drawn back from my chest at the first mention of my legal position. I yawned there in the darkness, but didn't really feel very sleepy, as I waited for some response.

"...Morgan?"

"Hmmm?"

"Are you— Are you in love with Lora Merrick?"

I had to think it over. "I don't know," I said sincerely. "I could do a hell of a lot worse, that's for sure."

"Have you ever kissed her?" Flax went on.

"That's none of your business," I said.

"Which means yes," said Flax. "If you hadn't, you'd have thrown me a pious denial..."

"Now look—" I said, then couldn't think of anything for her to look at.

"Has she ever kissed you...like this?" said Flax.

Her arm, the one not already about my waist, came up across my chest, and then her fingers were sliding into my hair, setting up a tingle-network down my spine, and she was pulling my head down toward hers. I went to resist, for a second, and then— Well, it wasn't as if Lora and I were *engaged* or anything...

Her lips tasted moist, hot and experienced. I drew back for air. Flax's head was back against my chest again, and her body was shivering slightly.

"I'll bet she never kissed like that," said Flax.

"...But what do *you* know about *electronics?*" I said in Lora's defense. "Now there's a girl who can—"

Flax was tugging my head down again. This time I didn't fight. I helped. We took another breather, and I found that I was shivering a little, myself.

"Of course, at the trial," I whispered, "I can always recommend leniency…"

"What trial?" said Flax, and started that head-tug again.

This time I kept my neck stiff. "Hot lips or not, I can't very well let you go scot-free. After all, *Lora* might have something to say about that! It's *her* mine, after all… And—uh—she has a temper, and…"

Flax's hand slid down from my head. "So you're adamant," she said fiercely. "Nothing will change your mind?"

"I'm sorry," I said.

Then her hand darted down to my belt and whisked out the .45, the muzzle of which was instantly pressed tightly up against my stomach. I sighed. "Now I'm *really* sorry."

"You have another gun," she said. "Drop it on the ground."

"You've got two hands," I said, uncooperatively.

"I need one to hang on. Drop it!"

I started to comply, then said, "What's to prevent my blasting you with it?"

"You're not the sort that shoots ladies," she said. "And this one I have might go off, you know."

"There's a story going around," I answered, "that an automatic pistol won't fire when it's pressed against a person like that. Shoves the slide back, you know…"

"Care to test that theory?" said Flax.

I dropped the pistol on the ground. "You know, there are wolves down there, lady."

"I'll find another tree," she said.

"You'd leave me weaponless in this feral forest?" I said. "You could leave me *one* of the guns, at least…"

Flax was already moving away from me on the branch, sidling out a ways to have clearance for jumping down. "I may need them both," she said simply. "After all, I'll be on the ground."

"Hope you break a leg," I muttered at the sound of her movement. There was a rustling of leaves, then a thump. "Are you dead, I hope?" I called down.

I heard her scrabbling for, then finding, the other gun. I thought of jumping down and surprising her, but she might just step back, tug a trigger, and surprise *me*. I sat where I was, despondently.

"See you at the mine, Morgan," her voice called to me. "*After* I get there, of course."

"Turn blue," I growled, into the darkness.

I heard her moving off through the bushes, and muttered a violent curse. Treed, betrayed and disarmed by a redhead! It wasn't my *first* such experience, but all the others had done it in a more metaphorical way...

I sat there, dangling my legs and thinking nasty things about Flax Dempster for awhile, then I sniffed. And sniffed again. Unless my nose had gone mad, I was smelling woodsmoke... Which meant fire. Which, in turn, meant Man!

Or a very scientific chimpanzee, of course.

The only trouble with the sense of smell is that it's not very directional, nor is it persistent. You can only smell an individual odor for a few minutes, and then some nasal gizmo goes *pffft,* and you're out of luck unless you can get a whiff of fresh air and start over again. But if I could spot the firelight... I started to climb.

After fifteen palm-shredding minutes, I found myself clasped to the uppermost—and thinnest—part of that triangular trunk, like a sailor in a crow's nest trying to sight a whale. Fortunately, the tree was a tall one, and I could see *over* a lot of the others. Black sky, glittering silver stars, and a distant arm of mountain range met my eyes. Then I saw the thin ribbon of smoke, lighted from beneath by the green flames that provoked it, tracing a wandering vertical course toward the stars.

I looked up into the heavens, and tried to find a guide. There was one tiny formation of stars in that unfamiliar layout that looked vaguely like a fishhook. The point was on an apparent line between my locale and the fire's. Well, there was a lot of forest between me and that fire, but I couldn't count on its being still burning at daylight, so—

I started to climb down, hoping the local carnivores were all well fed and asleep. Then I wondered...

The trees were close-spaced, after all, and Tarzan seemed to have no trouble maneuvering off the jungle floor...

What the hell. I slipped down the trunk to a point where its branches splayed nicely into those of the next tree between me and the starhook, and, straddling the limb, hand-hitched my way out there. The changeover was a little awkward, nearly plunging me a long ways to the ground, but I ended up hanging at arm's-length from the *other* tree, which was a help. I found some more footing there, and continued my arboreal excursion.

Two trees later, I was ready to risk being wolf bait on the ground again, until I hit a patch of really neighborly tree trunks, their main bodies barely ten feet apart. Them I could negotiate by holding overhead limbs with my hands and simply *stepping* from branch to branch with my feet. I began following this improved method of progress for the next seven trunks, and then I hit a hiatus, where even the lowest and longest tree branches didn't meet those of the tree ahead.

That killed the aerial route. I looked forward, and tried to spot the fire itself. Dimly, I detected a slight green flickering, probably reflected off some distant trees. Nothing to do but get to the ground and chance a barehanded struggle with one of those horned packs...

Then I saw something down below, and I stopped where I was and made sure I didn't even let one little finger rustle one tiny leaf.

There were creatures moving through the forest below me, and they weren't dumb animals, either. They carried spears, double-pronged, like the tails of the local wildlife. That made them intelligent, but not necessarily friendly. And besides, they didn't look too jolly, even discounting the weapons, as they padded toward that distant fire.

I had only an overhead view, so naturally couldn't get the full head-on effect, but the topsides were nothing to incite a chuckle. It was hard to tell if they were wearing hats, or not, but bareheaded or helmeted, *something* just above their faces sprouted twin horns, with a wicked forward-curve. From shoulder to elbow, they had bare flesh, but from elbow to wrist, the arms were matted with long dangling coats of hair, shaggy as a collie's throat. I couldn't be *certain* that they weren't wearing animal-hide wristlets, of course—*long* wristlets—but the humid jungle temperature made any but homegrown fur kind of ridiculous.

But it was their muzzles that bothered me the most. Even from above, I could see them, jutting forward, like the face of a boxer—the dog, not the fighter—and the gleam of up curved tusks that were their lower canines. With that sort of facial equipment, the spears were kind of superfluous, I felt, but I decided not to risk being impaled on either until I knew a little more of their intentions.

"Serve Flax right if she meets up with them," I thought. Then I remembered her two weapons. "Of course, it may just serve *them* right if they meet up with her..."

I sincerely hoped, all at once, that it was their own campfire they were approaching. Otherwise—it might be Lora and Binky, or Max and his pilot... Even *Max* shouldn't have to wake up to faces like that in the middle of the night.

I hung on up there, waiting until I was reasonably sure the last in the troupe had passed, then I crept back from my branch-tip to the tree trunk, and started a careful climb downward. If I could see them in their camp—if it *was* their camp—I might be able to tell whether or not they were friendly. I wasn't sure *how* I'd tell, exactly. Maybe I'd spot the chief pinning a rose on Mother of the Year, or something. Or pinning Mother of the Year on a rose, if my suspicions were correct.

I reached the ground, and stood against the trunk, panting for a moment, then I started moving forward toward the fire. Without the foliage of the trees between me and the ground, my way was suddenly clearer than it had been back at Flax's tree.

I could make out a distant collection of one-room-size cubical huts, alive with the dancing lights from the green fire. Keeping a tree or bush always between me and that encampment, I made my way through the woods toward it, crossing my fingers as if it were doing me some good.

The returning gang of warriors was just putting its spears against a kind of wooden rack near an oversized hut that was either the chief's home or the local sheriff's office. I inclined to the latter theory, seeing as there was a spear-holding fangface standing rigidly before the closed door of the place, and that it—unlike the other huts—had no windows. Probably even more likely the local pokey...

And a guard outside it. Therefore someone in it. Maybe someone from Earth? If it were, I ought to do something about getting him, her or them out of there, oughtn't I?

On the other hand, my efforts to penetrate the place might simply find me releasing the town drunk from a sleep-it-off incarceration. Assuming I didn't end up in the cell *with* him. Or dual-gored by one of those twin spearheads...

I took another look at the spear that guard held. In the leaping green firelight, it looked uncannily puny. It was not, I noted, a completely artificial construction. That is, the double head had not been added to a shaft. It was apparently the trimmed branch of a tree, cut off from the tree at its butt end, but simply trimmed of its rhombic red leaves at the other, like a water-dowser's rod.

Hell, I decided, after a squinting scrutiny of that double tip, you *couldn't* spear anyone with that. The worst you could do would be to *whip* him to death. Of course, *that* wasn't exactly a fun-way to perish, either...

The safest thing for me to do would be to simply move onward toward the east, and to give up any attempt to storm the jail. But, after all, it might just be Lora in there. Lora and Binky, that is, I added mentally.

It wasn't going to be easy. Unlike western movies, the rear part of the pokey was not on the fringe of the camp, where rescuers could cut through the wall and sneak the occupants out. On the contrary, the hut occupied the central section of the compound, edged out of being the main focus of the camp only by the fire. But the troupe I'd followed in had already split up and vanished into various dwellings, leaving the place deserted except for that guard. So with luck an open sneak to the back wall might not be observed.

I hated to risk it, though, just on the off chance that Lora was—that Lora and Binky were there. But could I turn and go on, without assuring myself that they weren't?

I couldn't, I decided, after much soul-searching.

Even if it turned out that the guy was simply an honor-guard in front of the chief's harem or something, I had to see who was inside that place. As I circled away from his visual area, to come up at the rear, I wondered if—should it be the harem—I could convince the caliph that I simply didn't *go* for hairy-forearmed girls with horns and fangs. Probably not. The chief would say, "Then what were you *doing* there?" and I'd say, "Looking for some friends," and *that* would be a nice foursome of famous last words!

All the huts seemed to face the fire, so I was glad the one I sought was the largest. Because, other than its size, it was the duplicate of any other place. I wouldn't want to bust in on someone's bedroom.

The rear wall, when I got to it, was very loosely thatched with layers of wide rhombic leaves, all dry and very coppery in their color, now. I tried shifting one, and it crisped to powder between my fingers with an unnerving crackle, but the jungle noises were still loud enough to cover it, if I worked slowly. At any moment, I expected the guard to come peeking around a corner, spear poised for tossing, or for flagellating, whichever it was.

I was very glad, and a little surprised, that the back wall yielded to my fingers so easily. A wall like that was hardly the type that would serve as a jail. Not unless the occupants were bound hand and foot. After three agonizing minutes, I had a hole large enough to poke my head into. After a silent prayer that there wasn't an axe waiting for my neck on the far side, I leaned in and looked.

It was blacker than a shuttered coal mine at midnight.

I not only could not see the interior, I couldn't even see my eyelashes when I squinted. So I tried listening. I held my breath and strained my ears. Then I heard it, soft unconscious breathing. And then my heart leaped as I heard a body shift slightly, and a palate vibrate in a familiar gargling growl. I hadn't spent two weeks on the Brunhilde with Binky Seers for nothing. I'd know that snore among a million. "Pssst!" I hissed. "Binky!"

There was a shuffling noise, followed by a rather vague "Mmmf," and then silence. Either he was gagged, or still asleep.

"Binky!" I persisted, a little louder.

A definite stirring this time. And then a voice, low and clear and very frightened.

"Morgan? Is that *you?*" said Lora Merrick.

"Sssh!" I cautioned. "Yes, it's me. Are you prisoners of these creatures?"

"Where did you go? We were so worried. We looked all over the area, and Binky found animal-tracks, and—"

"Will-you-for-pete's-sake-be *still!*" I urged desperately. "That guard'll hear you, and—"

"…Yes, Morgan?" she said, as I stopped.

"I—" I said tonelessly, "it looks like I'll be in there in a minute, Merrick…"

Dully, I pulled my head out of the hole, and turned to face the guard, who had just prodded me in the back with his spear-butt. He now had the supple-twig end pointed at me, and his manner was extremely menacing.

Even so, I would still have tried dodging that thing and coming at him with my fists, but he wasn't alone. About twelve of the villagers were with him, each toting a similar forked stick, all held threateningly on the horizontal.

And the horns, I noted with added dismay, weren't just worn Viking-fashion on a cap. They were their own.

"Morgan, what *is* it?" Lora's voice came to me, through the hole in the hut.

"It's part two of Life with Lora!" I called back over my shoulder. Then I was grabbed, bound, and cast into the hut with her and Binky.

CHAPTER SEVEN

HAVE they hurt you? Are you all right?" I said to Lora in the absolute darkness, the hole being already rethatched.

"Aw, I'm okay," Binky grunted. "They didn't do nothing 'cept tie us up and throw us in here. What we're mostly worried about is food and water."

"They took away our canteens and rations," Lora's voice explained, gloomily. "They brought us a bowl of some kind of fruit, but after one bite, I had to spit it out. It's almost completely saline, in a cupric way. Undoubtedly deadly for Earth organisms."

"You make me feel like something under a microscope," I complained. "But what happened to your pistols?"

"I tried to use mine when they surrounded us," Binky said disgustedly. "But they'd come in too close by the time I spotted them. One of them grabbed it, and it went off. So just like a bunch of kids, they all had to have a turn firing it—into the ground, though; they're not so dumb they don't recognize a weapon when they see it—and after all the rounds were spent, they tossed it away, and did the same with Lora's. Where's yours?"

I almost told him, then decided the hell with it. Lora might ask how Flax happened to be close enough to snag it. "...Lost it..." I laughed weakly. "Some hero, huh?"

"Didja notice all that stuff on their forearms?" Binky said conspiratorially. "Damnedest thing I ever saw!"

"You mean that shaggy growth of hair?" I said, puzzled by his bemusement.

"That's the stuff I mean," said Binky, "only, it ain't hair, Mr. Blane— It's rubber!"

"You're crazy!" I said, shaken by his pronouncement. "Why the hell would they have rubber for hair?"

"I think it's Crispin, Morgan," Lora said, softly. "Something to do with the planetary crust. Maybe they have electricity instead of blood—"

"Oh, *come* now!" I scoffed. "And maybe those horns are really radar antennae!"

"Quite possibly," she said, and I gave the subject up.

We lay there on the ground inside the hut for awhile, and I tried unsuccessfully to loosen the heavy thongs that bound my wrists and ankles into painful immobility. Giving a final futile tug, I turned my head toward where Lora's voice came from, and said, "Lora— Tell me something— If the rivers here are heavy with copper salts, and the trees and ground are spiked with the stuff, too— Who the hell needs a *mine*? So far as I can see, a mineralogist could exploit *any* old place on Crispin..."

"Probably a matter of convenience," said Lora, "or else my grandfather didn't know just how cupric the place was... See, Morgan, if it's to be profitable, the copper must be more or less readily available. In the water, it involves a distilling process to take out the salts, and then a tedious chemical process to reduce it to pure copper. Or in the trees—well—you've got to burn the wood and leaves, then do more chemistry to get the metal from the ashes. So I figure my grandfather found it in a better state. Copper is one ore that occurs in its natural state. It's a little heavier than iron, Morgan, and not quite as atomically active, so its pure state is found as often as its oxides—"

"Okay, okay," I interrupted. "I'll take your word for it, Lora…"

"You know," she said, after a moment, "this is the first occasion you've called me that. You usually say Merrick, as if I were a business associate, or a subordinate rank in your army or something."

"Habit," I said. "When you have gone out with as many girls as I have, you take to doing that. Saves embarrassing moments when you happen to have two or more with the same first names…" I paused, but Lora didn't say anything. Which was maybe just as well. "So," I went on, "what do we do about getting out of here?"

"We already tried rolling around and nibbling at these cords with our teeth," Binky said, discouraged. "They don't give way even a little bit."

"What do you think they plan to do with us?" Lora asked.

"If they're cannibals," I said, "let's hope we prove to be as poisonous to them as their planet is to us."

"Lotta good it'll do us if they get ptomaine *after* we've been run through their salami-slicer!" Binky growled. "If I could only get back to the Brunhilde!"

"Back?" I said. "What for?"

"That's where we were heading when a war-party of these rubber-haired ginks picked us up," Binky said. "First off, we were going there because it was the likely place for you to go if we got lost, but secondly, I thought of a way we could signal."

"How?" I said, fascinated.

"The atomic heater in the tail section," said Binky, "If I draw out the dampers, I may be able to rig it so it goes off, and the military base on the next planet will spot it on the detectors."

"You mean Radnor?" I said, then wished I hadn't.

"Morgan—" said Lora slowly, "where did you learn about Radnor? The last time I saw you, you didn't know the moon from the asteroid belt. Now you know the name of a far-flung military outpost in another galaxy…that's rather curious."

"Uh—" I said, thinking fast. I could say I'd read it someplace, or that they'd mentioned it, or that— But what the hell, you can go just so far in a deception before you're caught. I decided to tell all. "Lora, I didn't want to say this before— Didn't want to dim your hopes," I added quickly, putting my motivations on an altruistic level they didn't deserve. "But— Barton and that Dempster woman are on Crispin. She's the one took my gun…"

"They're here?!" Lora groaned. "That's terrible! If they get to the mine first, they can destroy any evidence that my grandfather ever was—*how* did she get your gun?"

I blurted, "Just reached out and snatched it."

"Just like that?"

"Yeah. Just like that."

"Oh."

"Uh…Yeah. Well, anyhow, she's got it, now. She and Barton came with pilots in separate Flickers from Radnor. Only the Flickers are the new ones, with the magnetic drive. So Flax— So this Dempster woman crashed, and her pilot got eaten by animals, but I have to assume that Barton's down, too. Whether dead or alive, I don't know…"

"Then she was alone with you," Lora said tonelessly.

"So what?" I snapped. "Weren't you alone with Binky? And what do you care who I'm alone with?"

"What do you care who *I'm* alone with?"

We lay there in silence awhile, then I said, "Look, we may be the main course at the next sound of the dinner chimes, Lora. It's foolish to quarrel…"

"Is it?" she said coolly.

"Damned right!" Binky's voice exploded. "You two can have your personal differences out later. Let's see about getting out of here, first!"

"What do we do?" I said sarcastically. "Butt our way out through the back wall and *hop* to safety?"

"That's not bad for a last resort," Binky said. "But if we could only get these cords off, we could maybe grab the guard, and scram before sunrise. Once the village is awake, we're sunk."

"Well," I said, "we don't have any knives, and you say that biting didn't do any good, so... There's one way left." I shifted my body over toward Binky. "Here, reach in my pants pocket, I've got some matches there."

"You think we can *burn* these things off?" Binky said. "My hands are behind my back, Mr. Blane..."

"So are mine," I growled.

"You just light the matches, and hold them till they singe your fingers. I'll try putting this cord in the flame. I'll guide it by the pain in my wrists."

"Don't be silly," Lora grunted, as she wriggled across toward us in the dark. "Binky can hold the matches, you hold your wrists out, and I'll watch what's happening and give directions."

"Fair enough," I said, and we got to work.

It was long, painful and tedious, most of the pain from a natural confusion about left and right when one's hands are behind the back, and another person holding the flame is facing the other direction, and the third party giving directions is at even another viewpoint. However, we had no trouble with up and down, which was a help.

All in all, it took maybe twenty minutes before the things grew carbonized enough to snap. Then, my hands free, I undid my ankles, then Binky's wrists, then he undid Lora's while I undid *his* ankles, and— At any rate, we were all free.

"Now what?" Binky whispered.

We hadn't been whispering before, but now that we were no longer bound, it seemed the thing to do.

"We could try going through that thatch, but they might have another guard posted, now. But there's one thing we can do: Right outside this wall, to the right of the door, is a whole rack of those pronged spears. If we just open the door and move fast enough, we may be able to terrorize the guard into silence with them."

"Why don't we just clout him?" Binky argued.

"Because if his head can grow these horns, it's probably bone-enforced for butting or goring, and a clout might get us nothing but his angry attention."

"Those spears looked mighty puny to me," Binky said.

"No punier than the guard's," I remarked. "Come on, gang. Let's move. It can't be too long till dawn, now."

The inside of the door was thatched, too. I pried a couple of the suppler leaves apart just wide enough for a peek. The broad back of our guard met my gaze. He was still rigidly holding his original stance.

"Okay, this is it," I said. "The nearest fringe of jungle is to our right when we exit. Soon's we get past the guard, that's the way we run. Got it?"

"Right," said Binky.

"Be careful, Morgan," said Lora.

Stealthily, I pressed the wood-and-thatch door open, and slipped out into the brilliant green firelight that illuminated the compound. The guard had not yet moved. I took a sidestep toward the spear-rack, and then I saw the muscles tighten across the upper part of his shoulders. An instant later, he'd spun to face me, that tusked boxer-face looking, beneath the glint of those horns, like a demon from a nightmare.

I took a step back, moving toward that rack, hoping he'd follow. He did. His double-pronged spear lowered to the horizontal, he took a step toward me.

And then Binky stepped out of the hut and, clasping his hands together, brought them at arm's length in a vicious curve that ended directly at the base of the warrior's skull with a dull crunching noise.

Binky jumped back, shaking his hands up and down and cursing under his breath. The warrior hadn't even been staggered. Instead, he turned, put a hand on Binky's chest, and shoved him backward to the ground, just at the moment when Lora came out the door.

The guard, seeing all of us loose, decided that reinforcements were in order, and he opened his mouth to yell. But by then I'd reached the racked spears, and had one hefted in my hand. Just as his head went back to sound the alarm, I flung it at him—

The slim, wobbly withe-ends struck him in the chest...and skidded off. The spear fell to the ground, a dud.

The moment of the impact had startled the guard. He looked down to see what it was that had struck him, and, seeing it, he glanced over and he saw me standing futilely beside the rack of these peculiarly impotent shafts.

Then the horned head went back, and the guard burst out with a sound that sounded very much like an Earth-type horse-laugh. In one of the nearby huts, someone began to stir. The whole village would be aroused if we didn't do something, fast. I grabbed the spear up from the ground.

"Run!" I yelled to Lora, who had just helped Binky to his feet. "The jungle, quick!"

I dashed past the still-chortling guard, grabbed Lora by the arm, and we took off for the distant tangle of trees.

Instantly, our guard roared something, a strange barking monosyllable that could only mean *"Halt!"* I turned my head to see what our alternative to obedience was.

The guard had this double pronged shaft of his held at the height of his waist, the delicate tips pointed toward me. It struck me, in that instant, that it was oddly like the way a man holds a rifle, not a spear...

Then the guard moved the tip, up and down, faster and faster, like a man wielding a long-handled paintbrush against an invisible fence. The tips became a blur, a shimmer of whirring green...

"Morgan, look out!"

Lora's hurtling body caught me in the side of the ribs, and we both staggered out of the way, just as a thin crackle of white light wormed violently between those trembling wooden tips, and then a glaring white thunderbolt materialized and flew past the spot where I'd just been standing.

"Hell's bells!" I gasped, grabbing Lora to me in a half-protective, half-protection-seeking embrace. *"A lightning-gun?!"*

There was no time to speculate, however, on the mystery of a primitive tribe with advanced weaponry. The guard was already vibrating that double-tip once more, and taking aim at us, a bigger target in our mutual clasp. And there were other fangfaces pouring out of huts now, all racing toward that rack. We'd be in a shower of lightning bolts in another moment.

"Well, if he can do it, so can I!" I said, pushing Lora away, and aiming the spear I'd snatched. Only I aimed it right at that rackful of other weapons. I whipped the air into a silken whimper with those tips, and then suddenly something numbing shot through me, from ankles to wrists, and even as I saw the rack explode into a July Fourth of green sparklers at the brunt of my hurled bolt, I was falling backward, every limb knotted into muscular spasms, and my shirt smoking and bursting into flame. Then the back of my head hit the ground, and I was momentarily away from it all...

I awoke to stinging pain, and sat up holding my head. My body was bare from the waist up, and my flesh was pink, with a few tiny white blisters on it. Lora was squatting beside me on the ground, looking anxious, while Binky stood guard, looking about the compound.

"Where *is* everybody?" I moaned, moving stiff arms and trying to flex some life back into my fingers.

"They've run off," Lora said. "You seared the hell out of them. I think they figure we're evil spirits, or some such thing. It seems that way."

"Just because I blasted their weapon-rack?" I asked.

"No, dopey," she said affectionately. "Because your *shirt* caught fire. Made on Earth, remember?"

"So what?" I mumbled, stupidly.

"So it burned *red*, that's what! These copper-bound people probably have never seen anything but green fire, Morgan."

"I'll be damned," I chuckled. "I guess it's a lucky thing that guy's second bolt *hit* me!"

"Morgan," Lora said, with impatience, *"that's* where his second bolt hit—"

She pointed toward the jungle behind me. I turned my head and saw a one-foot hole burnt into a triangular tree trunk, a few feet from the hole burnt by his first miss.

"Yipe!" I whispered reverently. "But what the hell set me on fire, then?"

"You did," said Lora. "Now we know why these natives have rubber-coated forearms. Insulation. It figures that on a highly magnetic planet there's a lot of natural danger from electricity. All the local creatures must have some sort of protection against electrocution. A natural grounding system, or rubberized arms, or even absorptive antennae as part of their metabolic cycles."

"Huh?" I said, lost, as usual.

"I mean that they either pass the electricity through themselves to the earth, or they fend it off, or they take it in and use it. Those are the only three possibilities. Which may explain the double tails on the local fauna. A sort of pickup antenna for each."

"Boy, this is a crazy place," I muttered, getting to my feet. "I wonder how this tribe ever got far enough ahead in science to make electric rifles?"

"They probably don't know beans about science," Lora said. "Any more than a caveman who could make fire with flint knew about oxidation or combustion. Don't you see that these guns are just a warlike application of a natural phenomenon? Natural, at any rate, to Crispin. Probably some prehistoric native saw a windstorm whipping tree branches about, and saw the resultant play of lightning bolts, so he cut one of them for himself, and—"

"You're taking the lightning part calmly enough," I remarked. "By me, that's the confusing part."

"Nothing simpler. Anytime you cut magnetic lines of force—which are plenty potent on Crispin—by a conductor, which these copper-glutted twigs are, you get an electric current. The things would be useless on Earth."

"Wow," I shook my head. "We're going to have to be plenty damn careful around here. We may destroy ourselves by just wiggling the wrong finger!"

"That's another thing," said Lora. "Binky and I have decided *not* to set off that atomic explosion, after all."

"No? Why not?" I said to Binky, still looking about.

Binky turned around. "Too much blast-wave, Mr. Blane. The wind from the blast would start the whole stinking jungle vibrating. We might just die by getting struck by lightning. And the jungle's the only place safe enough to have set the atomic engine off from. We couldn't stay on the lakeshore in the open when we did it. So—" He shrugged.

"So," I sighed, "let's scout around and see if we can't find our food and canteens, and then I guess we head for the mine again."

It took us nearly an hour to locate them. They were hanging, in their knapsacks, like trophies in one of the huts, probably the chief's. Then we drank some wonderful-tasting water, munched a quick plaster-cracker, and set off toward the mountains.

It was easy, now, since I'd spotted that fishhook-shaped star cluster between myself and the arm of mountain range. We just followed the hook.

We weren't starting a new program of night-travel, but we didn't much care to stick around the village till dawn. Superstitious terror can last only so long, then it gives way to suspicious curiosity, and finally to disdain, and— We didn't want to stick around for the awakening of intellect amongst the fangfaces. That was certain.

Just in case we struck another wolf pack, I took along some of the spears as had survived my attack on the rackful of them, wrapping the shredded remnants of my shirt—torn off by Lora when it caught fire—about the hafts of them as a pretty fair insulation. I hoped.

Lora, I noticed as we trekked into the underbrush, was oddly cool in her attitude, after her relief that I was alive had faded.

"Something eating you, Lora, huh?" I said, as we moved cautiously through the dark bushes.

"You may as well call me 'Merrick', again," she said. "I wouldn't want you making any *more* embarrassing errors about your '*many*' girl friends!"

"What the hell are you talking about?" I demanded.

"I'm talking about Flax Dempster's lipstick, of which I found generous traces on your *shirt!*" she snapped.

"Oh, that," I said. "...Sure it wasn't blood?"

"I *wish* it was!" she growled.

I decided to be silent till I could think of an excuse. It was a mighty quiet trip.

CHAPTER EIGHT

MORGAN, my darling! I love you," Lora breathed, as my arms encircled her slim loveliness, trembling and joyful in a whirl of white-lace wedding dress. The perfume of her hair was an ecstasy in my nostrils as I pressed her to me.

"Kiss me," I murmured huskily.

"Take off your shoes," said Lora.

"No, first, a kiss—" I pleaded, clutching her.

She pressed her hands against my chest, and turned the side of her face toward me as I tried forcing my lips on hers. "No, no!" she, cried, her dark brown eyes shut tight. "The shoes, the shoes, take them off...off...off..."

I sat up with a violent start, and rubbed my eyes.

The green flicker of the campfire reminded me instantly of where I still was. I looked about me. Binky was sitting on a small hillock, staring away from me into the darkness, the cloth-swathed haft of a lightning-spear in one hand. Lora lay asleep near me, one hand lying temptingly near my own. A dream. A lovely, beautiful, frustrating dream, damn it! I snorted, ruefully.

"What're you doing over there?"

I looked toward Binky. "Over where?"

He gestured, and looked frowningly intrigued.

I followed his moving finger, and saw that my bedding lay a good five feet from where I was sprawled. Was I a sleep-crawler? How the hell had I gotten over to Lora in my sleep, if not? I got up on hands and knees and scuttled back to the blanket where I belonged.

"The damnedest thing," I said to Binky, seating myself on my blanket and drawing my knees up to my chin. "I don't know *how* I got there…"

"I didn't hear a sound, either," Binky marveled, nibbling at the nail of his little finger. "You have some kind of commando training, or something?"

"Hell no. Just plain old infantry, Binky. How I got over to Lora, I have no idea… What're you looking at?"

I followed his gaze, and realized for the first time that Lora, too, was even further off her blanket, in the same direction I'd been from mine. "What the hell—?" I said, then stopped, watching my legs. "Binky! Binky, look at my legs!" I was shouting.

He looked as my legs slowly moved feet-first along the blanket, until I was sitting straight-legged on the earth.

"So?" he said.

"*I* didn't move them!" I said, staring at my feet. "They went by themselves!"

"Huh! ?" Binky came over quickly. "Do it again."

Obediently, I hoisted my knees to my chest, and sat waiting. Then I felt the rough surface of the blanket moving backward beneath the soles of my shoes, as my feet once more slid to the end of the bedding and off along the ground.

"Looked to *me* like you were moving them..." Binky said, suspiciously.

"No, honestly I— Look, you try it. Sit here, where I am." I scrambled up, and an uneasy Binky sat down carefully in my place, doubling up his legs before him as I had done.

"What—? Damnation!" he gasped, as his legs moved out before him, faster and faster, until he was straight-legged on the blanket. "That's the craziest thing I ever—"

"Ten-to-one it's this idiotic *planet* kicking up again!" I grumbled. "I'd better waken Lora; she's the physics expert in our group..." I turned my head. "Hey! Where's she *at!?*"

Binky and I both jumped to our feet, staring at the bare patch of blue grass where Lora had just been lying. Then, in the jungle undergrowth before our faces, there sounded a loud piteous cry of dismay.

"Morgan!"

It was Lora's voice.

Binky and I plunged into the bushes, racing crazily into the darkness to find her. I heard her voice up ahead of me, calling my name over and over.

"Coming!" I panted, dashing along. "Hang on, honey, I'm coming!"

Then I nearly stumbled over her on the earth. She was following my suggestion admirably. She was hanging on, all right, to the base of a sapling, her legs stretched out on the earth in the direction she'd been going.

"What is it?" I said, stooping down.

Then I sprawled flat on my face as a sensation hit my feet, not unlike having a rug jerked from under them. I caught tight hold of Lora to keep from being dragged away, just as Binky crashed out of the bushes, tried to pause, and was knocked flat in the same manner.

"Hey!" he cried, and then, before my horrified eyes, he started sliding feet-first along the ground, too far away for me to grab him. I watched, mute with fascination, until he arrested his rearward progress by grabbing at the knotted stem of a thornbush beside his path of departure.

"What's happening, Lora!?" I said.

"Shoes…" she gasped, hanging on for the two of us. "Kick off your shoes!"

It was startling to hear the very words of my dream thrown at me so sudden-like, but all at once I understood the reason for that subconscious dialogue I'd undergone. My body had felt that tugging at my feet, and had translated it into dream-plot for me. I began at once to pry at the counter of one shoe with the toe of the other, until I could kick it off. When I did so, it leaped away from the stockinged foot like something dropped from a great height, only sideways, and then vanished into the bushes beyond Binky.

"Magnetism!" I cried. "We're near a natural magnet of some kind… But why the shoes? I thought these were special non-magnetic ones, for use on a Lectralift…"

"They *are*," said Lora, who was busy kicking off her own footwear. "I don't understand it at all. The nails in the soles are supposed to be highly resistant to magnetism. This would…have to…Uh! There they go!…would have to be an enormously powerful one," she finished, as her shoes fled by themselves, and she hung on until I finally pried the other one of mine free and away.

In our stocking feet, we went over and helped Binky get rid of his. Then we got to our feet and brushed some of the dirt out of our clothes. I was beginning to feel pretty primitive, what with no shirt and now no shoes. Then I had a terrible thought.

"The canteens! They're nonmagnetic, too, but—?"

As one person, the three of us dashed back through the gloom to our campsite and looked. The tree-branch on which Binky had hung our gear was empty of everything but a few swaying remnants of carrying-straps. The terrific tugging had pulled away the canteens, and the assault packs, with their canned goods.

"Great!" I groaned, sitting down on the ground. "No food, no water, and a few weapons that may very well kill *us* when we try to use them!"

"We'll have to hope we find something edible, that's all," said Lora.

"That's *all!?*" I snarled. "That's *plenty!*"

"I didn't mean it in that sense," she said stiffly. "I meant that's all there's *left,* not that's all there's to *it!*"

"Lora," said Binky, "I think he's asking you to paste him one..."

"You *would* remember that!" I muttered at him. Then I look-ed at Lora. "Is my crabbing unreasonable, honey?"

She looked into my eyes, then sank down beside me. "No, I guess not. Not under the circumstances. And I haven't exactly been pleasant to you since our escape early yesterday morning, have I!"

"Like camping out with a gorgon!" I said, but not very earn-estly. Lora leaned forward on her hands, and brushed her lips lightly upon mine, then sat back.

"That was an apology," she explained.

I rubbed my hands together and grinned at her. "Seems to me," I said, leaning toward her, "I have *lots* of things to apologize for..."

"...Morgan..." she said, anxiously, but she didn't make a move to retreat. I took hold of her by the shoulders and planted a nice one, right on target.

"There!" I said, sitting back, "in the future, I want all your apologies to be like that one."

"I hope you don't mind," Binky said, "if I settle for a handshake?"

"Even if you apologize to *me?*" said Lora.

"Well, that'd make a difference, all right," Binky grinned. "Look, Mr. Blane," he added, more seriously, "it's almost dawn now, and we're all up; why don't we take off down the way we were just heading, long as it's in the direction we are going. Maybe the stuff's been stopped by a tangle of trees or something, and we can still get something to eat and drink."

"Good idea," I said, getting up. "Looks like all we have to carry is the blankets and spears."

"See, there *is* a bright side," said Lora, bending over to get her blanket. "And the spears'll serve as hike-staffs."

I brought down the palm of my hand where it'd do the most good. "Don't be sarcastic," I said, as she jumped up and clasped both hands to the injured section.

"My hour of revenge will come," she said ominously. "Just don't dare walk in front of me, that's all, boy!"

We started off for the mountains, with me bringing up the rear...

We came upon the foothills of the range in less than an hour, at which point we found the remains of most of our equipment. One of the canteens was dented but unsmashed, as it lay weirdly on the side of a black hunk of that magnetic rock, but try as we might, we couldn't even pry it loose with the three of us tugging at it. Finally, we were able to turn it enough on its own axis so that the neck pointed downwards, and were thus able to drink, using a thumb-on-the-hole method of withholding the precious liquid for each libation. We finished it off amongst us, since there was no way of bringing it along. From the canned goods we were able to get at a few of those thick dry wafers from those tins which were split by the impact, but we had to leave the others, since even the tiny two-inch can-opener provided with the kits was immovable against the rough black rock.

Thirst slaked, but slightly underfed, we began a painful bare-footed climb up the raw rock face of the slope. (Lora had insisted that we save the socks for night wear; they were no good for walking in, but they might keep our feet warm at what promised to be alpine temperatures.)

In an hour, we'd arisen barely one hundred feet above the straggling fingers of blue-and-red jungle that partially invaded the lower slopes of the range. And above that spot, the mountain wall was nearly vertical. We sat down, panting, on a sharp-edged projection of rock, and each nibbled moodily at a single dry cracker. Among us, we now had five left.

"Well, little heiress," I said, waving an arm in a slow sweeping curve from left to right, "there is your domain. I hope you're satisfied."

"The first thing I shall do after my coronation," said Lora, "is to have those dog-faced sharecroppers either file down their horns, or wear suitable pads upon them. I can't have my subjects gouging one another. It wouldn't be practical."

"And you might pass a decree about the water," I added.

"My first legal act shall be a law stating that no copper shall dissolve into, or otherwise pollute, the flowing streams of Crispin…" she said, then halted, swallowing.

I patted her shoulder. "I know. I'm a little blotter-throated myself. Let's not think about water for awhile."

It was a bad statement, psychologically. I immediately could think of nothing else.

"Well," said Binky, flicking a crumb or two from his lips, then dusting his palms off against one another, "we may as well start up again. We'll be needing a flat space to shelter on at nightfall."

" And if sunset catches us on a vertical section?" I asked, helping Lora regain her feet on the stone.

"Then we pray and keep climbing," said Binky.

"I hope that snow we saw at the top isn't riddled with more cupric pollution," I sighed, letting him take the lead so that Lora was between us.

"It shouldn't be," Lora said. "In the distillative process, even the most persistent solvents are usually left behind as crystallized—"

"Oh, climb girl, climb," I muttered.

Three hours later, we were barely twice as high as our last stop, but there was a wide ledge there, so we sank gratefully down upon it, and tried to catch our breaths.

From our new vantage point, I could see the other arm of the range, a dim bluer-than-sky haze on the horizon. We were on, we figured, the southwest part of the "X," so that had to be the northwest angle.

"Funny," I said, "the way these ranges are shaped. Of course, even from space, they're not perfectly *true* Xes, but near enough to make you wonder."

"On this planet, nothing would surprise me," said Lora. "It may be something to do with magnetism, or electricity, or even the crystalline shape of certain copper crystals..."

"Or a fantastic coincidence," said Binky. "Like the way the western continental outline of Europe and Africa almost duplicates the eastern continental outline of the Americas. As if the two of them were touching once, and split away."

"We'll probably never know," Lora sighed, and leaned her head against my shoulder tiredly, the long brown hair tangled and matted from the harrowing nature of our jungle journeying. I started to absently pluck a tiny piece of stiff twig out of her tresses, then stopped, listening.

"What's that!?" I said.

Binky and Lora sat up, instantly alert.

We all heard it. A dim, distant sigh of sound, like the noise made by the perpetually moving waves on a midnight beach.

"I think—" said Lora, then she pointed, excitedly, down toward the jungle at the far horizon. *"Look!"*

The blue-and-red growths were moving. We couldn't see the individual leaves, of course, but there was a color-shift as light-and-dark masses of these growths moved up and down, stirred by some unseen, unfelt force. Then, as this heaving, billowing motion spread across the treetops toward us, the sighing grew louder in my ears, and became a roar, a roar I finally recognized...

"Windstorm!" I cried, clambering to my feet. "Good grief! Will you *look* at that!"

At the far edge of jungle, the part caught most strongly in the growing motion of air, tiny sparks became visible. And what was a spark at that distance was something I wouldn't like to be close to. As the wind grew across the treetops, the thin line of sparkling electric discharges followed, coming closer and closer to where we stood.

"Do you think there's any danger?" I said to Lora.

She clung to my arm, gazing raptly at that beautiful growth of fierce energy. "I—I don't know," she said. "We should be safe up here, unless..."

"Unless—?"

"Unless the lightning is as affected by the magnetic field as our metal objects were..." she quavered.

"Oh, fine!" I moaned, shaking my head. "The day the forest has shooting practice, we decide to climb up on the damned *target!*"

"Better here than down there!" Binky hollered over the growing gale. I followed his gaze to the jungle, and saw what he meant. Trees, struck by other trees' discharges, were exploding into flaming green sparks, and their flying branches, even in near-death, were still vibrating and sending out flaming white thunderbolts of their own. Within a few minutes, all traces of blue-and-red were gone, hidden by a veritable canopy of raw lightning, that flared with blinding whiteness everywhere below us except the final fringe of forest down below the fall of the cliff. And then the wind, which began to pelt us with body-jolting blows, got even that final area to the vibratory point of electrical discharge.

Then the world went mad.

Searing snakes of lightning sprang toward the black rock below us, and struck like artillery shells. And then, the rock, split into boulders, started to topple, and—

Flew away *across* the jungle!

"The magnetic potential!" Lora cried, in my arms. "The lightning bolts are changing the potential of the rock when they hit it, and it's being *repelled* by the mountain!"

We'd given up hope of standing, and now the three of us lay flat on our bellies, watching the scene that was so unnervingly like an Apocalyptic end-of-the-world phase.

"Looks to me," said Binky, his voice a faint cry in the mingled sound of lightning, wind, and shattering rock, "like some of it's coming back for more…"

I looked out toward where the boulders were still flying, like an earth-bound asteroid swarm, and saw to my horror that a similar swarm was hurtling toward them from the opposite direction. "They reverse again?" I said, into Lora's ear, half-covering her tiny form with my body.

"I don't think so, Morgan… I think *those* stones are coming from the *other* arm of this range. The wind must be blowing over there, too—*Oh!*"

I had to keep from crying out, myself, at the sight she and I had just seen. The flying stones and boulders had met others in mid-flight above the jungle, and there was a smashing, crashing and sundering in mid-air that staggered my mind. It ended in an instant, then the shreds were falling horizontally back toward us. While other shreds headed for the farther arm of the X-shaped range.

And all the while, the canopy of lightning bloomed and hissed like a white bag full of vipers over the nearby jungle. All we could do was lie, cling and pray…I had a small inkling now of how the ranges had gotten their shapes, what with this electro-magnetic interplay of rock.

Now and then, a more ambitious bolt came up near where we cowered, and blasted off a section of cliffside. I could imagine us flying off into the air, riding one of those juggernauts to aerial destruction above the jungle floor— Or, avoiding that, smashing to death on that other range…

And then, quickly as it had come, it ended.

The distant electric flickerings died away, the wind became a sigh, a whisper, silence. The last jagged stab of lightning flared briefly against the mountainside, and the last few tiny pebbles spun giddily away to their destiny on the far range.

Shakily, we got to our feet. Lora, strangely enough, was smiling. I had a dim memory of some rather paternal affectionate kissing I'd indulged in while I held her, but it had been—I assured myself—solely to keep her spirits up. "You—uh—you okay?" I asked awkwardly.

She just nodded, and took my hand.

I looked at Binky, eager to change the subject. "What do you think? Can we make the top before sunset?"

Instead of answering, he continued to stare down below, at the ragged, smoking mat of jungle, and the raw, gouged places, in the cliffside. Then he turned to Lora.

"I was just wondering—" he said softly.

"Wondering what, Binky?" she asked, curiously.

He grinned, and shook his head ruefully. "Tell me, just what did your old grandfather have against you?"

CHAPTER NINE

WE HAD to spend a night on the mountainside, but we had a good-sized plateau for it, so it wasn't as bad as we'd feared. On the way, we caught sight of some birds, but they kept carefully away from our route, so I wasn't able to detect much detail. Except that all were bright crimson, from tail to beak, and the tail was split into two trailing scarlet plumes that didn't seem to impede their flight any.

And there were goat-like creatures on the crags, too. Though, since I'm no biologist, they may not have been goat-like at all. But the shaggy fur and horns made them seem as goatish as I could remember our Earth-animals to have been. The stubby tails, of course, were two-tipped.

Binky managed to bring one of them down with his spearblaster, or whatever it was, and we threw cupric caution to the winds—which were not, luckily, blowing—and roasted the flesh as best we could on a spit made from another spear, over a fire made from the third one. It was mostly an alternate of raw meat and charred meat, but we ate it anyhow, and to hell with cupric poisoning.

No reactions set in after dinner, so we set out again, with me wrapping my half-naked torso in a still-damp untanned pelt of this creature. Wool-side in, of course. The others, though I can't be certain it was due to the pelt-odor, made wonderful time keeping ahead of me on the climb.

When we got to the snow, we didn't bother trying to melt it; we just grabbed up handfuls of the wet, sticky stuff, and chewed ourselves a drink. It tasted swell.

I sat on a rock, shivering, my bare feet momentarily encased in my socks, and held clear of the sharp, icy surface we'd been climbing. The goat meat was coldly unappetizing, and the last military cracker had long since been wolfed dryly down. I couldn't help but wonder how I was to survive a barefoot trudge uphill through the snow that covered the mountainside above us, whose lower edge we had just reached.

Lora sat on another rock, Yogi-fashioned, with her legs folded neatly so that each bare foot rested snugly in the bend of each knee. I'd have done it, too, only I could never achieve that position. Not without cracking a tendon. I was busy being extremely jealous of her flexibility when Binky, who'd gone scouting around for maybe another goat, came clambering back toward us around a curve of cliffside.

"There's a pass!" he called excitedly. "We won't have to go over the top…"

"…Oh!" said Lora, with almost a disappointed sigh.

"For Pete's sake, lady!" I grumbled. "We weren't trying to plant a flag on the peak, you know. This was an attempt to get *beyond* the range, not *atop* it, remember?"

"Seems a shame, though, with it so close and all," she said, unfolding her legs with a fluid grace that kindled frustrated rage in my own.

Gingerly, I set my feet, still stockinged, down on the bare rock. "I don't care what you say, Lora. From here on, as long as these things last, I go with my socks on!"

"Maybe we all could," said Lora. "It may not be as hard climbing down. We can sort of sit-and-slide, possibly, bit by bit."

"Oh, no, we won't," I said. "I've lost a shirt, then my shoes, and pretty soon my socks, but I absolutely refuse to arrive at the mine with the trouser seat sheared off my—"

"Morgan!" said Lora.

"—bottom," I finished, stubbornly. "What did you think I was going to say?"

"Never mind," she said, and turned away, but I caught the flicker of a smile fighting to get onto her lips.

"What's the difference whether I say it, or you think it?" I asked, but she didn't answer, merely rolled her blanket, shouldered it, and made ready to leave. By common consent, Binky and I let her tote the sole remaining spear-thing, as a staff. In theory, she was the weaker sex, and needed it. I could have given her an argument on that, what with her agile limbs, and effortless output of energy. She was frisking at points where I was dead on my feet.

Wearily, I rolled my own blanket, slipped into my stinking animal-skin shirt, and followed trudgingly after her dancing feet as she moved along after Binky.

They'd suggested earlier that I might cut myself a less putrid garment out of my blanket, but cutting a head hole and wearing it poncho-fashion was awkward when climbing, with the perilous likelihood of stepping on the trailing front end and jerking your head against the cliff-face when you tried to straighten up, and cut it down to size I would not, asserting my rights to have an equal complement of bedding when the cool night fell. Of course, there was the alternative of sharing one of theirs, but Binky was too big, and Lora was too adamantly unwilling. So I walked in the rear and stank.

The path Binky had located through the pass was narrow, but at least level, so we made good time moving through it. Within four hours, we were on the other side of the range, looking down on a shimmering golden expanse of hot, glittering, waterless land. A desert. From the black foothills of the mountain ranges to the distant horizon, nothing moved, nothing stirred but the heat-disturbed air. The sky was kiln-blue turquoise over a planet-face of dazzling brass—

Brass...?

"Holy jumping Geronimo!" I cried, grabbing Lora into my arms. *'That's* the mine! The whole damned desert is made of copper!"

"But," she said, bewildered, "the map only showed a small point on it, marked 'Entrance to Mine'. I remember it clearly, Morgan..." She squinted in the sunlight, then shaded her eyes and peered down the slope toward the far-off foothills. "It was somewhere just about— *There!"* she cried triumphantly, and pointed.

I narrowed my eyes against the golden dazzle below, and tried to ascertain the locale of this thing she was trying to indicate, a sloppy approach to pinpointing when one is waggling the fingertip in ecstasy. "Hold that thing still, will you!" I growled, then at the same moment saw the square black object, barely bigger than a pinprick in that monstrous golden fabric of desert, almost nestled against the hills themselves. "You're crazy," I said uncertainly. "But let's go down and see, anyhow."

"Before we do," said Lora, pulling back from my embrace, "I have a request to make. Something must go, immediately."

"What?" I said.

"You have a choice," she grinned. "Me, or that goatskin. Simple as that."

It *was* getting pretty gamey, at that. I shrugged the stiff, odorous hide from my shoulders, and flexed my arms, "Okay, but if I die of sunburn, you're a murderess."

We scouted around, found a likely slope, and started a careful climb downward. I noticed that, however I tried keeping up with Binky and Lora, they always managed to stay ten feet or more below me.

"I got rid of the goatskin, remember?" I called down, after about half an hour of this.

"I know," Binky grinned back, "but the memory clings."

"You'd better take a shower when we get down," suggested Lora.

"In what, *copper?*" I snarled.

For answer, she pointed over to our left. I followed that finger, and saw what I hadn't noticed before. A thin column of silver shivered in the air alongside a distant cliff-face, turning to white clouds of spray at the base. Grandfather Merrick not only found himself a mine, but a waterhole for the miners.

"I hope it's not poison, too," I shouted at the top of Lora's head.

"It won't matter," she called back. "There'll be some kind of equipment near the mine, I think, and we can rig up a small water distillery if necessary."

"What about on my skin, though?" I yelled.

"If it's copper sulphate, it won't hurt a bit. In fact, such solutions are notoriously detrimental to the life of bacteria which cause offensive odors, and—"

"Climb!" I growled.

At about a hundred feet from the desert floor, we all paused to rest in the shade of an outcropping of black rock, eyeing that distant cataract with parched lips and sun-stung bodies. Despite the warmth, I had covered my shoulders and arms with my blanket, to keep off those skin-blistering yellow rays. At the moment, I felt like an any-minute-now case of heat exhaustion.

"That," I croaked, pointing toward what had been Lora's 'mine entrance,' down almost directly below our feet, "that doesn't look like no adit to me."

"Seems to be a shack," Binky observed, his voice raw and hoarse from the heat.

"Maybe," Lora said weakly, leaning her sun-pinkened face near to the cool shaded rock wall that supported our backs, "maybe my grandfather put the entrance inside... Wouldn't blame him...in this awful heat..."

"Maybe," Lora said weakly.

"I still think you're nuts," I said. "That whole desert there is copper. I recognize it."

"When'd *you* ever see copper...?" Lora asked.

"I'm a millionaire, remember?" I granted. "We sometimes have to break a nickel for the subway gum machines, you know."

"Oh, yeah, pennies. I forgot," she sighed, wearily. Her feet and body were hardly twinkling with energy now, I observed, but I didn't feel at all the satisfaction I should have. Instead, I was getting scared.

"You—You sure you can make it the rest of the way down, Lora?" I said, earnestly.

"Sure," she said, touching lightly upon my face with her fingertips. "As long as you're along, Morgan."

"You..." I said, trying weakly to joke, "you just love me for my money..."

She smiled gently, then nodded her head toward the vast expanse of burning orange-yellow desert. "And what about my almost-a-billion that I can sell this to the government for, assuming Barton's estimate was correct?"

"Oh, that... You mean you'll be rich, too? Well, in that case—" I turned my head, and looked into her dark brown eyes, inches from my own. "—In that case, maybe I could love you for yours, huh?"

Her face was suddenly serious, anxious. "And if the mine's a dud, Morgan? If all that desert is just sand?"

"Maybe—" I began, trying to wet dry lips with an almost-dryer tongue, "maybe I could love you anyway, Lora…"

"Morgan, I do love you," she said softly, watching me.

I slid an arm about her shoulders, and pulled her to me, gently. "And I love you, Lora," I said, and kissed her. Her lips were cracked, and so were mine, but I can't remember a more blissful encounter of same.

"And if he goes back on ya," Binky whispered, "I'll break every bone in his body, Miss."

"If I go back on her," I said, "you have my permission to do just that."

"Well," said Binky, "let's try to make the rest of the way, now. It's all downhill, anyhow, and not too steep to take quick-like, if we're—"

I looked at him. "What's up, Bink? Why'd you stop?"

"Oh, no," he said, his tone deep and woeful. "*Aw, no!* Not after all our trouble!"

I turned my head, slowly due to numerous stiff red sunburnt spots on my neck, and looked.

Settling gently down onto the desert floor beside the shack was a winged vehicle. A Flicker, working perfectly. And as I watched, the glassite dome flipped open, and three tightly-wedged people crawled out. Two men and a woman. I couldn't see the men from where I was, not that clearly. But one detail of the trio was unmistakable. The woman had red hair.

"I'll kill 'em!" Binky rasped. "I'll drop a rock on 'em. I'll set the damned shack on fire—"

"Easy, Binky," I said. "Don't strain yourself. The thing for us to do is get down there before they can gum things up. If we destroyed the shack, we might blot out evidence that we'd need ourselves."

"Besides—" Lora said, with a ghost of her usual smile, "the magnetic potential of this mountain prevents any of the rocks from being pried from its surface…"

"Shut up, darling," I said. "We're going to climb again. Come on, I'll help you."

A grueling half-hour later, we were standing on the floor of the desert, a hundred yards from the shack and that Flicker. I felt weak, woozy, drained of strength. But the shade, with the sun already past its zenith, was cooling and restful on the eastern side of the range. The crawling shadow of the range was already past the shack, and moving out into that vast, glowing desert.

I stooped down and picked up a pinch of the golden grain stuff and touched it to my tongue. I got that bitter-salty taste that I'd first learned of as a child.

"It's copper, Lora, or I don't know the flavor of pennies when I lick them," I said.

"Swell," said Binky, "Now, look, here's what we do. We get into that Flicker, all of us, and blast off for Radnor. When we get there, we—"

"We what?" I said. "Sick the military onto our friends? They haven't committed any planetary crime, which is all that the Space Force would care about. And the fraud they're undertaking we have no way of proving."

Binky's fertile imagination was not stopped, however. "Okay, so we take the Flicker and just *go* to Radnor. We don't tell anybody *anything,* not even those chumps are *here,* get it?"

"Binky, I'm ashamed of you," I grinned, "although I am perfectly in sympathy with your emotions. Nope, let's get on over there and— Make it, Lora?"

"Mm-hmm," she nodded. "A good glass of water'll fix up my trouble... Or maybe two."

"Come on, then," I said. Together, Binky and I helped her over the cooling copper "sand" to the door of the shack. Just as we reached it, it opened, and Maximilian Barton looked out at us.

"Thought I recognized you through the window," he nodded, "Come on in. Miss Dempster is famous for her hospitality."

I didn't miss the connotations of that statement, not for a minute. "You talk as if she owns this place..."

Barton stepped back, to let us enter.

"She does, Mr. Blane," he smiled. "Oh, there *were* some rather puzzling signs about the place that would give one suspicions to the contrary, but— As you can see, we thought we might need some kindling..."

As we got into the comparative gloom of the shack, I saw the other man—a stranger, probably Max's pilot—just finishing rending some bits of wood and stuff into bits with a short-handled axe. He was sweating hard, which seemed odd for a man of his build, even in a desert.

And then I knew what was bugging him. The axe. He must have carried it in. And, not too damned far away, the black magnetic mountain was exerting its steady, enormous tug. I had a funny thought, then, but Max interrupted my thinking.

"So you see, this place belongs solely to Flax, now."

I looked toward Flax. There was a soft smile on her lips, and her eyes were half-lidded, like those of a well-fed contented cat, though even greener.

"Congratulations," I muttered, as I helped Lora, almost a dead weight, into a chair. "Might I trouble you for some water for the lady?"

"Fraser—" Flax said to the big pilot, nodding.

He took a canteen from a sling at his hip, and held the mouth of it to Lora's lips. He seemed to be gripping it extra hard, which brought back my other thought in a hurry.

"Max, look, before we start discussing the pros and cons of ownership, I should tell you—"

"You may call me *Mis-ter* Barton, if you don't mind," said Max. "Your exalted financial position hardly gives you the right to take people's names and shorten them—"

"Max, for Pete's sake—" I growled, stepping toward him.

"Hold it!" said Flax, whipping up one of my stolen pistols from a kit bag on the floor.

"Look out!" I yelled, yanking Lora and chair and all out of the way.

The gun went off with a loud *"Blam!"* Ear-splitting in that small room, and Flax screamed in terror and dropped it.

"It jumped!" she cried, then gasped as the pistol slid swiftly along the floor and crashed up against the wall.

"What the devil—?" Max said, white-faced.

"That's what I'm trying to tell you, *fathead!*" I snapped. "That whole mountain range back there is *magnetic,* and if you or we ever want to see Radnor or Earth again, you'd better run like hell outside and peg down that *Flicker!*"

All quarrels momentarily forgotten, Max, Binky, Fraser the pilot and myself all dashed outside to save the ship. Where it had been was a shallow trench in the copper-sand. I turned my eyes to follow this smooth-walled gouge, made by the dragging belly of the Flicker, toward the side of the mountain.

And *there* was the Flicker! I looked a little to the left. And *there* was the Flicker! And there, and there, and there... I turned to Max, bitterly.

"How are you at jigsaw puzzles?" I muttered.

CHAPTER TEN

WE FILED back inside the shack, silently. Lora and Flax were watching us, their faces anxious.

"Our ticket to Radnor is now umpteen billion chunks on the cliff wall," I said, plopping down to a tired squat beside Lora's chair. "I'm open to suggestions."

Lora laid her hand on my shoulder, and let it linger there. Flax caught the gesture, and her already-green eyes glowed greener than a Crispin campfire.

"Maybe," she smiled sweetly at Lora, "my hospitality will wear thin."

"And maybe," I grunted, reaching up and replacing Lora's hand, which had risen an inch from my shoulder, "my patience will do the same."

"We still have the pistols," said Flax, sullenly.

"Oh, dry up," I said. "You can unhitch your corset and drop the *femme fatale* impersonations. This is serious stuff, you know. If someone doesn't come by looking for us, we're cooked—" I remembered the blistering heat outside. "Sorry."

"But," Max said, licking his lips and sinking down onto a lightweight plastic bench, "we can't just *sit* here…"

"We can *pace,*" Binky offered, with a wan smile.

"Could— Could I have a little of that water again?" Lora asked, in the ensuing silence. She knew it was a touchy request.

I looked up at Fraser, Max's pilot. "Can she?" I said.

He looked at Flax. She shrugged and turned away. Fraser came over and uncapped the canteen once more, holding it while Lora drank.

"Hey—" said Max, suddenly. "That's not the only canteen, is it?"

We all stared at Fraser. He swallowed, carefully, then blinked his eyes and said, "There was one more of 'm but it was in th' Flicker…"

"Don't worry," I said, seeing the anxious panic flash across Max's face. "There's a whole cataract of water about a two-mile hike down the cliff-face. Of course, it may be poisonous, but we can always distill it."

"But isn't that a long and tedious process?" he demanded.

"What's our hurry?" I shrugged. "We have nothing *but* time. I don't suppose one of you jokers brought a ham sandwich to this galactic picnic?"

Everybody looked at Fraser again. He flushed scarlet.

"There were some rations, but they was in the—"

"Flicker," Max nodded, miserably.

We sat a moment longer, then I said, "Say, tell me, Max, how did you three get a Flicker to *work* up on Crispin, anyhow? And how'd you meet up with Flax, who was last seen sneaking off into the woods with stolen property? And what took you so long to get here, with transportation like that?"

"Anything *else?*" Max said, with cold civility.

"Sure. How'd Fraser here ever get a pilot's license?"

"It was easy!" said Fraser, happily. "I got a perfect mechanical appetite. That means I can figure anything long as its s'posed t' *do* something! And I got a natural sense of good balance, and I got automatic response to vehicle stress, and I got perfect coordinature."

"And you went out to join the Space Force?" I marveled.

He stared, then grinned. "Oh, yeah," he said, snapping his fingers happily. "And I got drafted."

"That, solves that," I said, then turned to Max. "So how about you?"

Max sighed and gave in.

"Okay, we may as well trade stories as anything. It was simple enough. As soon as we got near Crispin, Fraser felt the force of the magnetic field affecting the Flicker. Don't ask me how: He's got extrasensory fingertips, or something. So he turned off the drive, and glided us in."

"Without," Flax said bitterly, "radioing the information to our ship, which dived blithely downward until the engine melted! Just like that!"

"Fraser couldn't think of *everything*, Flax," said her lawyer. "As far as I was concerned, his instantaneous action was commendable." He turned back to me. "But to continue— We landed with no damage, but he told me that he'd have to fix the engine to function on this planet. He couldn't tell me what was wrong, in scientific terms, but he *did* say that— What was it you said, Fraser?"

Fraser beamed, glad to be the center of attention.

"I said that the stuff what went round in the wires to give the push to the stuff in the fuel tank was getting bollixed by some other stuff on this place here that was pushing it the wrong way, so I had to pull a couple of wires and rig the Flicker to work without no power going into the wires except what it got anyhow from the planet, see?"

"That's what he said, all right," Max smiled.

"You mean he fixed the Flicker to work *from* the magnetic forces on Crispin instead of being burnt up by working *against* them!" I said. I caught Lora's admiring glance and flushed.

"Why, Morgan," she said softly, "you're learning!"

I grinned at her. "If *Fraser* can learn electronics, I'm going to have to learn it, too, or never hold my head up in public again."

"Aw, I didn't learn it. I got a gift," Fraser said.

"Yeah," said Flax. "One brain, minus instructions."

Fraser gave her a hurt look.

"So go on, Max," I said. "He fixed it. Then what? Why didn't you come here?"

"Because by then Fraser thought to radio to Flax's ship, to see if they'd made it. When they didn't answer, he got worried, so we took the Flicker up and started looking for wreckage. We found it, and landed, but there was no sign of either of them. Well, we couldn't just *leave*, after all, not without knowing."

"Why, Max," I said, with real surprise, "I never would have thought it of you."

"Don't pin a medal on him, yet, Morgan," said Flax, her words like razor-edged glass. "After all, how would it look if a lawyer handles an inheritance for a woman, gets her to sign him a power of attorney over her fortune, and then, in the course of taking her to examine her property, comes back without her...?"

"Oh—" I said. Max studiously avoided meeting Flax's eyes, and she never let off boring with them at the back of his perspiring neck.

"S-So," he went on, trying to discount her statement by ignoring it, "we took a look around. We found Ansel's parachute next. He'd been—uh—"

"If Ansel is Flax's pilot, skip this part. I not only found the parachute, I was there just after he'd been dragged, out of it. Go ahead from there, Max. We're right with you."

"By then, Fraser was getting tired, so we landed, and got some sleep. Meantime, Flax, who was somewhere in that woods, had seen us flying overhead. She moved off in the direction we'd taken past her point of view, hoping to get to an open area where she might signal if we came down again, and—"

"And I damned near broke my shin over a wing of their Flicker in the dark!" said Flax. "And do you know that those guys didn't want to *take* me?"

"Not take you?" I said. "Then why *find* you?"

"Not that *trip,* that's all," said Max, brushing a drop of sweat from his forehead. "The Flickers are only supposed to seat two people, you know. It might have been dangerous traveling with three. My intention was to have Fraser fly me here, then go back for her, and—"

"Ha!" said Flax.

"We were going to leave her food, and weapons, of course," Max smiled placatingly at her. It didn't work.

"Sure you were," she spat. "And in the meantime, you'd scoot around the shack here, while Old Fuzzbrain was winging back for me, and you'd make the wonderful discovery that it was *your* old grandfather that founded the Crispin Copper Mines!" She turned a baleful gaze from him to me. "Do you know that this crummy—"

"Ah-ah!" I said. "Don't forget: Fraser's here."

Her lips worked violently, but she shifted into a more genteel gear and went on, "This louse didn't even want me to leave *Earth* with him! Wouldn't let me see my own mine!"

"Whose mine!?" Lora exploded, but I grabbed her wrist just short of a tigerish spring at Flax.

"Easy," I said. "Let her tell it with her plot and motivations. We can always edit the final script."

"With parched, sunburnt fingers," Binky sighed. "Damn it, Mr. Blane, I'm so dry inside I could get relief licking a roll of dental floss!"

"If you have an extra, I'll join you," I said. Then I got to my feet. "Binky's right. Before we tell any more war stories about Crispin, we'd better go out and get some of that water before our corpuscles have to turn edgewise and *roll* through our veins."

"Well, who should go?" Max asked, looking around.

We stared at one another. I wasn't about to take off and leave Max to destroy any evidence he may have missed... Max wouldn't leave me alone to find it. For reasons of employment, Fraser and Binky couldn't be left, either of them, nor, for reasons of financial situations, could Lora and Flax. Of course, we could leave one person from one team, and one from an-other... But I didn't trust Flax and Lora not to scrap, and Lora wasn't exactly in top shape... Fraser could, in a pinch, destroy Binky with one hand. And if Max and I stayed, I couldn't guarantee peace, either. Besides which, our staying would have the end result of either having the women and our pilots carry-ing enough water for six people, which wasn't fair to the women, or if Max and I kept the women with us, then we'd have the same fight-problem between Binky and Fraser out at the cataract...

My head started to spin, so I gave it up. "Maybe," I said softly, "we had *all* better go."

"Morgan," Lora said softly, "we may as well sit here."

"Why?" I asked, looking down at her, her face bloodless be-neath the pink splotches of sunburn.

"Because," she smiled sadly, "we don't have anything to carry the water back in..."

"The canteen—" Max blurted, then stopped, recalling that the cataract fell down the side of the damnably magnetic mountain. It'd get to the cataract before *we* did, and it wouldn't be coming back.

"Old man Merrick must've had *something* to carry water in!" I argued. "He couldn't just sit here and desiccate!"

"He had something," said Flax, with a scornful smile at her lawyer. "A nice one-gallon earthenware jug."

"Swell," I said. "Where's it at?"

She jerked a thumb at the floor. I looked. Amongst the splinters of the signboard Fraser had been chopping when we'd entered, I detected shards of pottery.

"*Why*, Max!" I groaned. "For Pete's sake, why?"

"It—" he murmured, much subdued, "it had his name painted on the side…"

"Then you *admit* this place is Lora's!" I yelled in triumph.

Max stepped back, startled. "I didn't—I mean—I didn't mean to imply that it was *her* grandfather's name…"

"Whose else's? Flax's? Yours'! And if so, why the carnage?"

Max sat down, angry, now. "You'll never prove it in court. You have three witnesses, I have three witnesses."

"Don't count too hard on *me*, honey," said Flax.

"You're just as involved as I am—" he said furiously.

"Let's not forget one thing, huh?" Binky interrupted groaningly. "If we don't get some water, we never even *get* to court!"

"He's right," said Lora. "Maybe— Maybe the only thing for us to do is to all go over to the cataract and drink, as much as we can hold."

"Then sweat it out hiking back," Flax muttered. "And if we get thirsty in the middle of the night, we can slip into our bunny-fur sandals and skip two miles to the waterfall! No, thank you."

"*I* know!" said Fraser, startling all of us. "How come we don't just go to the water and *stay* there?"

"Out of the mouths of boobs," said Flax. "Why don't we?"

After a few seconds' thought, and feeling very foolish, I admitted I didn't know any reason why not. We all began gathering our gear together for the trip. Lora, however, was worried.

"Morgan," she said, leaning close to me and whispering, as I made a pack out of my blanket with some cords I'd found, "there's just one thing: Why didn't my *grandfather* put this shack nearer the cataract? It would have been tough on *him* being this far, wouldn't it? It doesn't make sense."

I paused, thinking. "Maybe the noise bothered him? Those cataracts don't *tiptoe* down cliffsides, you know…"

"Perhaps you're right," she said, the frown leaving her face. "Maybe he just couldn't sleep nights."

She turned away just before her worried frown reappeared, this time on *my* face. Why *hadn't* old Merrick camped nearer? However, I was too thirsty by then to think it out. Whatever the reason was, if Merrick had found it out and survived, then we should be able to.

It was only when we were all halfway to the cataract that I remembered one tiny detail: Old Merrick *hadn't* survived…

CHAPTER ELEVEN

SAY, what if the water's poisonous?" Max asked, as we got nearer to the thundering column of falling water. "We can't bring distilling apparatus out here: The mountain'll snatch it up!"

"If it's poisonous, we may as well go ahead and drink it," Flax murmured. "It'll be quicker than death by thirst."

"Hey, I don't wanna drink no poison!" Fraser complained.

"Why not?" Flax said with a shrug. "Socrates did."

"But he had brains," I pointed out.

"Ain't *I* got brains?" Fraser said, looking unhappy.

"You've got something better," I said. *"Sense!"*

"Oh, I don't know," said Flax. "After all, if he had any sense, he—"

"Wouldn't have come to Crispin, yeah," I finished for her. "Where does that leave you?"

"Last in line at the waterhole," she said. "I hope."

"Hey, lady!" Fraser said, dodging suddenly away from Lora, who was being helped along by Binky and me, "watch the points on that crutch. You want I should break 'em off shorter for you, maybe?" he said helpfully.

"No, thanks," said Lora, quickly. "This is just fine."

Fraser shrugged, and joined the trudge waterward.

The "crutch," of course, was the spear-gadget we'd brought with us all the way from that village. Binky and I had thought it best to have some kind of weapon handy, in case any more trouble arose. Max's bunch had naturally left the pistols and canteens safely behind at the shack, away from the pull of Mount X, as I'd come to think of it. I wasn't about to demonstrate the fact that we were armed, not to Max Barton, not yet. But Earth-deserts, barren by day, have an uncomfortable way of coming to life at night. We might meet only the Crispin equivalent of rabbits and prairie dogs. But then again, I didn't relish stumbling over a Crispin rattlesnake, horned viper, gila monster, or tarantula...

The pool at the base of the falls was finally reached, and we all paused on the brink, eyeing one another. Who would be the lucky person to get the first swig?

"Why don't we do it by the numbers?" Binky suggested. "You know: We all get on hands and knees by the water, and do a one-for-the-money, two-for-the-show—"

"And everybody chickens out on *Four,*" Flax said.

"Whatever may be in it," Lora said, "it can't be as poisonous as all that! I'll just take a sip, and if it's bad-tasting, I'll spit it out."

"And if it's cyanide?" said Flax. "That works awfully fast, you know."

"Cyanide's not a copper compound—" Lora said.

"*Must* the poison be copperish?" Flax asked, calmly.

"She's got a point, there, Lora," I said. "We'd better be careful..."

"Damn it to hell!" Flax groused, sitting down on the ground, which was black rock, like the mountain, "I can just see us all found here, years from now: Six mummies frozen in a position of violent discussion!"

"Or six skeletons, in the throes of cupric poisoning," I added.

"Okay," said Flax. "So one of us drinks, and the other five watch him for ill effects…"

"And why a '*him*'?" Max inquired politely. "I'd always heard it said: Ladies first."

"To hell with all of you," said Binky, and with that, he dropped down to the brink, plunged his face into the water, and began drinking. I watched the rhythmic movements of his windpipe, as the liquid was swallowed gulp by gulp, and waited to see if he suddenly went prone. Or into convulsions.

Neither happened. After a minute's guzzling, Binky lifted his face from the water, dripping wet, and rolled over on the bank with a contented sigh.

"How is it?" I asked.

"It's cold, and it's wet, and if it's poison, I can't taste it," he said.

The next minute or so resembled a Roman Orgy, except that the liquid imbibed was hardly the kind to get even the strictest teetotaler upset. For a long time afterwards, we all just lay on our backs on the bare black rock, and gave satisfied groans as our systems attempted to shuttle the liquid from our alimentary canals to slightly withered cells elsewhere in our bodies.

The desert before us, with its billion facets of pure orange-yellow metal, picked up and amplified the starlight from the black sky, and turned itself into a shimmering sea of pale golden light. It was like watching a marsh mist that had a slight case of jaundice. And then, in the distance, I saw the first moving shape…

"Hold it, folks," I whispered, sitting up. "We have company!"

The group bobbed up around me, and looked where I was looking. Great black shapes were gliding smoothly toward us.

"Mr. Blane—" said Binky, his voice low and nervous. "I just thought: This is probably a waterhole for the animals in this desert!"

"Stop reading my mind," I said. "Come on, people, let's get out of here, fast. I don't know what those things are, but the smallest ones are bigger than Fraser, and that's enough for me."

We all scrambled to our feet. I grabbed Lora, and Binky grabbed up the "crutch." I put a hand on his arm.

"Not unless we *have* to!" I cautioned him. "Hey, where's the insulation?"

He mumbled something vaguely vile, and said, "The henna job copped it for a washcloth, to take the travel-stains off her face. I couldn't think of an excuse why not."

"Damn!" I said. Then, "Look, better let *me* take it, then, Bink. I've *already* lost my shirt."

"Morgan," Lora said urgently, "you *can't!* If we're on the desert when you use it, the copper under your feet will act as a conductor, and boost the current!"

"In that case," I said, noting the departing backs of Max's group, "let's just follow their example and run like hell!"

We took off swiftly, trotting at the heels of Max, his pilot, and his redheaded insubordinate, in the direction of the shack. I glanced back and saw that the dark shapes were growing more numerous, lumbering silently across the metallic "sand" toward the waterhole.

"Small wonder the shack's way to hell and gone, Lora," I said, keeping a good hold on her arm as we ran. "Your grandfather was averse to getting stepped on in his sleep!"

"But what *are* those things?" Lora asked, frightened.

"Hard to say, in this kind of light," I panted, as we hurried through the darkness, "but whatever they are, they're big, they're fast, and there are hundreds of them. Let's not stand around to check whether or not they're friendly."

"Wait a minute—" Binky gasped, grasping my arm. "The blankets, Mr. Blane! I don't know what I was thinking of, but we can use them!"

"Oh, damn!" I said, stopping and jerking my rolled pack of blanket-and-cord off my shoulders. "Of course! Here, wrap this around the haft of that thing, Bink!"

He took the blanket, still folded, and twisted it about the end of the spear-gadget, holding it tightly with both hands. "Now we should be a match for these things," he said.

Suddenly, up ahead of us in the dark, Flax screamed. Then the other trio came rushing back to us, frantic.

"More of them, coming from in front of us!" Max cried. "We're trapped between two herds…"

I looked beyond him. Sure enough, a tide of shuffling black forms was rolling toward us over the starlit desert floor, silent, ponderous and ominous…

"Too many, Bink!" I said, as he started to lower the flexible tips of the spear-gadget to the horizontal. "Come on, everybody, straight in toward the mountain wall. We can climb up out of range."

We turned at right angles to our previous path and rushed toward the silent black bulk of the mountain, as the shadowherd drew nearer and nearer.

"What if they can climb, too?" Max shouted as we ran.

"Then *we* climb *faster!*" I yelled back. "Hurry, damn it!"

We stumbled from the metallic sands onto the sharp-edged surface of the lower mountain slopes, and rushed blindly forward into the shadows. My feet, bereft of even my socks, now, were lanced with shooting stabs of pain as they sprang over that jagged black rocky surface. Binky and I each had one of Lora's arms, half-carrying her so that her feet barely touched the ground at all.

We were downwind of the cataract, now, and some of the cold wet spray was collected into shallow puddles on the stone beneath our hurrying feet, making our haste somewhat treacherous. I was just about to shout a word of caution to the others when my own feet splashed into a collection of these puddles, and I skidded and fell, inadvertently dragging Lora with me. Binky, with Lora torn free of his grasp, stumbled onward a few steps, then went down heavily to the rocks, his hands still clutching the blanket-insulated haft of that spear-gadget, which began to whir at the double-tipped end from the shock of his fall...

Then a wiggling, writhing, pencil-thick spark leaped the gap between those vibrating tips, and an eye-searing white thunderbolt zigzagged at a wild angle into the air of the black desert night and blasted a towering shard of Mount X into enormous boulders.

Boulders which instantly were whirled off into the night by their reversed polarity, toward wherever the northeast angle of the range lay.

"What happened? What was that?" Flax cried out from ahead of us. But I was watching the north horizon, waiting for the results of that accidental rushing of the horizontal-avalanche season... Then I saw the white sparks in the distance as those boulders struck home. Would the impact dislodge more rock from over there? ...An ominous buzzing came through the air, and I had my answer. The return-flight of rocks crashed deafeningly into the mountain wall nearly overhead, and a shower of electrical radiance cascaded down at us as another batch of boulders was knocked loose, re-polarized, and sent flying. It was some holocaust and we were right in the center.

Within minutes, utter electric chaos was broken loose in the hitherto calm desert night. Slower-moving bulks of rock were met by already-returning masses of magnetic stone in mid-air, and shattered into sparkling fragments of death-dealing speed and power. Out on the sands, the black herds were milling about in terror, giving loud roaring cries of confusion, and moving at a fast gallop over the shifting copper sands, striking one another head-on, caroming off broad sides, falling down with hideous squealing noises. And then a bunch of them, falling into a panicky formation, started coming our way, fast, looking, under the intermittent flashes of energy that now lit the sky, like escapees from a madman's nightmare. I caught a glimpse of flat, dull-eyed faces, long limp mouths swaying ponderously from underslung jaws, and high, spiral horns on the broad bony foreheads...

"Binky!" I yelled. "Behind us— The herd!"

He got groggily to his feet, and turned toward the onrushing menace, trying to level the weapon again. Then I saw that he'd let the blanket fall away, and was going to use the thing while standing barefoot in a puddle, yet!

"No!" I yelled, springing to my feet and launching myself at him in an urgent dive that struck the shaft from his hands before I plunged face-first onto the hard black rock.

The next flash I saw was mine alone to view, as my head smacked upon the side of a boulder, and consciousness exploded into silent blackness...

CHAPTER TWELVE

FIRST there was warmth, and then the feeling of something soft beneath me, and then my eyes snapped open and I was staring at the interlocked plastic ceiling of the shack. I blinked my eyes, and felt a painful tug somewhere on my right temple. Carefully, I brought my fingers to the spot and touched lightly.

"It's a lump," said a voice. "Egg-shaped, purple and slightly softer than your thick skull."

I raised my head with an effort and saw Flax Dempster sitting on that plastic bench near the foot of the cot where I lay. Hot yellow sunlight was streaming remorselessly in through the faded glassine window and tiny chinks in the walls, where the prefabricated parts had been warped apart. Flax's green eyes were bright, but her face was drawn with tension.

"What happened?" I said, trying to sit up.

Flax came over and sat on the edge of the cot, pushing me back into place, gently. "You brained yourself slightly, that's all. But that lightning-stick thing landed butt-first in a cleft of rock and threw a bolt that turned the whole damned herd around again. Most of them galloped over the horizon and got away."

"Most of them?" I frowned, squinting in the brightness.

"Light bother you? Here—" Flax tugged a loose piece of canvas that served as a curtain over the glassine, and the room's golden glow abated somewhat. "Some of them had fractured their skulls from running into one another. They were still there this morning, so Fraser and Binky rigged up a spit and roasted some of the meat. Then Madame Curie suggested making water bags out of the skins, or something, and lugging fresh drink back here to us. Want some?"

She lifted the metal canteen with an effort, and I heard a wonderful sloshing inside it. She didn't wait for my answer, just twisted off the cap and held it to my lips with one hand, the other supporting my head. I swallowed the cold liquid gladly, then wiped my lips with the back of my wrist as she replaced the cap.

"Isn't that hard to handle, in the magnetic field?" I asked, as she set the canteen back into a small pocket of wall, where it couldn't be dragged across the floor as the gun had been the evening before.

"I do you a favor, maybe you'll do me one," she said, with a brief wink of one eye.

"I don't have my checkbook with me—" I started, then bit the words off before finishing, as a sudden taut whiteness appeared beneath her eyes. "Sorry," I said contritely, "that was uncalled for."

"Yes, it was," she said, and turned away her face, though she remained seated on my bedside.

"Say," I went on, hoping a subject-change might relieve the boo feeling that had sprung up between us, "where are the others?"

"Listen," said Flax, grinning wryly, and tilting her head toward the Mount X side of the shack. I attuned my ears in that direction and did as bidden.

Faintly, I caught a sound of heavy thuds, and shouts, some of them shouts of laughter. "What gives?" I said, "It sounds like Jones Beach in July."

"They're playing Blast-the-Flicker, with that lightning-stick," Flax drawled, with a weary head shake.

"What! But why?" I demanded. "This is no time for childish games—"

"Oh, it's not a game," Flax said, anticipating my statement. "Fraser, with his high mechanical 'appetite', thinks he might be able to fix it to fly solo, by itself, to Radnor, with a Send Help message scratched on the chassis, or whatever. So then Lora Merrick said—" Flax widened her eyes in a devastatingly accurate mimicry of Lora's usual I've-*got*-it! expression, clapped her hands together, and went on, "'*Say,* folks! If *we* can *blast* the *Flicker*-parts, then *they'll* reverse po-*lar*-ity and fly *loose,* and *then*—'"

"Hold it," I said, chuckling despite myself. "She doesn't really sing-song like that, Flax!"

"Well, she comes close enough to it to turn my tummy, slightly," Flax said, shaking her head. "Anyhow, they're out there, now, indulging in an electronic skeet shoot. They electrify a Flicker-chunk, then when it flies off the wall toward the other range, they blast it down in mid-air, and all dive on it before it can skid along the ground back to the wall it just left. More fun than ducking for apples!"

Outside, I heard a crackling boom, then a shrill squeal of male and female laughter, another boom, then the sounds of frantic running about and general horseplay.

"Sounds jolly," I admitted. "But you shouldn't pick on Lora, Flax. Didn't she tell you we were engaged?"

"No, but I suspected something of the sort," Flax said, moodily. "Chalk up another conquest for cowlike eyes!"

"Aw, come on, don't be like that," I said.

"Why not?" Flax spun to face me. "Honestly, Morgan, I don't know what you see in her. All she knows is electronics, and all you know is the New York theater. I can just see you two on an opening night. You'll be trying to watch the performance, and she'll be putting a bee in your ear about the ingenuity of the inventor of the revolving stage..."

"Aw, layoff, will you," I said softly. "Why, I've never felt this way about anyone before. This is the real thing, Flax."

"How do you know?" she said, staring into my eyes in a very disconcerting manner. "That session we had in the treetops wasn't exactly a dud."

"Listen, then—" I said, and started telling her about Lora. How anxious I'd been when we'd been originally separated, how I'd risked my life investigating that fangface prison to find her, how worried I'd felt when she was so weak on the down-journey toward the shack— "Didn't you ever feel like that, Flax?" I said, finishing. "What else is it but love?"

"It's manhood, stupid," said Flax, bitterly, folding her arms. "The urge to protect the helpless. Yes, I've felt it, too, that feeling, Morgan. I used to have a kitten. It was constantly falling down behind the stove, tripping over its own whiskers, and lolling around with sick eyes when it had a bad piece of salmon for dinner— And I went out of my way to take care of it, but I hardly felt obliged to *propose!*"

"You're jealous, aren't you!" I remarked.

"Why shouldn't I be?" she said angrily. "Damn it, Morgan, *I* like you, too. And here you are, going head-over-heels about a little ball of fluff with a transistor for a heart!"

"Now, now," I said, soothingly. "You feel this way at the moment, because I'm young, and available, and—"

"Don't flatter yourself, Morgan Blane," said Flax. "At the *moment,* you have a three-day scraggly growth of black prickles on your face, a sunburnt nose, and you smell like you've been wallowing in sheepdip!"

I remembered my goatskin jacket with chagrin. "I meant to take a shower," I said. Then, "Well, if it's not my looks, it must he my money."

"What money?" Flax snapped. "What good is your damned checkbook in this desert?"

"We might get back…" I said slowly.

"Okay!" she raged, standing up and glaring at me, her hands balled into fists, and arms ramrods at her sides. "So when we get back, *then* you accuse me of mercenary motives, not before!" Crystal tears suddenly sparkled in those bright green eyes. "In the meantime, shut up, you louse!"

"Hey, Flax..." I said, concerned. "I didn't mean to—" My hand reached out and took hold of hers. She was trembling, violently, and breathing fast, through flaring nostrils...

Then she dropped down again upon the bed, sitting and looking into my eyes. A queer tingling sensation began at the back of my neck as I looked into those eyes—

"Flax..." I said hoarsely. "What—?"

Her hands, cool and firm, slipped down at either side of my throat, as if she would strangle me. Then they slid back of my neck, and her lips were suddenly pressing on mine, with a fierce warmth that startled me. My arms, of their own volition, came up around her and pulled her tightly to me.

That kiss scared me. I was shaking when she pulled her lips away from mine and buried her face against the pillow behind my head, her cheek hot against my own, and her flaming hair like golden silk across my face. I held onto her, not knowing quite what to do. It had been such a *hungry* kiss, with such inexpressible yearning in it.

Like an idiot, I kept stroking her back with one hand and murmuring, "Easy, easy," over and over into her ear.

"Hold me, Morgan," she sobbed, "hold me."

What the hell. I held her. After a moment, I couldn't bear much more propinquity. I was hotter than the desert climate could account for.

"Is—Is this just a way of ensuring leniency, or something, when we get back?" I said. I couldn't think straight.

Flax lifted her head and stared into my eyes. "Is that what you really think, Morgan?" Her voice was suddenly very tired. I couldn't meet her gaze.

"I don't know what to think anymore," I grunted, uneasily.

"Well," she said, sitting up and pushing back her hair, "that's progress of sorts, anyhow."

I took hold of her hand, and kept hold of it, not saying anything. She watched me, curiously, then said, "You have the oddest expression. What are you thinking?"

I grinned. "I was just realizing what I like about you, Flax… You're—You're *resilient.*"

"Why, Mis-ter Blane!" she said, with feigned shock, and a very prudent straightening of the front of her blouse collar.

"Not *that way!*" I laughed. "I mean your personality. Do you know I've never seen anyone bounce back as nicely as you do. I've done nothing but be nasty to you—"

"Agreed," said Flax without hesitation.

"Even at our first meeting, I implied something or other about you…"

"You implied that I was no stranger to harsh expletive. Well, it's true. I don't *use* such bad language, but I doubt if there's any word you could employ that I wouldn't be able to recognize. No harm in that, is there?"

"No, none," I admitted. "But you're kind of courageous, too. It took nerve to run off into the jungle like you did, when you left me that time. Even with those guns."

"Want to know a secret?" she said, abruptly.

I nodded, interested.

"I wasn't running off because of what you'd said about having me arrested. I took off because I didn't trust myself alone with you any longer: You bring out the beast in me."

I laughed. "You don't exactly blunt my fangs, either."

"Too bad," said Flax, staring with a secret smile at the ceiling, "that you're so mad about Lora Merrick…"

I realized with a start that I'd quite forgotten Lora for the moment. "…Oh, yeah," I whispered. "Lora."

"Your fiancée, remember?" Flax goaded me.

I lay back and looked at her, quite beautiful in the just-bright-enough diffused sunlight of that single room. "You're a very intriguing person, Flax," I said. "Tell me, how did you get into this setup, anyhow?"

"The way I told you. Or, rather, the way you guessed. Max Barton offered me a billion dollars. I didn't say no. Would you have?"

"It wasn't honest," I evaded.

"Answer the question," Flax prodded.

"Well—" I said. "I can't say. After all, I'm rich enough already…"

"Nice, the way you skirt the issue," said Flax. "What if you were me, Morgan, and you got a chance like Barton offered. Could you simply say you wouldn't?"

"Maybe not," I admitted. "How about your real grandfather? Still alive?"

She shook her head. "Died in the Second World War."

"So there's no chance that Max had you fooled about this so-called inheritance?" I said.

"What are you doing," she said suddenly, "trying to find excuses for me? Can't you like me unless I'm perfect, Morgan?"

"What are you talking about?" I said guiltily, quite aware what she meant.

"That you, in your holier-than-thou way, are on the brink of taking a shine to me," she said wearily. "Only I have to meet the Blane Standard, don't I? If you can convince yourself that I was Max's dupe, fine. You are just dying for me to lie and say I've been the innocent victim of this shyster lawyer. And the part that kills me is that you'll *know* it's not *true!* But some fussy little part of your ego wants to hear me *say* it, anyway."

I sat up on the cot. "Now, Flax, I didn't—"

"Lie down!" she said. I did. "Well, Morgan, I'm *not* going to lie just to make things easy on your stilted conscience! The truth is that Max asked me to do something crooked, I knew it was crooked, and I said, *'Swell! When do we start?'*"

I said, "Oh," very softly, then lay there, silent.

"So if you ever get over this infantile crush you have for that fluffy feline physicist and want me instead, you take me as I am, or not at all. I'm a *crook*, Morgan… Morgan, did you hear me? I'm involved in attempted larceny, of my own free will."

"Are—Are you sorry?" I said, hopefully.

"Not in the least," said Flax. "I won't even give you *that* satisfaction."

"What satisfaction?" I demanded.

"Charity. Reclaiming the poor misguided girl. Taking her from her evil path toward crime and— Nope, you take me, crookedness and all, and maybe I'll repent later. But I won't even guarantee it."

"You stinker," I said, softly.

"Look who's talking," she laughed. "B.O. Blane!"

"Come here," I said, and grabbed her, pulling her down to me again. Her lips were still hungry against mine, but a lot of the desperation was gone from her attitude. She laid her cheek against mine once more, and whispered gently, "I hope that damned Flicker's in at least a million pieces..."

Then I realized that I hadn't been hearing that blasting noise for some time. I looked toward the door, which was partway open, and saw shadows approaching over the copper-sand surface.

"Whoops!" I said, sitting up. "Take ten, Flax."

She broke away and stared at me, oddly. "Why the long guilty face, Morgan? Aren't you a free agent?"

"I don't want to startle her, is all," I said. "I'd rather explain it to her than have her just bust in and get the wrong impression—"

"The wrong impression?" said Flax, with an arch of one trim eyebrow.

"All right, all right," I muttered. "The *right* impression, then. Better?"

"Much."

The foursome came in the door, all of them carrying bits and pieces of electronic parts, fighting the tug of the mountain. They looked over at us, then stacked the junk against the wall, where it stacked easily enough due to the pull from the mountain out beyond it.

Lora, even more sunburnt, but nowhere near as weak-looking as the night before, stared at me, a funny look on her face.

I wondered for a frantic instant if it were lipstick-smears again, then remembered that Flax hadn't been wearing any, and relaxed a bit.

"How— How's your head, Morgan?" Lora asked.

"Purple," I said, "but relatively painless."

"That's good," she said. "Do you want some meat? We cooked up some of the flesh of those buffalo, or whatever they were. It's not bad…"

"It tastes like an old innersole boiled in butter," said Binky, "But it hasn't poisoned any of us."

The conversation seemed normal enough, but there was a tremor of high tension in that room. I looked at the group, closely. Max seemed as usual, a little nettled and nervous, but Binky, Fraser and Lora seemed uncomfortable.

"Lora…" I said. "What's the matter?"

She faltered a smile, which faded instantly, then took a hesitant step toward me, and said, "Morgan, I—"

The air outside was suddenly split by a piercing roar of sound, a roar that grew louder and louder, from a high-pitched screech to a thunderous boom. I vaulted out of the cot and stumbled to the doorway beside Flax, the others already having dashed outside to see the cause of the disturbance. My mind was alive with unnerving images of magnetic avalanches, stampeding herds, flying thunderbolts, or even charging fangfaces. But it was none of these.

Settling with ponderous grace down into a whirling cloud of blast-disturbed copper sand, I beheld the stately gray needle of a Space Force Battleship, its wide tail vanes extending flat-bottomed hydraulic rods to cushion the shock of landing. As it came to rest, and the dazzling copper cloud began to settle back to the desert floor, from the side opposite Mount X long metal darts sprang out, diving into the shifting sands and pulling a network of long cables taut against the tug of the magnetic mountainside.

"I'll be damned," I said to Flax. "They must have been here before!"

We raced out to the ship, and stood waiting with the others as the circular airlock swung open, and a pair of uniformed men descended to the ground in a most efficient manner.

As the men, officers, reached us, Fraser came smartly to attention and saluted. They returned the salute, then the older one, a captain, said, "At ease," and looked over the rest of us. "Which of you," he said, "is Maximilian Barton?"

Max, his eyes bugging with surprise, said, "*I* am, Captain..."

The officer nodded, bleakly. "I have a warrant for your arrest."

"*What?!*" Max bleated. "What for?"

"It says for fraud," the captain explained. "The authorities back on Earth thought we'd find you here. Seems you registered a claim on a copper mine belonging to someone else, Mr. Barton."

"But they— How could they— It's not true!" he said.

"The Government Assayer's office says different," said the captain, unsmilingly. "Just after your claim came in and was registered, they got a pre-dated claim to the identical spot, made out by one Ira Merrick."

"Grandfather!" Lora exclaimed. "He sent a duplicate copy to the claims office!"

"Well—it's—it's a coincidence, that's all!" Max blustered. "Apparently, two people discovered the same strike of copper, and—"

"And drew up exactly the same map?" said the captain. "Your map is a duplicate of his, drawn on the same type of paper, penned by the same hand. *His.*"

"Then she *lied!*" Max said, desperately, spinning and pointing a finger at Flax. "She came to me with that map and said that it was *her* grandfather who had discovered it—"

The captain turned to Flax, his eyes narrowed with suspicion. "Is that true, Miss?" he said.

Flax's eyes locked on mine, helplessly.

"Of course not!" I blurted.

"Who the hell are you?" the captain said to me, in a curt voice.

"Tell him, Lora!" I said, passing the buck.

"He's the man who brought me up here to save the mine, that's all!" she said, with a stubborn jut of her jaw at the captain. "His name is Morgan Blane, and he's got millions of dollars!"

"Well, la-de-da!" said the captain, unimpressed. "But— Are you vouching for this woman, Mr. Blane?"

I looked at Flax, then at Lora, then back at the captain. "S-Sure!" I said. "She— She was working for *me*, all along!"

"He's crazy!" Max shouted. "She was not!"

"How do you know?" said the captain.

"Because she was working for *me*—" Max blurted, then stopped, aghast.

"I think you'd better come along, Mr. Barton," said the captain. He turned to Flax, "And you, too, Miss."

"Why?" I said. "You haven't got a warrant for her, have you?"

"Well, no," said the captain, "but I thought—"

"You're just the arresting officer, remember," I cautioned him. "It's not your place to pass judgment. If the courts want her, they'll have to send her a subpoena."

"He's lying!" Max shouted. "He's in love with her!"

"Is that true?" said the officer.

"*Yes!*" I snapped, avoiding Lora's eyes. "And that *proves* she's innocent! Would a guy with a few million bucks go around falling in love with *crooks?*"

"Morgan!" came a cry from Lora. I looked over at her, bracing myself for the pain, the shock on her face. When my gaze reached her face, I had to blink and look twice. I could see nothing but relief and elation.

"You're not mad?" I said.

"No!" she cried, happily.

"That's what I was going to tell you, back in the shack, Morgan. I—I'm in love with someone else!"

"Who, for Pete's sake?" I exclaimed.

"With the most beautiful electronic mind I've met in the entire universe!" she sighed, turning and taking her newfound love by the hand.

"Fraser?!" I gasped.

"Yes," she said, "isn't it wonderful?"

"It's— It's *perfect!"* I laughed, staring stupidly from her to Flax, who seemed as happily stupefied as I was.

"Okay, okay," said the captain. "Break it up. What I want to know is: Who's coming with me?"

"All of us!" I said. "And the sooner, the better."

The captain just stared.

"It was nice of Lora to drop the charges against me," Flax murmured, snuggling close to me. We were in subspace, riding Earthward in a military vessel that had been taking some rotating troops home from duty.

"I had to twist her arm, slightly," I grinned. "Not in the physical sense, of course. I wouldn't dare, not with that behemoth she's affianced to standing by. I just told her I'd sue her for the price of the Brunhilde if she didn't layoff."

"She has a fortune," Flax said, with a frown. "Why should that stop her?"

"She intends to save every penny of it," I said. "That's why she stopped."

"Would you tell me something, Morgan?" said Flax, nestling her face behind mine.

"Sure. What?"

"Well, if those military men had been on Crispin before, how come *they* didn't spot that desert of copper?"

"Oh, that," I chuckled. "Seems we were wrong about the stuff. It's copper, all right, but a Crispin variation, an isotope, stable—as Lora explained it—that won't carry a current of electricity to save its life. I should have figured there was something funny about it when it never once reacted to the magnetic field of that mountain range."

Flax goggled at me. "Then where's her fortune coming from?"

"Fraser," I said. "It seems that *he's* the guy who went and *invented* the Lectralift drive! He gets half a million bucks for each one they build."

"Why the little gold-digger!" Flax exclaimed.

"Look who's talking," I said, and kissed her. "Can the captain of a spaceship perform a wedding ceremony?" I muttered.

"That's what he told me when I asked him," she grinned.

Once again I was treed by a redhead. Of course, there's a lot to be said for outdoor living…

THE END

If you've enjoyed this book, you will not want to miss these terrific titles…

ARMCHAIR SCI-FI, FANTASY, & HORROR DOUBLE NOVELS, $12.95 *each*

D-1   **THE GALAXY RAIDERS** by William P. McGivern
             SPACE STATION #1 by Frank Belknap Long

D-2   **THE PROGRAMMED PEOPLE** by Jack Sharkey
             SLAVES OF THE CRYSTAL BRAIN by William Carter Sawtelle

D-3   **YOU'RE ALL ALONE** by Fritz Leiber
             THE LIQUID MAN by Bernard C. Gilford

D-4   **CITADEL OF THE STAR LORDS** by Edmund Hamilton
             VOYAGE TO ETERNITY by Milton Lesser

D-5   **IRON MEN OF VENUS** by Don Wilcox
             THE MAN WITH ABSOLUTE MOTION by Noel Loomis

D-6   **WHO SOWS THE WIND…** by Rog Phillips
             THE PUZZLE PLANET by Robert A. W. Lowndes

D-7   **PLANET OF DREAD** by Murray Leinster
             TWICE UPON A TIME by Charles L. Fontenay

D-8   **THE TERROR OUT OF SPACE** by Dwight V. Swain
             QUEST OF THE GOLDEN APE by Ivar Jorgensen and Adam Chase

D-9   **SECRET OF MARRACOTT DEEP** by Henry Slesar
             PAWN OF THE BLACK FLEET by Mark Clifton.

D-10   **BEYOND THE RINGS OF SATURN** by Robert Moore Williams
             A MAN OBSESSED by Alan E. Nourse

ARMCHAIR SCIENCE FICTION CLASSICS, $12.95 each

C-1   **THE GREEN MAN**
             by Harold M. Sherman

C-2   **A TRACE OF MEMORY**
             By Keith Laumer

C-3   **INTO PLUTONIAN DEPTHS**
             by Stanton A. Coblentz

ARMCHAIR MASTERS OF SCIENCE FICTION SERIES, $16.95 each

M-1   **MASTERS OF SCIENCE FICTION, Vol. One**
             Bryce Walton—"Dark of the Moon" and other tales

M-2   **MASTERS OF SCIENCE FICTION, Vol. Two**
             Jerome Bixby: "One Way Street" and other tales

If you've enjoyed this book, you will not want to miss these terrific titles…

ARMCHAIR SCI-FI & HORROR DOUBLE NOVELS, $12.95 each

D-11 **PERIL OF THE STARMEN** by Kris Neville
THE STRANGE INVASION by Murray Leinster

D-12 **THE STAR LORD** by Boyd Ellanby
CAPTIVES OF THE FLAME by Samuel R. Delaney

D-13 **MEN OF THE MORNING STAR** by Edmund Hamilton
PLANET FOR PLUNDER by Hal Clement and Sam Merwin, Jr.

D-14 **ICE CITY OF THE GORGON** by Chester S. Geier and Richard Shaver
WHEN THE WORLD TOTTERED by Lester del Rey

D-15 **WORLDS WITHOUT END** by Clifford D. Simak
THE LAVENDER VINE OF DEATH by Don Wilcox

D-16 **SHADOW ON THE MOON** by Joe Gibson
ARMAGEDDON EARTH by Geoff St. Reynard

D-17 **THE GIRL WHO LOVED DEATH** by Paul W. Fairman
SLAVE PLANET by Laurence M. Janifer

D-18 **SECOND CHANCE** by J. F. Bone
MISSION TO A DISTANT STAR by Frank Belknap Long

D-19 **THE SYNDIC** by C. M. Kornbluth
FLIGHT TO FOREVER by Poul Anderson

D-20 **SOMEWHERE I'LL FIND YOU** by Milton Lesser
THE TIME ARMADA by Fox B. Holden

ARMCHAIR SCIENCE FICTION CLASSICS, $12.95 each

C-4 **CORPUS EARTHLING**
by Louis Charbonneau

C-5 **THE TIME DISSOLVER**
by Jerry Sohl

C-6 **WEST OF THE SUN**
by Edgar Pangborn

ARMCHAIR SCIENCE FICTION & HORROR GEMS SERIES, $12.95 each

G-1 **SCIENCE FICTION GEMS, Vol. One**
Isaac Asimov and others

G-2 **HORROR GEMS, Vol. One**
Carl Jacobi and others

If you've enjoyed this book, you will not want to miss these terrific titles…

ARMCHAIR SCI-FI, FANTASY, & HORROR DOUBLE NOVELS, $12.95 each

D-21 **EMPIRE OF EVIL** by Robert Arnette
         THE SIGN OF THE TIGER by Alan E. Nourse & J. A. Meyer

D-22 **OPERATION SQUARE PEG** by Frank Belknap Long
         ENCHANTRESS OF VENUS by Leigh Brackett

D-23 **THE LIFE WATCH** by Lester Del Rey
         CREATURES OF THE ABYSS by Murray Leinster

D-24 **LEGION OF LAZARUS** by Edmond Hamilton
         STAR HUNTER by Andre Norton

D-25 **EMPIRE OF WOMEN** by John Fletcher
         ONE OF OUR CITIES IS MISSING by Irving Cox

D-26 **THE WRONG SIDE OF PARADISE** by Raymond F. Jones
         THE INVOLUNTARY IMMORTALS by Rog Phillips

D-27 **EARTH QUARTER** by Damon Knight
         ENVOY TO NEW WORLDS by Keith Laumer

D-28 **SLAVES TO THE METAL HORDE** by Milton Lesser
         HUNTERS OUT OF TIME by Joseph E. Kelleam

D-29 **RX JUPITER SAVE US** by Ward Moore
         BEWARE THE USURPERS by Geoff St. Reynard

D-30 **SECRET OF THE SERPENT** by Don Wilcox
         CRUSADE ACROSS THE VOID by Dwight V. Swain

ARMCHAIR SCIENCE FICTION CLASSICS, $12.95 each

C-7   **THE SHAVER MYSTERY, pt. 1**
         by Richard S. Shaver

C-8   **THE SHAVER MYSTERY, pt. 2**
         by Richard S. Shaver

C-9   **MURDER IN SPACE** by David V. Reed
         by David V. Reed

ARMCHAIR MASTERS OF SCIENCE FICTION SERIES, $16.95 each

M-3   **MASTERS OF SCIENCE FICTION, Vol. Three**
         Robert Sheckley, "The Perfect Woman" and other tales

M-4   **MASTERS OF SCIENCE FICTION, Vol. Four**
         Mack Reynolds, "Stowaway" and other tales

If you've enjoyed this book, you will not want to miss these terrific titles...

ARMCHAIR SCI-FI & HORROR DOUBLE NOVELS, $12.95 each

D-31   **A HOAX IN TIME** by Keith Laumer
INSIDE EARTH by Poul Anderson

D-32   **TERROR STATION** by Dwight V. Swain
THE WEAPON FROM ETERNITY by Dwight V. Swain

D-33   **THE SHIP FROM INFINITY** by Edmond Hamilton
TAKEOFF by C. M. Kornbluth

D-34   **THE METAL DOOM** by David H. Keller
TWELVE TIMES ZERO by Howard Browne

D-35   **HUNTERS OUT OF SPACE** by Joseph Kelleam
INVASION FROM THE DEEP by Paul W. Fairman,

D-36   **THE BEES OF DEATH** by Robert Moore Williams
A PLAGUE OF PYTHONS by Frederik Pohl

D-37   **THE LORDS OF QUARMALL** by Fritz Leiber and Harry Fischer
BEACON TO ELSEWHERE by James H. Schmitz

D-38   **BEYOND PLUTO** by John S. Campbell
ARTERY OF FIRE by Thomas N. Scortia

D-39   **SPECIAL DELIVERY** by Kris Neville
NO TIME FOR TOFFEE by Charles F. Meyers

D-40   **RECALLED TO LIFE** by Robert Silverberg
JUNGLE IN THE SKY by Milton Lesser

ARMCHAIR SCIENCE FICTION CLASSICS, $12.95 each

C-10   **MARS IS MY DESTINATION**
by Frank Belknap Long

C-11   **SPACE PLAGUE**
by George O. Smith

C-12   **SO SHALL YE REAP**
by Rog Phillips

ARMCHAIR SCIENCE FICTION & HORROR GEMS SERIES, $12.95 each

G-3   **SCIENCE FICTION GEMS, Vol. Two**
James Blish and others

G-4   **HORROR GEMS, Vol. Two**
Joseph Payne Brennan and others

If you've enjoyed this book, you will not want to miss these terrific titles…

ARMCHAIR SCI-FI & HORROR DOUBLE NOVELS, $12.95 each

D-41   **FULL CYCLE** by Clifford D. Simak
           IT WAS THE DAY OF THE ROBOT by Frank Belknap Long

D-42   **THIS CROWDED EARTH** by Robert Bloch
           REIGN OF THE TELEPUPPETS by Daniel Galouye

D-43   **THE CRISPIN AFFAIR** by Jack Sharkey
           THE RED HELL OF JUPITER by Paul Ernst

D-44   **WE THE MACHINE** by Gerald Vance
           PLANET OF DREAD by Dwight V. Swain

D-45   **THE STAR HUNTER** by Edmond Hamilton
           THE ALIEN by Raymond F. Jones

D-46   **WORLD OF IF** by Rog Phillips
           SLAVE RAIDERS FROM MERCURY by Don Wilcox

D-47   **THE ULTIMATE PERIL** by Robert Abernathy
           PLANET OF SHAME by Bruce Elliot

D-48   **THE FLYING EYES** by J. Hunter Holly
           SOME FABULOUS YONDER by Phillip Jose Farmer

D-49   **THE COSMIC BUNGLARS** by Geoff St. Reynard
           THE BUTTONED SKY by Geoff St. Reynard

D-50   **TYRANTS OF TIME** by Milton Lesser
           PARIAH PLANET by Murray Leinster

ARMCHAIR SCIENCE FICTION CLASSICS, $12.95 each

C-13   **SUNKEN WORLD**
           by Stanton A. Coblentz

C-14   **THE LAST VIAL**
           by Sam McClatchie, M. D.

C-15   **WE WHO SURVIVED (THE FIFTH ICE AGE)**
           by Sterling Noel

ARMCHAIR MASTERS OF SCIENCE FICTION SERIES, $16.95 each

MS-5   **MASTERS OF SCIENCE FICTION, Vol. Five**
           Winston K. Marks—Test Colony and other classics

MS-6   **MASTERS OF SCIENCE FICTION, Vol. Six**
           Fritz Leiber—Deadly Moon and other classics

TERROR BENEATH THE CLOUDS OF JUPITER!

Something mysterious was going on in Jupiter's gigantic "Red Spot." Earth space ships were sent there, only to vanish without a trace. It was a mystery that defied explanation. But how was this scientific wonder connected to these strange disappearances? Two determined members of the Planetary Exploration Forces took up the task of finding out. As they hurtled headlong through the void, little did they realize that their fates would soon lie in the hands of a menacing alien race…

Here is a nail-biting tale of outer space adventure, direct from the pages of "Astounding Stories." Read on as veteran sci-fi author Paul Ernst spins a web of interplanetary intrigue in this grand science fiction thriller.

CAST OF CHARACTERS

BRAND BOWEN

His job was dangerously simple: search for his missing comrades by flying his spacecraft directly into one of the most dangerous spots in the solar system.

GRECA

She was as beautiful and alluring as any woman in the galaxy. Unfortunately, her entire race of people was captive to a monstrous alien race.

DEX HARLOW

He loved flying through space on dangerous missions, but this time it got him a lot more than he bargained for.

THE ROGAN LEADER

His race was a vile alien horde from the depths of outer space. Were his sinister ambitions limited to the conquest of Jupiter, or would Earth itself soon to be in his crosshairs?

COMMANDER STONE

As the chief of the Planetary Exploration Forces, he had the grim duty of sending his best men into space, knowing full well they would probably never return.

THE RED
HELL OF
JUPITER

By
PAUL ERNST

ARMCHAIR FICTION
PO Box 4369, Medford, Oregon 97501-0168

CHAPTER ONE
The Red Spot

Commander Stone, grizzled chief of the Planetary Exploration Forces, acknowledged Captain Brand Bowen's salute and beckoned him to take a seat.

Brand, youngest officer of the division to wear the triple-V for distinguished service, sat down and stared curiously at his superior. He hadn't the remotest idea why he had been recalled from leave: but that it was on a matter of some importance he was sure. He hunched his big shoulders and awaited orders.

"Captain Bowen," said Stone. "I want you to go to Jupiter as soon as you can arrange to do so, fly low over the red area in the southern hemisphere, and come back here with some sort of report as to what's wrong with that infernal death spot."

He tapped his radio stylus thoughtfully against the edge of his desk.

"As you perhaps know, I detailed a ship to explore the red spot about a year ago. It never came back. I sent another ship, with two good men in it, to check up on the disappearance of the first. That ship, too, never came back. Almost within the second of its arrival at the edge of the red area all radio communication with it was cut off. It was never heard from again. Two weeks ago I sent Journeyman there. Now *he* has been swallowed up in a mysterious silence."

An exclamation burst from Brand's lips. Sub-Commander Journeyman! Senior officer under Stone, ablest man in the expeditionary forces, and Brand's oldest friend!

Stone nodded comprehension of the stricken look on Brand's face. "I know how friendly you two were," he said soberly. "That's why I chose you to go and find out, if you can, what happened to him and the other two ships."

Brand's chin sank to rest on the stiff high collar of his uniform.

"Journeyman!" he mused. "Why, he was like an older brother to me. And now…he's gone."

There was silence in Commander Stone's sanctum for a time. Then Brand raised his head.

"Did you have any radio reports at all from any of the three ships concerning the nature of the red spot?" he inquired.

"None that gave definite information," replied Stone. "From each of the three ships we received reports right up to the instant when the red area was approached. From each of the three came a vague description of the peculiarity of the ground ahead of them: it seems to glitter with a queer metallic sheen. Then, from each of the three, as they passed over the boundary—nothing! All radio communication ceased as abruptly as though they'd been stricken dead."

He stared at Brand. "That's all I can tell you, little enough, God knows. Something ominous and strange is contained in that red spot: but what its nature may be, we cannot even guess. I want you to go there and find out."

Brand's determined jaw jutted out, and his lips thinned to a purposeful line. He stood to attention.

"I'll be leaving tonight, sir. Or sooner if you like. I could go this afternoon: in an hour—"

"Tonight is soon enough," said Stone with a smile. "Now, who do you want to accompany you?"

Brand thought a moment. On so long a journey as a trip to Jupiter there was only room in a space ship—what with supplies and all—for one other man. It behooved him to pick his companion carefully.

"I'd like Dex Harlow," he said at last. "He's been to Jupiter before, working with me in plotting the northern hemisphere. He's a good man."

"He is," agreed Stone, nodding approval of Brand's choice. "I'll have him report to you at once."

He rose and held out his hand. "I'm relying on you, Captain Bowen," he said. "I won't give any direct orders: use your own discretion. But I would advise you not to try to land in the red area. Simply fly low over it, and see what you can discern from the air. Good-by, and good luck."

Brand saluted, and went out, to go to his own quarters and make the few preparations necessary for his sudden emergency flight.

The work of exploring the planets that swung with Earth around the sun was still a new branch of the service. Less than ten years ago, it had been, when Ansen devised his first crude atomic motor.

At once, with the introduction of this tremendous new motive power, men had begun to build space ships and explore the sky. And, as so often happens with a new invention, the thing had grown rather beyond itself.

Everywhere amateur space flyers launched forth into the heavens to try their new celestial wings. Everywhere young and old enthusiasts set Ansen motors into clumsily insulated shells and started for Mars or the moon or Venus.

The resultant loss of life, as might have been foreseen, was appalling. Eager but inexperienced explorers edged over onto the wrong side of Mercury and were burned to cinders. They set forth in ships that were badly insulated, and froze in the absolute zero of space. They learned the atomic motor controls too hastily, ran out of supplies or lost their courses, and wandered far out into space—stiff corpses in coffins that were to be buried only in time's infinity.

To stop the foolish waste of life, the Earth Government stepped in. It was decreed that no space ship might be owned or built privately. It was further decreed that those who felt an urge to explore must join the regular service and do so under efficient supervision. And there was created the Government bureau designated as the Planetary Exploration Control Board, which was headed by Commander Stone.

Under this Board the exploration of the planets was undertaken methodically and efficiently, with a minimum of lives sacrificed.

Mercury was charted, tested for essential minerals, and found to be a valueless rock heap too near the sun to support life.

Venus was visited and explored segment by segment; and friendly relations were established with the rather stupid but peaceable people found there.

Mars was mapped. Here the explorers had lingered a long time: and all over this planet's surface were found remnants of a vast and intricate civilization—from the canals that laced its surface, to great cities with mighty buildings still standing. But of life there was none. The atmosphere was too rare to support it; and the theory was that it had constantly thinned through thousands of years till the last Martian had gasped and died in air too attenuated to support life even in creatures that must have grown greater and greater chested in eons of adaptation.

Then Jupiter had been reached: and here the methodical planet by planet work promised to be checked for a long time to come. Jupiter, with its mighty surface area, was going to take some exploring! It would be years before it could be plotted even superficially.

Brand had been to Jupiter on four different trips; and, as he walked toward his quarters from Stone's office, he reviewed what he had learned on those trips.

Jupiter, as he knew it, was a vast globe of vague horror and sharp contrasts.

Distant from the sun as it was, it received little solar heat. But, with so great a mass, it had cooled off much more slowly than any of the other planets known, and had immense internal heat. This meant that the air—which closely approximated Earth's air in density—was cool a few hundred yards up from the surface of the planet, and dankly hot close to the ground. The result, as the cold air constantly sank into the warm, was a thick steamy blanket of fog that covered everything perpetually.

Because of the recent cooling, life was not far advanced on Jupiter. Too short a time ago the sphere had been but a blazing mass. Tropical marshes prevailed, crisscrossed by mighty rivers at warmer than blood heat. Giant, hideous fernlike growths crowded one another in an everlasting jungle. And among the distorted trees, from the blanket of soft white fog that hid all from sight, could be heard constantly an ear-splitting chorus of screams and bellows and whistling snarls. It made the blood run cold just to listen—and to speculate on what gigantic but tiny-brained monsters made them.

Now and then, when Brand had been flying dangerously low over the surface, a wind had risen strong enough to dispel the fog banks for an instant; and he had caught a flash of Jovian life. Just a flash, for example, of a monstrous lizard-like thing too great to support its own bulk: or a creature all neck and tail, with ridges of scale on its armored hide and a small serpentine head weaving back and forth among the jungle growths.

Occasionally he had landed—always staying close to the space ship, for Jupiter's gravity made movement a slow and laborious process, and he didn't want to be caught too far from security. At such times he might hear a crashing and splashing and see a reptilian head loom gigantically at him through the fog. Then he would discharge the deadly explosive gun which was Earth's latest weapon, and the creature would crash to the ground. The chorus of hissings and bellowings would increase as he hastened slowly and laboriously back to the ship, indicating that other unseen monsters of the steamy jungle had flocked to tear the dead giant to pieces and bolt it down.

Oh, Jupiter was a nice planet! mused Brand. A sweet place—if one happened to be a two-hundred-foot snake or something!

He had always thought the entire globe was in that new, raw, marshy state. But he had worked only in one comparatively small area of the northern hemisphere; had never been within thirty thousand miles of the red spot. What might lie in that ominous crimson patch, he could not even guess. However, he reflected, he was soon to find out, though he might never live to tell about it.

Shrugging his shoulders, he turned into the fifty story building in which was his modest apartment. There he found, written by the automatic stylus on his radio pad, the message: "Be with you at seven o'clock. Best regards, and I hope you strangle. Dex Harlow."

Dex Harlow was a six-foot Senior Lieutenant who had been on many an out-of-the-way exploratory trip. Like Brand he was just under thirty and perpetually thirsting for the bizarre in life. He was a walking document of planetary activity. He was still baked a brick red from a trip to Mercury a year before: he had a scar on his forehead, the result of jumping forty feet one day on the moon when he'd meant to jump only twenty; he was minus a finger which had been irreparably frost-bitten on Mars; and he had a crumpled nose that was the outcome of a brush with a ten-foot bandit on Venus who'd tried to kill him for his explosive gun and supply of glass, dyite-containing cartridges.

He clutched Brand's fingers in a bone-mangling grip, and threw his hat into a far corner.

"You're a fine friend!" he growled cheerfully. "Here I'm having a first rate time for myself, swimming and planing along the Riviera, with two more weeks leave ahead of me—and I get a call from the Old Man to report to you. What excuse have you for your crime?"

"A junket to Jupiter," said Brand. "Would you call that a good excuse?"

"Jupiter!" exclaimed Dex. "Wouldn't you know it? Of course you'd have to pick a spot four hundred million miles away from all that grand swimming I was having!"

"Would you like to go back on leave, and have me choose someone else?" inquired Brand solemnly.

"Well, no," said Dex hastily. "Now that I'm here, I suppose I might as well go through with it."

Brand laughed. "Try and get you out of it! I know your attitude toward a real jaunt. And it's a real jaunt we've got ahead of us, too, old boy. We're going to the red spot. Immediately."

Dex's sandy eyebrows shot up. "The red spot! That's where Coblenz and Heiroy were lost!"

"And Journeyman," added Brand. "He's the latest victim of whatever's in the hell-hole."

Dex whistled. "Journeyman too! Well, all I've got to say is that whatever's there must be strong medicine. Journeyman was a damn fine man, and as brave as they come. Have you any idea what it's all about?"

"Not an idea. Nobody has. We're to go and find out— if we can. Are you all ready?"

"All ready," said Dex.

"So am I. We'll start at eleven o'clock in one of the Old Man's best cruisers. Meanwhile, we might as well go and hunt up a dinner somewhere, to fortify us against the synthetic pork chops and bread we'll be swallowing for the next fortnight."

They went out; and at ten minutes of eleven reported at the great space ship hangars north of New York, with their luggage, a conspicuous item of which was a chess board to help while away the long, long days of spacial travel. Brand then paused a little while for a final check-up on directions.

They clambered into the tiny control room and shut the hermetically sealed trap-door. Brand threw the control switch and precisely at eleven o'clock the conical shell of metal shot heavenward, gathering such speed that it was soon invisible to human eyes. He set their course toward the blazing speck that was Jupiter, four hundred million miles away; and then reported their start by radio to Commander Stone's night operator.

The investigatory expedition to the ominous red spot of the giant of the solar system was on.

CHAPTER TWO
The Pipe-like Men

Brand began to slacken speed on the morning of the thirteenth day (morning, of course, being a technical term: there are no horizons in space for the sun to rise over). Jupiter was still an immense distance off; but it took a great while to slow the momentum of the space ship, which, in the frictionless emptiness of space, had been traveling faster and faster for nearly three hundred hours.

Behind them was the distant ball of sun, so far off that it looked no larger than a red-hot penny. Before them was the gigantic disk of Jupiter, given a white tinge by the perpetual fog blankets, its outlines softened by its thick layer of atmosphere and cloud banks. Two of its nine satellites were in sight at the moment, with a third edging over the western rim.

"Makes you think you're drunk and seeing triple, doesn't it?" commented Dex, who was staring out the thick glass panel beside Brand. "Nine moons! Almost enough for one planet!"

Brand nodded abstractly, and concentrated on the control board. Rapidly the ship rocketed down toward the surface. The disk became a whirling, gigantic plate; and then an endless plain, with cloud formations beginning to take on definite outline.

"About to enter Jupiter's atmosphere." Brand spoke into the radio transmitter. Over the invisible thread of radio connection between the space ship and Earth, four hundred million miles behind, flashed the message.

"All right. For God's sake, be careful," came the answer, minutes later. "Say something at least every half hour, to let us know communication is unbroken. We will sound at ten second intervals."

The sounding began: *peep*, a shrill little piping noise like the fiddle of a cricket. Ten seconds later it came again: *peep*. Thereafter, intermittently, it keened through the control room—a homely, comforting sound to let them know that there was a distant thread between them and Earth.

Lower the shell rocketed. The endless plain slowly ceased its rushing underneath them as they entered the planet's atmosphere and began to be pulled around with it in its revolution. Far to the west a faint red glow illumined the sky.

The two men looked at each other, grimly, soberly.

"We're here," said Dex, flexing the muscles of his powerful arms.

"We are," said Brand, patting the gun in his holster.

The rapid dusk of the giant planet began to close in on them. The thin sunlight darkened; and with its lowering, the red spot of Jupiter glared more luridly ahead of them. Silently the two men gazed at it, and wondered what it held.

They shot the space ship toward it, and halted a few hundred miles away. Watery white light from the satellites, "that jitter around in the sky like a bunch of damned waterbugs," as Dex put it, was now the sole illumination.

They hung motionless in their space shell, to wait through the five-hour Jovian night for the succeeding five hours of daylight to illumine a slow cruise over the red area that, in less than a year, had swallowed up three of Earth's space ships. And ever as they waited, dozing a little, speculating as to the nature of the danger they faced, the peep, peep of the radio shrilled in their ears to tell them that there was still a connection—though a very tenuous one—with their mother planet.

"Red spot ten miles away," said Brand in the transmitter. "We're approaching it slowly."

The tiny sun had leaped up over Jupiter's horizon; and with its appearance they had sent the ship planing toward their mysterious destination. Beneath them the fog banks were thinning, and ahead of them were no clouds. For some reason there was a clarity unusual to Jupiter's atmosphere in the air above the red section.

"Red spot one mile ahead, altitude forty thousand feet," reported Brand.

He and Dex peered intently through the port glass panel. Ahead and far below, their eyes caught an odd metallic sheen. It was as though the ground there were carpeted with polished steel that reflected red firelight.

Tense, filled with an excitement that set their pulses pounding wildly, they angled slowly down, nearer to the edge of the vast crimson area, closer to the ground. The radio keened its monotonous signal.

Brand crawled to the transmitter, laboriously, for his body tipped the scales here at nearly four hundred pounds.

"We can see the metallic glitter that Journeyman spoke of," he said. "No sign of life of any kind, though. The red glow seems to flicker a little."

Closer the ship floated. Closer. To right and left of them for vast distances stretched the red area. Ahead of them for hundreds of miles they knew it extended.

"We're right on it now," called Brand. "Right on it— we're going over the edge—we're—"

Next instant he was sprawling on the floor, with Dex rolling helplessly on top of him, while the space ship bounced up twenty thousand feet as though propelled by a giant sling.

The peep, peep of the radio signalling stopped. The space ship rolled helplessly for a moment, then resumed an even keel. Brand and Dex gazed at each other.

"What the hell?" said Dex.

He started to get to his feet, put all his strength into the task of moving his Jupiter-weighted body, and crashed against the top of the control room.

"Say!" he sputtered, rubbing his head. "Say, what *is* this?"

Brand, profiting by his mistake, rose more cautiously, shut off the atomic motor, and approached a glass panel again. "God knows what it is," he said with a shrug. "Somehow, with our passing into the red area, the pull of gravity has been reduced by about ten, that's all."

"Oh, so that's all, is it? Well, what's happened to old Jupe's gravity?"

Again Brand shrugged. "I haven't any idea. Your guess is as good as mine."

He peered down through the panel, and stiffened in surprise.

"Dex!" he cried. "We're moving! And the motor is shut off!"

"We're drawing down closer to the ground, too," announced Dex, pointing to their altimeter. "Our altitude has been reduced five thousand feet in the last two minutes."

Quickly Brand turned on the motor in reverse. The space ship, as the rushing, reddish ground beneath indicated, continued to glide forward as though pulled by an invisible rope. He turned on full power. The ship's progress was checked a little. A very little! And the metallic red surface under them grew nearer as they steadily lost altitude.

"Something seems to have got us by the nose," said Dex. "We're on our way to the center of the red spot, I guess—to find whatever it was that Journeyman found. And the radio communication his been broken somehow…"

Wordlessly, they stared out the panel, while the shell, quivering with the strain of the atomic motor's fight against whatever unseen force it was that relentlessly drew them forward, bore them swiftly toward the heart of the vast crimson area.

"Look!" cried Brand.

For over an hour the ship had been propelled swiftly, irresistibly toward the center of the red spot. It had been up about forty thousand feet. Now, with a jerk that sent both men reeling, it had been drawn down to within fifteen thousand feet of the surface; and the sight that was now becoming more and more visible was incredible.

Beneath was a vast, orderly checkerboard. Every alternate square was covered by what seemed a jointless metal plate. The open squares, plainly land under cultivation, were surrounded by gleaming fences that hooked each metal square with every other one of its kind as batteries are wired in series. Over these open squares progressed tiny, two legged figures, for the most part following gigantic shapeless animals like figures out of a dream. Ahead suddenly appeared the spires and towers of an enormous city!

Metropolis and cultivated land! It was as unbelievable, on that raw new planet, as such a sight would have been could a traveler in time have observed it in the midst of a dim Pleistocene panorama of young Earth.

It was instantly apparent that the city was their destination. Rapidly the little ship was rushed toward it; and, realizing at last the futility of its laboring, Brand cut off the atomic motor and let the shell drift.

Over a group of squat square buildings their ship passed, decreasing speed and drifting lower with every moment. The lofty structures that were the nucleus of the strange city loomed closer. Now they were soaring slowly down a wide thoroughfare; and now, at last, they hovered above a great open square that was thronged with figures.

Lower they dropped. Lower. And then they settled with a slight jar on a surface made of reddish metal; and the figures rushed to surround them.

Looking out the glass panel at these figures, both Brand and Dex exclaimed aloud and covered their eyes for a moment to shut out the hideous sight of them. Now they examined them closely.

Manlike they were: and yet like no human being conceivable to an Earth mind. They were tremendously tall—twelve feet at least—but as thin as so many animated poles. Their two legs were scarce four inches through, taper-less, boneless, like lengths of pipe; and like two flexible pipes they were joined to a slightly larger pipe of a torso that could not have been more than a foot in diameter. There were four arms, a pair on each side of the cylindrical body, that weaved feebly about like lengths of rubber hose.

Set directly on the pipe-like body, as a pumpkin might be balanced on a pole, was a perfectly round cranium in which were glassy, staring eyes, with dull pupils like those of a sick dog. The nose was but a tab of flesh. The mouth was a minute, circular thing, soft and flabby looking, which opened and shut regularly with the creature's breathing. It resembled the snout-like mouth of a fish, of the sucker variety; and fish-like, too, was the smooth and slimy skin that covered the beanpole body.

Hundreds of the repulsive things, there were. And all of them shoved and crowded, as a disorderly mob on Earth might do, to get close to the Earthmen's ship. Their big dull eyes peered in through the glass panels, and their hands—mere round blobs of gristle in the palms of which were set single sucker disks—pattered against the metal hull of the shell.

"Gawd!" said Brand with a shudder. "Fancy these things feeling over your body…"

"They're hostile, whatever they are," said Dex. "Look out: that one's pointing something at you!"

One of the slender, tottering creatures had raised an arm and leveled at Brand something that looked rather like an elongated, old-fashioned flashlight. Brand involuntarily ducked. The clear glass panel between them and the mob outside gave him a queasy feeling of being exposed to whatever missile might lurk in the thing's tube.

"What do we do now?" demanded Dex with a shaky laugh. "You're chief of this expedition. I'm waiting for orders."

"We wait right here," replied Brand. "We're safe in the shell till we're starved out. At least they can't get in to attack us."

But it developed that, while the slimy looking things might not be able to get in, they had ways of reaching the Earthmen just the same!

The creature with the gun-like tube extended it somewhat further toward Brand.

Brand felt a sharp, unpleasant tingle shoot through his body, as though he had received an electric shock. He winced, and cried out at the sudden pain of it.

"What's the matter—" Dex began. But hardly had the words left his mouth when he, too, felt the shock. A couple of good, hearty Earth oaths exploded from his lips.

The repulsive creature outside made an authoritative gesture. He seemed to be beckoning to them, his huge dull eyes glaring threateningly at the same moment.

"Our beanpole friend is suggesting that we get out of the shell and stay awhile," said Dex with grim humor. "They seem anxious to entertain us—*ouch!*"

As the two men made no move to obey the beckoning gesture, the creature had raised the tube again; and again the sharp, unpleasant shock shot through them.

"What the devil are we going to do?" exclaimed Brand. "If we go out in that mob of nightmare things—it's going to be messy. As long as we stay in the shell we have some measure of protection."

"Not much protection when they can sting us through metal and glass at will," growled Dex. "Do you suppose they can turn the juice on harder? Or is that bee-sting their best effort?"

As though in direct answer to his words, the blob-like face of the being who seemed in authority convulsed with anger and he raised the tube again. This time the shock that came from it was sufficient to throw the two men to the floor.

"Well, we can't stay in the ship, that's certain," said Brand. "I guess there's only one thing to do."

Dex nodded. "Climb out of here and take as many of these skinny horrors with us into hell as we can," he agreed.

Once more the shock stung them, as a reminder not to keep their captors waiting. With their shoulders bunched for abrupt action, and their guns in hand, the two men walked to the trap-door of the ship. They threw the heavy bolts, drew a deep breath—and flung open the door to charge unexpectedly toward the thickest mass of creatures that surrounded the ship!

In a measure their charge was successful. Its very suddenness caught some of the tall monstrosities off guard. Half a dozen of them stopped the fragile glass bullets to writhe in horrible death on the red metal paving of the square. But that didn't last long.

In less than a minute, thin, clammy arms were winding around the Earthmen's wrists, and their guns were wrenched from them. And then started a hand-to-hand encounter that was all the more hideous for being so unlike any fighting that might have occurred on Earth.

With a furious growl Dex charged the nearest creature, whose huge round head swayed on its stalk of a body fully six feet above his own head. He gathered the long thin legs in a football grip, and sent the thing crashing full length on its back. The great head thumped resoundingly against the metal paving, and the creature lay motionless.

For an instant Dex could only stare at the thing. It had been so easy, like overcoming a child. But even as that thought crossed his mind, two of the tall thin figures closed in behind him. Four pairs of arms wound around him, feebly but tenaciously, like wet seaweed.

They began to constrict and wind tighter around him. He tore at them, dislodged all but two. His sturdy Earth leg went back to sweep the stalk-like legs of his attackers from under them. One of the things went down, to twist weakly in a laborious attempt to rise again. But the other, by sheer force of height and reach, began to bear Dex down.

Savagely he laced out with his fists, battering the pulpy face that was pressing down close to his. The big eyes blinked shut, but the four hose-like arms did not relax their clasp. Dex's hands sought fiercely for the thing's throat. But it had no throat: the head, set directly on the thin shoulders, defied all throttling attempts.

Then, just as Dex was feeling that the end had come, he felt the creature wrench from him, and saw it slide in a tangle of arms and legs over the smooth metal pavement. He got shakily to his feet, to see Brand standing over him and flailing out with his fists at an ever tightening circle of towering figures.

"Thanks," panted Dex. And he began again, tripping the twelve-foot things in order to get them down within reach, battering at the great pulpy heads, fighting blindly in that expressed craving to take as many of the creatures into hell with him as he could manage. Beside him fought Brand, steadily, coolly, grim of jaw and unblinking of eye.

Already the struggle had gone on far longer than they had dreamed it might. For some reason the grotesque creatures delayed killing them. That they could do so any time they pleased, was certain: if the monsters could reach them with their shock-tubes through the double insulated hull of the space ship, they could certainly kill them out in the open.

Yet they made no move to do so. The deadly tubes were not used. The screeching gargoyles, instead, devoted all their efforts to merely hurling their attenuated bodies on the two men as though they wished to capture them alive.

Finally, however, the nature of the battle changed. The tallest of the attackers opened his tiny mouth and piped a signal. The ring of weaving tall bodies surrounding the two opened and became a U. The creatures in the curve of the U raised their shock-tubes and, with none of their own kind behind the victims to share in its discharge, released whatever power it was that lurked in them.

The shock was terrific. Without the glass and metal of the ship to protect them, out in the open and defenceless, Brand and Dex got some indication of its real power.

Writhing and twitching, feeling as though pierced by millions of red hot needles, they went down. A swarm of pipe-like bodies smothered them, and the fight was over.

CHAPTER THREE
The Coming of Greca

The numbing shock from the tubes left the Earthmen's bodies almost paralyzed for a time; but their brains were unfogged enough for them to observe only too clearly all that went on from the point of their capture.

They were bound hand and foot. At a piping cry from the leader, several of the gangling figures picked them up in reedy arms and began to walk across the square, away from the ship. Brand noticed that his bearers' arms trembled with his weight: and sensed the flabbiness of the substance that took the place in them of good solid muscle. Physically these things were soft and ineffectual indeed. They had only the ominous tubes with which to fight.

The eery procession, with the bound Earthmen carried in the lead, wound toward a great building fringing the square. In through the high arched entrance of this building they went, and up a sloping incline to its tower-top. Here, in a huge bare room, the two were unceremoniously dumped to the floor.

While three of the things stood guard with the mysterious tubes, another unbound them. A whole shower of high pitched, piping syllables was hurled at them, speech which sounded threatening and contemptuous but was otherwise, of course, entirely unintelligible, and then the creatures withdrew. The heavy metal door was slammed shut, and they were alone.

Brand drew a long breath, and began to feel himself all over for broken bones. He found none; he was still nerve-wracked from that last terrific shock, but otherwise whole and well.

"Are you hurt, Dex?" he asked solicitously.

"I guess not," replied Dex, getting uncertainly to his feet. "And I'm wondering why. It seems to me the brutes were uncommonly considerate of us—and I'm betting the reason is one we won't like!"

Brand shrugged. "I guess we'll find out their intentions soon enough. Let's see what our surroundings look like."

They walked to the nearest window-aperture, and gazed out on a startling and marvelous scene.

Beneath their high tower window, extending as far as the eye could reach, lay the city, lit by the reddish glare of the peculiar metal with which its streets were paved. For the most part the metropolis consisted of perfectly square buildings pierced by many windows to indicate that each housed a large number of inmates. But here and there grotesque turrets lanced the sky, and symbolic domes arched above the surrounding flat metal roofs.

One building in particular they noticed. This was an enormous structure in the shape of a half-globe that reared its spherical height less than an eighth of a mile from the building they were in. It was situated off to their right at the foot of a vast, high-walled enclosure whose near end seemed to be formed by the right wall of their prison. They could only see it by leaning far out of the window; and it would not have come to their attention at all had they not heard it first—or, rather, heard the sound of something within it: for from it came a curious whining hum that never varied in intensity, something like the hum of a gigantic dynamo, only greater and of a more penetrating pitch.

"Sounds as though it might be some sort of central power station," said Brand. "But what could it supply power for?"

"Give it up," said Dex. "For their damned shock-tubes, perhaps, among other things—"

He broke off abruptly as a sound of sliding bolts came from the doorway. The two men whirled around to face the door, their fists doubling instinctively against whatever new danger might threaten them.

The door was opened and two of their ugly, towering enemies came in, their tubes held conspicuously before them. Behind came another figure; and at sight of this one, so plainly not of the race of Jupiter, the Earthmen gasped with wonder.

They saw a girl who might have come from Earth, save that she was taller than most Earth women—of a regal height that reached only an inch or two below Brand's own six foot one. She was beautifully formed, and had wavy dark hair and clear light blue eyes. A sort of sandal covered each small bare foot; and a gauzy tunic, reaching from above the knee to the shoulder, only half shielded her lovely figure.

She was bearing a metal container in which was a mess of stuff evidently intended as food. The guards halted and stepped aside to let her pass into the room. Then they backed out, constantly keeping Dex and Brand covered with the tubes, and closed and barred the door.

The girl smiled graciously at the admiration in the eyes of both the men—a message needing no inter-planetary interpretation. She advanced, and held the metal container toward them.

"Eat," she said softly. "It is good food, and life giving."

For an instant Brand was dumbfounded. For here was language he could understand—which was incredible on this far-flung globe. Then he suddenly comprehended why her sentences were so intelligible.

She was versed in mental telepathy. And versed to a high degree! He'd had some experience with telepathy on Venus; but theirs was a crude thought-speech compared to the fluency possessed by the beautiful girl before him.

"Who are you?" he asked wonderingly.

"I am Greca"—it was very hard to grasp names or abstract terms— "of the fourth satellite."

"Then you are not of these monsters of Jupiter?"

"Oh, no! I am their captive, as are all my people. We are but slaves of the tall ones."

Brand glanced at Dex. "Here's a chance to get some information, perhaps," he murmured.

Dex nodded; but meanwhile the girl had caught his thought. She smiled—a tragic, wistful smile.

"I shall be happy to tell you anything in my power to tell," she informed him. "But you must be quick. I can only remain with you a little while."

She sat down on the floor with them—the few bench-like things obviously used by the tall creatures as chairs were too high for them—and with the informality of adversity the three captives began to talk. Swiftly Brand got a little knowledge of Greca's position on Jupiter, and of the racial history that led up to it.

Four of the nine satellites of Jupiter were now the home of living beings. But two only, at the dawn of history as Greca knew it, had been originally inhabited. These were the fourth and the second.

On the fourth there dwelt a race, "like me," as Greca put it—a kindly, gentle people content to live and let live.

On the second had been a race of immensely tall, but attenuated and physically feeble things with great heads and huge dull eyes and characters distinguished mainly for cold-blooded savagery.

The inhabitants of the fourth satellite had remained in ignorance of the monsters on the second till one day "many, many ages ago," a fleet of clumsy ships appeared on the fourth satellite. From the ships had poured thousands of pipe-like creatures, armed with horrible rods of metal that killed instantly and without a sound. The things, it seemed, had crowded over the limits of their own globe, and had been forced to find more territory.

They had made captive the entire population of the satellite. Then—for like all dangerous vermin they multiplied rapidly—they had overflowed to the first and fifth satellites—the others were uninhabitable—and finally to the dangerous surface of Jupiter itself. Everywhere they had gone, they had taken droves of Greca's people to be their slaves, "and the source of their food," added Greca, with a shudder; a statement that was at the moment unintelligible to the two men.

Brand stared sympathetically at her. "They treat them very badly?" he asked gently.

"Terribly! Terribly!" said Greca, shuddering again.

"But you seem quite privileged," he could not help saying.

She shook her dainty head pathetically. "I am of high rank among my people. I am a priestess of our religion, which is the religion of The Great White One who rules all the sky everywhere. The Rogans" (it was the best translation Brand could make of her mental term for the slimy tall things that held them captive) "—the Rogans hold my fate over the heads of my race. Should they rebel, I would be thrown to the monster in the pen. Of course the Rogans could crush any revolt with their terrible tubes, but they do not want to kill their slaves if they can help it. They find it more effective to hold their priestesses in hostage."

Brand turned from personal history to more vital subjects.

"Why," he asked Greca, "are the shining red squares of metal laid everywhere over this empire of the Rogans?"

"To make things light," was the reply. "When the Rogans first came to this mighty sphere, they could hardly move. Things are so heavy here, somehow. So their first thought was to drive my enslaved people to the casting and laying of the metal squares and the metal beams that connect them, in order to make things weigh less."

"But how do the plates function?"

Greca did not know this, save vaguely. She tried to express her little knowledge of the scientific achievements of the savage Rogans. After some moments Brand turned to Dex and said:

"As near as I can get it, the Rogans, by this peculiar red metal alloy, manage to trap and divert the permanent lines of force, the magnetic field, of Jupiter itself. So the whole red spot is highly magnetized, which somehow upsets natural gravitational attraction. I suppose it is responsible for the discoloration of the ground, too."

He turned to question the girl further about this, but she had got nervously to her feet already.

"I'll be taken away soon," she said. "I was brought in here only to urge you to eat the food. I must be interpreter, since the Rogans speak not with the mind, and I know their hateful tongue."

"Why are they so anxious for us to eat?" demanded Dex with an uneasy frown.

"So you will be strong, and endure for a long time the—the ordeal they have in store for you," faltered the girl at last. "They intend to force from you the secret of the power that drove your ship here, so they too may have command of space."

"But I don't understand," frowned Brand. "They must already have a means of space navigation. They came here to Jupiter from the satellites."

"Their vessels are crude, clumsy things. The journey from the nearest satellite is the limit of their flying range. They have nothing like your wonderful little ships, and they want to know how to build and power them."

She gazed sorrowfully at them and went on: "You see, yours is the fourth space ship to visit their kingdom; and that makes them fearful because it shows they are vulnerable to invasion. They want to stop that by invading your planet first. Besides their fear, there is their greed. Their looking-tubes reveal that yours is a fruitful and lovely sphere, and they are insatiable in their lust for new territories. Thus they plan to go to your planet as soon as they are able, and kill or enslave all the people there as they have killed and enslaved my race."

"They'll have a job on their hands trying to do that!" declared Dex stoutly.

But Brand paled. "They can do it!" he snapped. "Look at those death-tubes of theirs. We have no arms to compete with that." He turned to Greca. "So the Rogans plan to force the secret of our motors from us by torture?"

She nodded, and caught his hand in hers.

"Yes. They will do with you as they did with the six who came before you—and who died before surrendering the secret."

"So! We know now what happened to Journeyman and the others!" burst out Dex. "I'll see 'em in hell before I'll talk!"

"And me," nodded Brand. "But that doesn't cure the situation. As long as ships disappear in this red inferno, so long will the Old Man keep sending others to find out what's wrong. The Rogans will capture them as easily as they captured us. And eventually someone will happen along who'll weaken under torture. Then—"

He stopped. A dread vision filled his mind of Earth depopulated by the feebly ferocious Rogans, of rank on rank of Earth's vast armies falling in stricken rows at the shock of the Rogans' tubes.

Greca caught the vision. She nodded. "Yes, that is what would happen if they found ways of reaching your globe."

"But, God, Brand, we can't allow that!" cried Dex. "We've got to find a way to spike the guns of these walking gas-pipes, somehow!"

Brand sighed heavily. "We are two against hundreds of thousands. We are bare-handed, and the Rogans have those damned tubes. Anyway, we are on the verge of death at this very moment. What under heaven can we do to spike their guns?"

He was silent a moment: and in the silence the steady hum from the domed building outside came to his ears.

"What's in that big, round topped building, Greca?" he asked quietly.

"I do not know, exactly," replied the girl. "There is some sort of machinery in it, and to it go connecting beams from all the square metal plates everywhere. That is all I know."

Brand started to question her further, but her time was up. The two guards poked their loathsome pumpkin heads in the doorway and contemptuously beckoned her out. She answered resignedly, in the piping Rogan tongue, and went with them. But she turned to wave shyly, commiseratingly at the two men; and the expression in her clear blue eyes as they rested on Brand made his heart contract and then leap on with a mighty bound.

"We have an ally in her," murmured Brand. "Though God only knows if that will mean anything to us..."

CHAPTER FOUR
In the Tower

"What I can't figure out," said Dex, striding up and down the big bare room, "is why we're needed to tell them about the atomic motor. They've got our ship, and three others besides. I should think they could learn about the motor just by taking it apart and studying it."

Brand grinned mirthlessly, recalling the three years of intensive study it had taken him to learn the refinements of atomic motive power. "If you'd ever qualified as a space navigator, Dex, you'd know better. The Rogans are an advanced race; their control of polar magnetism and the marvelously high-powered telescopes Greca mentions prove that; but I doubt if they could ever analyze that atomic motor with no hint as to how it works."

Silence descended on them again, in which each was lost in his own thoughts.

How many hours had passed, the Earthmen did not know. They had spent the time in fruitless planning to escape from their tower room and go back to the ship again. Though how they could get away in the ship when the Rogans seemed able to propel it where-ever they wished against the utmost power of their motor, they did not attempt to consider.

One of Jupiter's short nights had passed, however—a night weirdly made as light as day by red glares from the plates, which seemed to store up sunlight, among their other functions—and the tiny sun had risen to slant into their window at a sharp angle.

Suddenly they heard the familiar drawing of the great bolts outside their door. It was opened, and a dozen or more of the Rogans came in, with Greca cowering piteously in their midst and attempting to communicate her distress to Brand.

At the head of the little band of Rogans was one the prisoners had not seen before. He was of great height, fully two feet taller than the others; and he carried himself with an air that proclaimed his importance.

The tall one turned to Greca and addressed a few high-pitched, squeaky words to her. She shook her head; whereupon, at a hissed command, two of the Rogans caught her by the wrists and dragged her forward.

"They have come to question you," Greca lamented to Brand. "And they want to do it through me. But I will not! I will not!"

Brand smiled at her though his lips were pale.

"You are powerless to struggle," he said. "Do as they ask. You cannot help us by refusing, and, in any case, I can promise that they won't learn anything from us."

The tall Rogan teetered up to the prisoners on his gangling legs, and stared icily at them. Crouched beside him, her lovely body all one mute appeal to the Earthmen to forgive her for the part she was forced to play, was Greca.

At length the Rogan leader spoke. He addressed his sibilant words to Greca, though his stony eyes were kept intently on the Earthmen.

"He says," exclaimed Greca telepathically, "to inform you first that he is head of all the Rogan race on this globe, and that all on this globe must do as he commands."

Brand nodded to show he understood the message.

"He says he is going to ask you a few questions, and that you are to answer truthfully if you value your lives:"

"First, he wants to know what the people of your world are like. Are they all the same as you?"

Dex started to reply to that; but Brand flung him a warning look. "Tell him we are the least of the Earth people," he answered steadily. "Tell him we are of an inferior race. Most of those on Earth are giants five times as large as we are, and many times more powerful."

Greca relayed the message in the whistling, piping Rogan tongue. The tall one stared, then hissed another sentence to the beautiful interpreter.

"He wants to know," said Greca, "if there are cities on your globe as large and complete as this one."

"There are cities on Earth that make this look like a— a—" Brand cast about for understandable similes— "like a collection of animal burrows."

"He says to describe your planet's war weapons," was the next interpretation. And here Brand let himself go.

With flights of fancy he hadn't known he was capable of, he described great airships, steered automatically and bristling with guns that discharged explosives powerful enough to kill everything within a range of a thousand miles. He told of billions of thirty-foot giants sheathed in an alloy that would make them invulnerable to any feeble rays the Rogans might have developed. He touched on the certain wholesale death that must overtake any hostile force that tried to invade the planet.

"The Rogan shock-tubes are toys compared with the ray-weapons of Earth," he concluded. "We have arms that can nullify the effects of yours and kill at the same instant. We have—"

But here the Rogan leader turned impatiently away. Greca had been translating sentence by sentence. Now the tall one barked out a few syllables in a squeaky voice.

"He says he knows you are lying," sighed Greca. "For if you on Earth have tubes more effective than theirs why weren't you equipped with them on your expedition here to the red kingdom?"

Brand bit his lips. "Check," he muttered. "The brute has a brain in that ugly head."

The Rogan leader spoke for a long time then; and at each singsong word, Greca quivered as though lashed by a whip. At length she turned to Brand.

"He has been telling what his hordes can do, answering your boasts with boasts of his own. His words are awful! I won't tell you all he said. I will only say that he is convinced his shock-tubes are superior to any Earth arms, and that he states he will now illustrate their power to you to quell your insolence. I don't know what he means by that..."

But she and the Earthmen were soon to find out.

The Rogan leader stepped to the window and arrogantly beckoned Brand and Dex to join him there. They did; and the leader gazed out and down as though searching for something.

He pointed. The two Earthmen followed his leveled arm with their eyes and saw, a hundred yards or so away, a bent and dreary figure trudging down the metal paving of the street. It was a figure like those to be seen on Earth, which placed it as belonging to Greca's race.

The tall leader drew forth one of the shock-tubes. Seen near at hand, it was observed to be bafflingly simple in appearance. It seemed devoid of all mechanism—simply a tube of reddish metal with a sort of handle formed of a coil of heavy wire.

The Rogan pointed the tube at the distant figure.

Greca screamed, and screamed again. Coincident with her cry, as though the sound of it had felled him, the distant slave dropped to the pavement.

That was all. The tube had merely been pointed: as far as Brand could see, the Rogan's "hand" had not moved on the barrel of the tube, nor even constricted about the coil of wire that formed its handle. Yet that distant figure had dropped. Furthermore, fumes of greasy black smoke now began to arise from the huddled body; and in less than thirty seconds there was left no trace of it on the gleaming metal pavement.

"So that's what those things are like at full power!" breathed Dex. "My God!"

The Rogan leader spoke a few words. Greca, huddled despairingly on the floor, crushed by this brutal annihilation of one of her country-men before her very eyes, did not translate. But translation was unnecessary. The Rogan's icy, triumphant eyes, the very posture of his grotesque body, spoke for him.

"That," he was certainly saying, "is what will happen to any on your helpless planet who dare oppose the Rogan will!"

He whipped out a command to the terror-stricken girl. She rose from her crouching position on the floor; and at length formulated the Rogan's last order:

"You will explain the working of the engine that drove your space ship here."

Dex laughed. It was a short bark of sound, totally devoid of humor, but very full of defiance. Brand thrust his hands into the pockets of his tunic, spread his legs apart, and began to whistle.

A quiver that might have been of anger touched the Rogan leader's repulsive little mouth. He glared balefully at the uncowed Earthmen and spoke again, evidently repeating his command. The two turned their backs to him to indicate their refusal to obey.

At that, the tall leader pointed to Dex. In an instant three of the guards had wound their double pairs of arms around his struggling body. Brand sprang to help him, but a touch of the mysterious discharge from the leader's tube sent him writhing to the floor.

"It's no use, Brand," said Dex steadily. He too had stopped struggling, and now stood quietly in the slimy coils of his captors' arms. "I might as well go along with them and get it over with. I probably won't see you again. Good luck!"

He was borne out of the room. The Rogan leader turned to Brand and spoke.

"He says that if your comrade does not tell him what he wants to know, your turn will come next," sobbed Greca. "Oh! Why does not The Great White One strike these monsters to the dust!"

She ran to Brand and pressed her satiny cheek to his. Then she was dragged roughly away.

The great door clanged shut. The heavy outer fastenings clicked into place. Dex had gone to experience whatever it was that Journeyman and the rest had experienced in this red hell. And Brand was left behind to reflect on what dread torments this might comprise; and to pray desperately that no matter what might be done to his shrinking body he would be strong enough to refuse to betray his planet.

CHAPTER FIVE
The Torture Chamber

Swiftly Dex was carried down the long ramp to the ground floor, the arms of his captors gripping him with painful tightness. Heading the procession was the immensely tall, gangling Rogan leader, clutching Greca by the wrist and dragging her indifferently along to be his mouthpiece.

They did not stop at the street level; they continued on down another ramp, around a bend, descending an even steeper incline toward the bowels of Jupiter. Their descent ended at last before a huge metal barrier which, at a signal from the leader, drew smoothly up into the ceiling to disclose a gigantic, red-lit chamber underlying the foundations of the building.

In fear and awe, Dex gazed around that huge room.

It resembled in part a nightmare rearrangement of such a laboratory as might be found on Earth; and in part a torture chamber such as the most ferocious of savages might have devised had they been scientifically equipped to add contrivances of supercivilization to the furthering of their primitive lust for cruelty.

There were great benches—head-high to the Earthman—to accommodate the height of the Rogan workmen. There were numberless metal instruments, and glass coils, and enormous retorts; and in one corner an orange colored flame burnt steadily on a naked metal plate, seeming to have no fuel or other source of being.

There was a long rack of cruelly pointed and twisted instruments. Under this was a row of long, delicate pincers, with coils on the handles to indicate that they might be heated to fiendish precision of temperatures. There were gleaming metal racks with calibrated slide-rods and spring dials to denote just what pull was being exerted on whatever unhappy creature might be stretched taut on them. There were tiny cones of metal whose warped, baked appearance testified that they were little portable furnaces that could be placed on any desired portion of the anatomy, to slowly bake the selected disk of flesh beneath them.

Dex shuddered; and a low moan came from Greca, whose clear blue eyes had rested on the contents of this vast room before in her capacity as hostage and interpreter for the inhuman Rogans.

And now another sense of Dex's began to register perception on his brain.

A peculiar odor came to his nostrils. It was a musky, fetid odor, like that to be smelled in an animal cage; but it was sharper, more acrid than anything he had ever smelled on Earth. It smelled—ah, he had it!—*reptilian*. As though somewhere nearby a dozen titanic serpents were coiled ready to spring!

Looking about, Dex saw a six-foot square door of bars in one wall of the laboratory—like the barred entrance to a prison cell. It was from the interstices of this door that the odor seemed to emanate; but he had no chance to make sure, for now the Rogan leader approached him.

"I will first show you," he said, through his mouthpiece, Greca, "what happens to those who oppose our orders. We have a slave who tried to run away into the surrounding jungles three suns ago..."

A man was dragged into the chamber. He was slightly taller and more stockily muscled than an Earthman might be; but otherwise, in facial conformation and general appearance, he might have come here straight from New York City. Dex felt a great pang of sympathy for him. He was so plainly one of humankind, despite the fact that he had been born on a sphere four hundred million miles from Dex's.

The fellow was paralyzed with horror. His eyes, wide and glazed, darted about the torture room like those of a trapped animal. And yet he made no move to break away from the clutch of the two Rogans who held him. He knew he was helpless, that wild-eyed glance told Dex. Knew it so thoroughly that not even his wildest terror could inspire him to try to make a break for freedom, or strike back at the implacable Rogan will.

At a nod from the leader, the man was stripped to the waist. Here Dex started in amazement. The man's broad chest was seamed and crisscrossed by literally hundreds of tiny lateral scars, some long healed, and some fresh incisions.

He was dragged to a metal plate set upright in the wall, and secured to it by straps of metal. Evidently the miserable being knew what this portended, for he began to scream—a monotonous, high-pitched shriek that didn't stop till he was out of breath.

The Rogan leader stared at him icily, then depressed a small lever set in the wall beside him. The plate against which the captive was bound began to shine softly with a blue light. The slave twisted in his bonds, screaming again. Rhythmic shudders jerked at his limbs. His lips turned greenish white. The shudders grew more pronounced till it seemed as though he were afflicted with a sort of horrible St. Vitus dance. Then the tall Rogan pulled back the lever. The slave hung away from his supporting shackles, limp and unconscious.

Dex moistened his lips. An electric shock? No, it was something more terrible than that. Some other manifestation of the magnetic power the Rogans had harnessed—a current, perhaps, that depolarized partly the atoms of the body structure? He could only guess. But the convulsed face of the unfortunate victim showed that the torment, whatever it was, was devilish to the last degree!

"That will be the next to the last fate reserved for you," the Rogan informed Dex, through Greca. "Death follows soon after that—but not too soon for you to see and feel what waits for you behind the barred door!" And he nodded toward the cage-entrance affair, from which came the musky, reptilian stench.

"Now that you have seen something of what will happen to you if you refuse to tell us what we want to know, we shall proceed," said the leader.

He pointed toward one of the gargantuan work benches, and two of the Rogans slid down from it a contrivance that looked familiar to Dex. An instant's scrutiny showed him why it was familiar: it was a partly dismantled atomic motor.

In spite of the ordeal that faced him, Dex felt a thrill of elation as he looked at the motor. In its scattered state, it told a mute story: a story of long and intensive study by the Rogans, which had yielded them no results! Only too obviously, the intricate secret of atomic power had not let itself be solved.

On the heels of the elation that filled his heart, came a sickening realization of his dilemma. He could not have told the Rogans what they wanted to know even if he had wished to! He himself didn't know the principles of the atomic engine. As Brand had remarked, he was no space navigator; he was simply a prosaic lieutenant, competent only at fighting, not at all versed in science.

He knew, though, that it would do no good to assert his ignorance to the Rogans. They simply wouldn't believe him.

"You will rebuild this engine for us," ordered the tall leader, "showing us the purpose of each part, and how the power is extracted from the fuel. After that you will set it running for us, and instruct us in its control."

Dex braced himself. His final moment had come.

By way of indicating his refusal he looked away from the dismantled motor and said nothing. The Rogan repeated his command. Dex made no move. Then the leader acted.

He said something to the Rogan guards who had been standing by all this while, alert against an outbreak from their prisoner. Dex was caught up, carried to one of the metal racks, and thrown down on its calibrated bed. Loops of metal, like handcuffs, were snapped around his wrists and ankles; and a metal hoop was clamped over his throat, pinning him to the torture rack. Resistance would have been useless, and Dex submitted quietly.

The contrivance, with him on it, was wheeled toward the barred door. It was halted at a spot marked on the floor, about thirty feet from the bars. The Rogan leader stepped alongside the rack, with Greca trembling beside him.

Dex closed his eyes for a moment, grimly marshaling strength of will to go through the trial that was just beginning.

The Rogan leader depressed another lever in the rock wall. The barred door slid slowly up, to reveal the receding darknesses of some great cave, or room, that adjoined the laboratory. Dex rolled his eyes so that he could watch the doorway; and, in a cold perspiration, waited for whatever might appear.

It was not long in coming!

The reptilian smell suddenly grew stronger. There was a booming hiss, a savage bellowing. A clattering of vast scales rattled out as some body weighing many tons was dragged over rock flooring. Then, before Dex's staring eyes appeared a huge, wedge-shaped head, at sight of which he bit his lips to keep from crying aloud.

Often enough he had seen one of those terrific heads looming in the fog of the northern hemisphere of Jupiter. He did not know the genus of the vast monster that bore it, but he did know it for the fiercest of the lizard giants that roamed the Jovian jungles. A creature larger than a terrestrial whale, with great long neck and heavy long tail dragging yards behind it, it would find the puny bulk of a man nothing but a morsel in its jaws!

Again the gigantic thing hissed and bellowed. And then its huge head came through the six-foot door and its neck uncoiled to send the gaping jaws within a foot of Dex. There it struggled to reach him, prevented by the small doorway that restrained the bulk of its enormous body, its head only inches away from the cleverly measured spot to which the metal rack had been wheeled.

Dex stared, hypnotized, into the dull, stony eyes of the beast, gasping for breath in the stench of its exhalations. The jaws snapped shut, fanning his cheek. He fought for self-control. Steady! Steady! The slimy Rogans had no intention of feeding him to the thing yet. Not till they had made more determined efforts to wring from him the secret of the motor. They were just prefacing actual physical torture with hellish mental torture, that was all.

That he was right in his guess was proved in a few moments. He heard a louder hiss from the great lizard so near him. Opening his eyes, he saw the Rogan leader in the process of forcing the serpentine neck to withdraw foot by foot back into the doorway, using his shock-tube as a sort of distant prod.

The monster swayed its ugly flat head back and forth, hissing deafeningly at the sting of the tube, now and again lunging with its vast unseen body at the too narrow entrance that kept it from entering the laboratory. Dex could hear the foundation walls of the building creak at the onslaught of that tremendous weight.

If it would only break through, he thought savagely. But it wasn't going to. In a short while it was cowed by the deadly tube, and withdrew its head awkwardly from the chamber. The barred door slid into place, and the Rogan leader once more turned his attention to his prisoner.

"You will be wheeled within reach of the creature as the last step of your fate," Dex was informed. "Meanwhile, we shall start with something less deadly…"

A cogged wheel beside him was turning a notch. Dex felt the sliding bed of the rack crawl slightly under him. Intolerable tension was suddenly placed on his arms and legs. The leader stared at a spring dial; and moved the wheel another notch. The rack expanded again, stretching Dex's body till his joints cracked.

"You will tell us what we want to know," said the Rogan, glaring coldly down at him.

Dex compressed his lips stubbornly. He couldn't tell them if he wanted to, and, by God, he wouldn't if he could.

Another notch, the wheel was turned; and in spite of himself, Dex groaned. One more notch, while the metal slide-rods beneath him lengthened a fraction of an inch…

CHAPTER SIX
The Inquisition

Blind, animal fear caught Dex and shook him in its grip. Then rage filled his heart, driving out the fear as a gale dissipates fog. With pain-dimmed eyes he glared at the gangling, hateful figure that gazed down on him with icy eyes. If he could only blast that monstrous, physically feeble but mentally ferocious thing to bits! Annihilate it! Blow it to the four corners of Jupiter! And all the other Rogans with it!

And with this thought he suddenly saw, through the red mists of rage, the shock-tube that was dangling indifferently from the Rogan leader's hand.

Instantly the red mists began to clear away. Another change took place in the tortured lieutenant's mind. The blind hot rage faded into more deadly, cold wrath. A plan began to bud into thought. It was a futile plan, really. It could not possibly accomplish anything vital. But it *might* give him a chance for a little revenge before his life was snuffed out—might give him a chance to strike a blow for the dead Journeyman and the other gallant explorers who had perished here in this chamber before him.

He closed his eyes to hide the hate and calculation in them. The tall Rogan leaned lower over the rack.

"You are ready to do as I command?" he demanded.

"Yes," whispered Dex. "Yes."

In the beautiful Greca's eyes, as she translated his assent, was horror. But then, faintly, her mind caught the thought that lay beneath the Earthman's apparent surrender. She veiled her own eyes with long lashes, lest they betray the captive's plan to the alert Rogan. Her lips moved silently; perhaps she was praying to her Great White One.

"Release him," the Rogan ordered, triumph in his bird-like, shrill voice. The metal hoops were unfastened. Dex stretched his outraged body, wincing with the pain of movement; then felt life and strength returning to him.

"Come with us to the motor," commanded the Rogan, his dull eyes glinting in anticipation of learning the coveted secret that should add one more planet to the Rogan's tyranny.

Dex walked to the dismantled atomic engine with him. He walked slowly, pretending more stiffness and weakness than he really owned to. No use in letting his captors know that his resilient muscles were so quickly throwing off the torment of the rack.

As he walked he kept his gaze covertly on that shock-tube that dangled in the leader's grasp. The rest of the guard had none; they had laid their weapons down on a far bench on their entrance to the chamber, depending on the one with which their leader was armed.

Eagerly the Rogans crowded around Dex and the motor that had thus far baffled them. They bent down from their twelve-foot heights to bring their staring goggle-eyes closer to the lesson in atomic motive power, till Dex was in a sort of small dome of Rogans, with their long, pipe-like legs forming the wall around him, and their thin torsos inclining forward to make a curved ceiling over him.

The Rogan leader drew Greca within the circle to interpret the Earthman's explanations.

Dex moved a trifle, to bring himself nearer the tall leader. Again he glanced covertly at the shock-tube.

"The first thing to tell about our motor," said Dex, stalling for time, "is that it utilizes the breaking up of the atom as its source of power."

He edged closer to the Rogan leader.

"You see those electrodes?" he said, pointing to two copper castings in a chamber between the fuel tank and the small but enormously powerful turbine that whirled with the released atomic energy. The Rogan leader blinked assent. His small, horrible mouth was pursed with his concentration of thought.

"The electrodes partially break down the atoms of fuel passing from the tank," explained Dex, desperately attempting scientific phraseology for a matter as far over his head as the remote stars. He raised his hand a trifle, bringing it nearer the Rogan's tube...

"Is that the outlet from the tank?" inquired the Rogan, pointing with the tube, and so raising it out of Dex's reach.

"Yes," mumbled Dex, sick with disappointment: he'd been on the point of leaping for the weapon. He sidled close again. Greca bit her lips lest she cry out with suspense.

"The partially disintegrated atoms pass into the turbine chamber," he went on, "and are there completely broken down by heat, which has been generated by the explosive energy of the atoms passing in before them."

"I warn you to speak true," said the leader, suddenly removing his gaze from the specimen motor and staring icily down at Dex. Dex's hand dropped abruptly from its place near the tube. Again his fingers had come within a foot of it.

"We will get ahead faster," piped the Rogan, an edge of suspicion sounding in his shrill voice, "if I conduct the explanation. I will ask questions for you to answer. What is the fuel used?"

"Powdered zinc," Dex answered promptly. No harm in admitting that. The Rogans must already know it; zinc was common to Jupiter, as Earth spectroscopes had showed long since; and they had no doubt analyzed it by now. The chances were that the leader was merely testing him, to see if he were sincere in his ostensible surrender.

That his guess was right, he read in the fishy, dull eyes. The Rogan leader nodded at his answer, and some of the lurking suspicion in his gaze died down.

"How is it prepared?"

Now this marked the beginning of the end, Dex knew. The preparation of the powdered metal was half the secret of atomic power—and Dex hadn't the faintest idea what it was! This questions-and-answers affair was going to pin him down in short order!

"How is it prepared?" repeated the Rogan leader inexorably. "Tell us, or—"

But at that instant Dex attained his objective.

Once more his hand had crawled slowly toward the tube—till, once more, it was within reach. Then, more bold as his position grew more desperate, he straightened up—and, with a lightning move, had wrenched it from the sucker-disk that held it!

He shouted his triumph. He had it! *Now* let the devils put him back on the torture bed if they could! *Now* let them try to make him betray his planet!

There was an alarmed squeak from the Rogan leader, and in an instant the huge laboratory was in an uproar. The Rogan guards whipped their hose-like arms toward the Earthman. Dex, with a sweep of his hands, knocked the pipe-stem legs of two of the guards from under them, leaped over their bodies, and stood at bay in a corner—guarding the bench on which the guards had laid their tubes when they filed into the laboratory.

The air resounded with the shrill calls of the excited Rogans. Then they began to close in on him, all the while eyeing the tube in his hand with terror written large on their hideous faces.

Dex's eyes blazed with the light of vengeful exultation. For the death of Journeyman and the rest, for the coming inevitable death of himself and Brand, he was going to pay—at least in part—with the captured tube of death in his hand! It was a lovely thought, and for a few seconds he delayed acting in order to savor it.

Then, with a smile of pure happiness, he leveled the tube at the nearest Rogan in order to shrivel him to nothingness as he had seen the slave shrivelled in the street.

The Rogan did not fall! Full in the face of the death tube he teetered forward, his arms reaching savagely toward the Earthman.

Dex stared incredulously. Cold fear crept into his heart. He pointed the tube more accurately, and squeezed harder on the coil handle. Still nothing happened. The Rogans warily drew closer.

Perspiration began to trickle down Dex's cheeks. In God's name, why didn't the tube work? He had thought all he had to do was point it and squeeze down on the handle. But evidently there was more to the trick than that!

He groaned. He had staged all this elaborate play for a weapon as useless to his untrained mind as one of Earth's explosive guns, with the safety-lock clamped on, would have been to an abysmal Venusian savage!

By now the nearest Rogan was within reaching distance of him. One of its two pairs of slimy arms uncoiled toward him. The other pair strained to reach around him and get to the weapons on the bench by his side.

With a cry, Dex dashed the useless shock-tube down on the reaching arms. As long as he didn't know how to work it anyway, he might as well use it as a club.

The Rogan squeaked with pain; the arms recoiled. Dex jerked the tube back over his shoulder for another blow…

There was a shriek from the doomed wretch fastened to the metal plate. The slave that had been tortured before Dex's eyes as an object lesson! He had been returned to consciousness a short time since, and had been writhing and shuddering against the plate.

Dex flashed a glance at him over his shoulder, as he shrieked, and cried aloud himself at what he saw.

The tortured slave was rapidly disappearing! Another shriek left his lips, to be broken off halfway. In an instant nothing was left of the struggling body but a wisp of greasy black smoke!

Dex stared stupidly at the tube in his hand. Then, as a squeak of agony sounded from a Rogan in front of him, his mind grasped what had happened. Somehow its mechanism had been jarred into functioning when he dashed it against the groping arm. In some way its death dealing power had been unleashed. With a cry of exultation, Dex began to use it!

The Rogan in front of him, squealing, collapsed on the floor, dwindling swiftly into nothingness. Dex turned the mysterious death against another teetering creature. It too went up in oleaginous smoke.

The Rogan leader came next. Dex whirled the tube in his direction, and saw him go down. Then he sprang to annihilate still another grotesque monster who had almost reached the bench on which were the other tubes. He shouted and raved as this fourth Rogan crumbled. Torture him, would they! Plan to capture Earth, would they! He'd kill off the whole damned population with this tube!

The Rogan survivors, squeaking in panic, gave over their attempts to retrieve the tubes. They dove for various hiding places—under benches, behind retorts, anywhere to get away from the terror running amuck in their midst. And after them sprang Dex, mad with his sudden miraculous success, to ferret them out one by one and blow them into hell with their own horrible death-engine.

In his ecstasy of rage, Dex overlooked the Rogan leader. He had seen that attenuated monstrosity go down, and had assumed he was dead. But such was not the case. In the corner Dex had vacated when he sprang after the fleeing guard, the tall leader twisted feebly and sat up.

One of his four arms was missing, a smoking stump showing where the annihilating ray from the tube had blasted it off at the shoulder. But he was far from dead. With cold purpose in his great staring eyes, he moved snakily toward the bench Dex had now left unguarded.

The Earthman got another Rogan; whirled to track down still another. Promptly the leader sank motionless to the floor. The Rogan leader continued his crawling. He reached the bench, fumbled up and along its surface for the nearest tube.

Dex, unconscious of the sure fate gathering behind him to strike him down, dashed past a great glass tank behind which Greca was huddling in mortal fear, and charged down on two more of the squeaking guards.

Then, suddenly, some sixth sense warned him that something was wrong. He whirled toward the corner he had left.

The Rogan leader, two of his surviving arms propping feebly against the bench, was pointing a shock-tube squarely at him!

Dex fell to the floor to escape the first discharge of the tube, and leveled his own. He felt the thing grow hot in his hand, saw a blinding blue-white fire leap into being in the space between them as the rays from the two tubes met and absorbed each other. He shifted, to get out of the line and blast the creature he had too hastily reckoned as dead. But he was not quick enough. A fraction before him, the Rogan leader shifted.

Dex felt a terrible burning sensation all over his body, as the ray from his tube met the conflicting ray less squarely, and allowed a little of it to reach him. He shrieked as the slave had shrieked when he felt the annihilating current from the plate sweeping through his body.

A black fog seemed to close in around the Earthman's senses. He crashed to the floor, with a glimpse of the leering triumph on the Rogan's face as the last picture to stamp itself in his failing consciousness.

The tall Rogan, obviously in agony from his blasted arm, squeaked a faint order. The four guards who were left issued fearfully from their hiding places and came to him.

He pointed his tube at Dex Harlow, lying unconscious on the floor. There he hesitated an instant, his soft little mouth slobbering in his rage and pain. Then he let the tube sink slowly off its line.

He gave another command. The four guards picked the Earthman up and carried him to the metal torture-plate on which the slave had met his death. The tall leader's eyes gleamed with vicious hatred as the limp body was fastened to the metal.

Mouthing and squealing with the pain of his seared arm-stump, he wobbled toward the lever, a mere turn of which would readily convert the plate into a bed of agony.

CHAPTER SEVEN
In the Power-House

Alone in the prison room, after Dex had been dragged away to be subjected to the Rogan inquisition, Brand gnawed at his fingers and paced distractedly up and down the stone flooring. For a while he had no coherent thought at all; only the realization that his turn came next, and that the Rogans would leave no refinement of torment untried in their effort to wring from him the secret of the atomic engine.

He went to the window, and absent-mindedly stared out. The whining hum from the great domed building off to the right, like the high-pitched droning of a swarm of gargantuan bees, came to his ears. He listened more intently, and leaned out of the window to look at the building.

Under that dome, it came to him again, was, in all probability, the mainspring of the Rogan mechanical power. If only he could get in there and look around! He might do some important damage; he might be able to harass the enemy materially before the time came for him to die.

He leaned farther out of the window, and examined the hundred feet or so of sheer wall beneath him. He saw, scrutinizing it intently, that the stone blocks that composed it were not smooth cut, but rough hewn, with the marks of the cutters' chisels plainly in evidence. Also there was a considerable ridge between each layer of blocks where the

Rogans' mortar had squeezed out in the process of laying the wall.

Never in sanity would a man have thought of the thing Brand considered then. To attempt to clamber down that blank wall, with only the slight roughness of the protruding layers of mortar to hang on to, was palpable suicide!

Brand shrugged. He observed that to a man already condemned to death, the facing of probable suicide shouldn't mean much.

With scarcely an increase in the beating of his heart, he swung one leg out over the broad sill. If he fell, he escaped an infinitely worse death; if he didn't fall, he might somehow win his way into that domed building whence the hum came.

Cautiously, clutching at the rough stone with finger tips that in a moment or two became raw and bleeding masses, he began his slow descent. As he worked his way down, he slanted to the right, toward the near wall of the retaining yard whose end was formed by the round structure that was his goal.

Beneath him and to the left the broad street swarmed with figures: the tall ones of the Rogans and the shorter, sturdier ones of slaves. Any one of those dozens of grotesque pedestrians might glance up, see him, and pick him off with the deadly tubes. Under his fingers the mortar crumbled and left him hanging, more than once, by one hand. For fully five minutes his life hung by a thread apt to be severed at any time. But—he made it. Helped by the decreased gravity of the red spot, and released from inhibiting fear by the fact that he was already, figuratively, a dead man, he performed the incredible.

With a last slithering step downward, he landed lightly on the near wall of the enclosure, and started along its broad top toward his objective.

Now he was in plain sight of any one who might be looking out the windows of the tower building or from the dome ahead of him; but this was a chance he had to take, and at least he was concealed from the swarms in the street. Making no effort to hide himself by crawling along the top of the wall, he straightened up and began to run toward the giant dome.

Hardly had he gone a dozen steps when he suddenly understood the meaning of the high-walled enclosure to his right!

Off in a far corner rose a slate colored mound that at first glance he had taken for a great heap of inanimate dirt. The mound began to move toward him—and metamorphosed into an animal, a thing that made Brand blink his eyes to see if he were dreaming, and then stop, appalled, to look at it.

He saw a body that dwarfed the high retaining walls to comparative insignificance. It had a tree-like tail that dragged behind it; and a thirty-foot, serpentine neck at the end of which was a head like a sugar barrel that split into cavernous jaws lined with backward-pointing teeth. Two eyes were set wide apart in the enormous head, eyes that were dead and cold and dull, yet glinting with senseless ferocity. It was the sort of thing one sees in delirium.

With increasing energy the creature made for him, till finally it was approaching his sector of the wall at a lumbering run that was rapid for all its ungainliness.

It was apparent at a glance that the snaky neck, perched atop the lofty shoulder structure, would raise the head with its gaping jaws to his level on the wall! Brand ran. And after him thudded the gigantic lizard, its neck arching up and along the wall to reach him.

A scant five yards ahead of the snapping jaws, Brand reached his goal, the dome, and clambered over its curved, metal roof away from the monster's maw.

He stopped to pant for breath and wipe the sweat from his streaming face. "Thank God it didn't get me," he breathed, looking back at the bellowing terror that had pursued him. "Wonder why it's there? It's too ferocious to be tamed and used in any way: it must be kept as a threat to hold the slaves in hand. It certainly looks well fed..."

He shuddered; then he began to explore the dome of the building for a means of entrance.

There was no opening in the roof. A solid sheet of reddish metal, like a titanic half-eggshell, it glittered under him in an unbroken piece.

He crept down its increasingly precipitous edge till he reached a sort of cornice that formed a jutting circle of stone around it. There he leaned far over and saw, about ten feet below him, a round opening like a big port-hole. From it were streaming waves of warm, foul air, from which he judged it to be a ventilator outlet.

He scrambled over the edge of the cornice, hung at arm's length, and swung himself down into the opening. And there, perched high up under the roof, he looked down at an enigmatic, eery scene.

That the structure was indeed a strange sort of power-house was instantly made evident. But what curious, mysterious, and yet bewilderingly simple machinery it held!

In the center was a titanic coil of reddish metal formed by a single cable nearly a yard through. Around this, at the four corners of the compass, were set coils that were identical in structure but a trifle smaller. From the smaller coils to the larger streamed, unceasingly, blue waves of light like lightning bolts.

Along a large arc of the wall was a stone slab set with an endless array of switches and insulated control-buttons. Gauges and indicators of all kinds, whose purpose could not even be guessed at, were lined above and below, all throbbing rhythmically to the leap of the electric-blue rays between the monster coils.

Almost under Brand's perch a great square beam of metal came through the building wall from outside, to be split into multitudinous smaller beams that were hooked up with the bases of the coils. Across from him, disappearing out through the opposite wall, was an identical beam.

"The terminals for the metal plate system that extends over the whole red spot," murmured Brand. "This building *is* important. But what can I do to throw sand in the gears before I'm caught and killed?"

He surveyed the great round room below him more thoroughly. Now he saw, right in the center of the huge control board, a solitary lever, that seemed a sort of parent to all the other levers and switches. It was flanked by a perfect army of gauges and indicators; and was covered by a glass bell which was securely bolted to the rock slab.

"That looks interesting," Brand told himself. "I'd like to see that closer, if I can climb down from here without being observed... Why"—he broke off—"where is everybody...?"

For the first time, in the excitement and concentration of his purpose, the emptiness of the place struck him. There was no sign of light in the great building—no workmen or slaves anywhere. There was just the great coils, with the streamers of blue light bridging them and emitting the high-pitched, monotonous hum audible outside the dome, and the complicated control board with its quivering indicator needles and mysterious levers. That was all.

"Must be out to lunch," muttered Brand, his eyes going fascinatedly toward that solitary, parent lever under its glass bell. "Well, it gives me a chance to try some experiments, anyway."

It was about fifty feet from his perch to the floor; but a few feet to one side was a metal beam that extended up to help support the trussed weight of the roof. He jumped for this, and quickly slid down it.

He started on a run for the control board; but almost immediately he stopped warily to listen: it seemed to him that he had caught, faintly, the squeaking, high tones of Rogan conversation.

Miraculously, the sound seemed to come from a blank wall to his left. He crept forward to investigate…

The mystery was solved before he had gone very far. There was an opening in the wall leading off to an annex of some kind outside the dome building. The opening was concealed by a set-back, so that at first glance it had seemed part of the wall itself. From this opening drifted the chatter of Rogans.

Brand stole closer, finally venturing to peer into the room beyond from an angle where he himself could not be seen. And he found that his whimsical reference to "lunch" had contained a ghastly element of fact!

In that annex were several dozen of the teetering, attenuated Rogans, and an equal number of slaves. And the relation of the slaves and the Rogans was one that made Brand's skin crawl.

Each Rogan had stripped the tunic from the chest of his slave. Now, as Brand watched, each drew a keen blade from his belt, and made a shallow gash in the shrinking flesh. There were a few stifled screams—some of the slaves were women—but for the most part the slashing was endured in stoical silence. When red drops began to ooze forth, the Rogans stooped and applied their horrible little mouths to the incisions...

"The slimy devils!" Brand whispered hoarsely, at sight of that dreadful feeding. "The inhuman, monstrous vermin!"

But now one or two of the Rogans had begun to utter squeaks of satiation; and Brand hastened away from there and toward the control board again. He hadn't an idea of what he might accomplish when he reached it; he didn't know but that a touch of the significant looking parent-lever might blast him to bits; but he did know that he was going to raise absolute hell with something, somewhere, if he possibly could.

Swiftly he approached the great master-lever, protected by its bell of glass. (At least it looked like glass, for it was crystal clear and reflected gleamingly the blue light from the nearby coils). He tapped it experimentally with his knuckles...

At once pandemonium reigned in the great vaulted building. There was a siren-like screaming from a device he noticed for the first time attached under the domed roof. A clanging alarm split the air from half a dozen gongs set around the upper walls.

Squealing shouts sounded behind Brand. He whirled, and saw the Rogans, interrupted in their terrible meal, pouring in from the annex and racing toward him. Rage and fear distorted their hideous faces as they pointed first to the big lever and then at the escaped Earthman. They redoubled their efforts to get at him, their long unsteady legs covering the distance in great bounds.

Brand swore. Was he to be caught again before he had accomplished a certain thing? When he had already managed to win clear to his objective?

He hammered at the glass bell with his fists, but realized with the first blow that he was only wasting time trying to crack it bare-handed. He glanced quickly about and saw a metal bar propped up against the control board near him.

He sprang for it, grasped it as a club, and returned to the glass bell. Raising his arms high, he brought the thick metal bar down on the glass with all his strength.

With a force that almost wrenched his arms from their sockets, the bar rebounded from the glass bell, leaving it uncracked.

"Unbreakable!" groaned Brand.

Desperately he tried again, whirling the bar high over his head and bringing it smashing down. The result was the same as before as far as breaking the bell was concerned. But—a little trickle of crushed rock came from around the bolts in the slab to which the bell was fastened.

A third time be brought the bar down. The glass bell sagged a bit sway from the slab...

He had no chance for more assaults on it. The nearest Rogans had leaped for him. Slimy arms were coiling around him, while the loathsome sucker-disks tore at his unprotected face and throat.

Savagely Brand lashed out with the bar. It caved in a pair of the long, skinny legs, bringing a bloated round head down within reach. He smashed it with the bar, exulting grimly as the blow crumpled bone and flesh almost down to the little mouth which was yet carmine from its recent feeding.

The process seemed a sound one to Brand, unable as he was to reach the Rogans' heads that towered six feet above his own. Methodically, swinging the bar with the weight of his body behind it, he repeated the example. First a crash of the bar against a pair of legs, then the crushing in of the Rogan's head when he toppled with agonized squeals to the floor.

Again and again he crushed the life out of a Rogan with his one-two swing of the deadly bar. They were thinning down, now. They were wavering in their charges against the comparatively insignificant being from another planet who was defending himself so fiercely.

Finally one of their number turned and ran toward an exit, waving his four arms and adding his high-pitched alarms to the incessant ringing of the gongs and shrieks of the warning siren up under the roof. The rest rushed the Earthman in a body.

Steadily, almost joyfully, Brand fought on. He had expected to be annihilated by one of the Rogan shock-tubes long before now; but as yet there was no sign of any. Either these Rogan workmen were not privileged to carry the terrible things, or they were too occupied to think of going and getting them; anyhow, Brand was left free to wield his bar and continue crushing out the lives of the two-legged vermin that attacked him.

With almost a shock of surprise, he saw finally that he had battered their number down to three. At that he took the offensive himself. He rammed the bluntly pointed end of the bar almost through one writhing torso, broke the back of a second with a whistling blow, and tripped and exterminated the third almost in as many seconds. The creatures, without their death-tubes, were as helpless as crippled rats!

Panting, he turned again toward the loosened glass bell, and battered at it with the precious bar. Gradually the bolts that held it to the stone slab were wrenched out, till only one supported it. But at this point, from half a dozen set-back doorways, streams of infuriated Rogans began pouring into the building and toward him.

The one that had fled had come back with help.

CHAPTER EIGHT
Tremendous Odds

Like living spokes of a half-wheel, with the Earthman as the hub, the Rogans converged toward Brand, a howling roar outside indicating that there were hundreds more waiting to jam into the dome as soon as they were able. There were still no shock-tubes in evidence: evidently the worker who had gone for help had gathered the first Rogan citizens he had encountered on the streets. But the very numbers of the mob spelled defeat for Brand.

However, there was still the great lever behind him to yank away from its switch-socket. The glass bell was almost off now. With a last mad blow, he knocked loose the remaining bolt that held it. The bell clattered to the floor.

A concerted shriek came from the crowding Rogans as they saw the Earthman's hand close on the lever. Whatever effect the throwing of that master-switch could have, there was no doubt that they were extremely anxious to prevent it!

And now, in the rear of the crowding columns, appeared Rogans taller than the others, with an authoritative air, who waved before them, eager to unleash their power, batteries of the death-tubes.

Resigning himself to annihilation in the next instant, Brand pulled down hard on the lever.

The effect wrought by the throwing of that great switch was almost indescribable.

In a flash, as though all had been struck at once by a giant's hand, every Rogan in the mob shot toward the floor, long thin legs caving under him as if turned to water. Writhing feebly, they endeavored to get up, but could not; and, still weakly ferocious, began to creep toward the Earthman like huge-headed worms.

Brand himself had been thrown to the floor with the falling of that switch. He had felt as though an invisible ocean had been poured on him, weighting him down intolerably. To move arms or legs required enormous effort; and to get up on his feet again was like rising under a two-hundred-pound pack.

The movement of the switch, he saw, had cut off the gravity reducing apparatus of the Rogans—whatever that might consist of. They were now, abruptly, subjected to the full force of gravity exerted by Jupiter's great mass. They could no more stand erect on their tottering, lofty legs than they could fly.

But, though greatly handicapped by the gravity pull, they were still not entirely helpless. Like huge, long insects they continued to worm their way toward Brand, using their four arms and their boneless legs to help urge them over the flooring. And in their rear the Rogan guards struggled to lift their tubes and level them at the escaped prisoner.

Prompt to avoid that, Brand went down on his hands and knees. Thus he was shielded by the foremost crawling Rogans: the ones in the rear, with the tubes, could not raise themselves high enough to bore down over their fellows' heads at the Earthman.

Squatting on his knees, Brand awaited the first resolute crawlers. And, on his knees, whirling the now thrice weighty bar at heads that were conveniently low enough to be accessible, he began his last stand.

In the Rogans came, evidently determined, at any sacrifice of life, to get the Earthman away from that vital control board. And to right and left, crouching low to escape the tubes of the guards slowly crawling forward from the rear, Brand laid about him with the bar.

He got a little sick at the havoc he was wreaking on these slow-moving, gravity-crippled things: but remembrance of their grisly feeding habits, and the torture they must by now have inflicted on Dex, kept him flailing down on soft heads with undiminished effort.

With the gravity pull what it was, the Earthman was immeasurably stronger than any individual Rogan. For a time the contest was all in his favor. It was like killing slugs in a rose garden!

Nevertheless, these slugs were, after all, twelve feet long and possessed of intelligence, besides being hundreds in number. After a while the tide of battle began to turn in their favor.

Brand began to feel his arms ache burningly with the sustained effort of wielding a weapon that now weighed about twenty-five pounds. He knew he couldn't keep up the terrific strain much longer. And, in addition, he could see that the armed Rogans in the rear were steadily forging ahead among the unarmed attackers, till they soon must be in a position to blast him with their weapons.

Brand brought down his bar, with failing force but still deadly effect, on the loathsome face of the nearest Rogan, grunting with satisfaction as he saw it crumple into a shapeless mass. He thrust it, spear-like, into another face, and another.

Then, abruptly, he found himself weaponless.

Raising it high to bring it down on an attacker who was almost about to seize him, he felt the metal bar turn white hot, and dropped it with a cry as it seared the skin from the palms of his hands. Some Rogan guard in the rear had managed to train his tube on the bar; and in the instant of its rising had almost melted it.

Weaponless and helpless, Brand crawled slowly back before the tortuously advancing mob, keeping close enough to them to be shielded from the tubes of the rear guards. Without his club he knew the end was a matter of seconds.

He had an impulse to leap full into the mass of repulsive, crawling bodies and die fighting as his fists battered at the gruesome faces. But a second impulse, and a stronger one, was the blind instinct to preserve his life as long as possible.

Hesitantly, almost reluctantly, acting on the primitive instinct of self-preservation, he continued to back away from the advancing horde; away from the switch and toward the rear of the dome.

With the instant of his withdrawal, a Rogan turned toward the lever to push it back up into contact and release the red kingdom from the burden of Jupiter's unendurable gravity. And now ensued a curious struggle. The lever, placed for the convenience of creatures twelve feet or more tall, was about five feet from the floor. And the Rogan couldn't reach it!

Stubbornly he heaved and writhed in an effort to raise his inordinately heavy body from the floor to a point where one of the weaving arms could reach the switch. But the pipe-stem legs would not bear its weight. Each time it nearly reached the lever, only to fall feebly back again in a snarl of tangled limbs.

Meanwhile, Brand had flashed a quick look back over his shoulder to see, in the wall behind him, a metal door he hadn't noticed before. He found time for a flashing instant to wonder why there were no Rogans entering from that doorway, too; but it was a vain wonder, and it faded from his mind as the ever advancing, groping monsters before him kept crowding him back.

Instinctively he changed his course a trifle, to edge toward the metal door. Perhaps, behind it, there was sanctuary for a few moments. Perhaps he could force it open, spring out, and bar it again in the faces of the pursuing mob. It sounded improbable, but at least it offered him a slim chance where before no chance had seemed possible.

He reached the door at last, fumbled behind him and felt, high over his head, a massive sliding bolt.

In the spot Brand had left, the struggle to throw the gravity-lever back into closed contact position went on. The Rogan who was fruitlessly trying to reach up to it paused and said something to one near him. That one halted, and began to crawl toward him.

The two of them tried to reach it, one bracing the other and helping him pry his body up from the implacable pull of Jupiter's uninsulated mass. The top Rogan reached a little higher. The flesh sucker-disk that served as a hand almost grasped the lever, but failed by only a few inches.

A third Rogan crawled up. And now, with two arching their backs to help the other, the thing was done. The hose-like, groping arm went up and pushed the lever back into place.

The blue streamer began to hum and crackle from coil to coil again. The invisible weight that pressed down was released as once more the giant planet's gravity was nullified. The Rogans got eagerly to their feet and began to race toward Brand in their normal long bounds.

Brand, just cautiously rising, when the power went back on, found himself leaping five feet into the air with the excess of his muscular effort. And in that leap he saw the Rogans in the rear straighten up and point their tubes. However, also in that leap, his fumbling hand shot back the bolt that securely shut the metal door.

With a shout of defiance he jumped out of the door and slammed it shut after him, feeling it grow searing hot an instant later under the impact of the rays from the tubes that had been trained on him.

A stinging shock reached him through the metal, flinging him to the ground. He rolled out of its range and leaped to his feet to race away from there. Then, with a gasp, he flattened his body back against the wall of the dome building.

He was in the enclosure that held the gigantic, lizard-like thing that had nearly got him on his escape from the tower room.

He wheeled frantically to go back and face the Rogan death-tubes. Anything rather than wait while that mammoth heap of tiny-brained ferocity ran him down and tore him to shreds! But even as he turned, he heard the bolt shoot home on the inside of the door; heard vengeful squeals of triumph from his pursuers.

At the other end of the enclosure, near the foot of the tower building, the great lizard eyed him unblinkingly, its tremendous jaws gaping to reveal a cavernous mouth that was hideously lined with bright orange colored membrane. Then, squatting lower with every step it took, like a mountainous cat about to spring on its prey, it began to stalk on its tree-like legs toward the tiny creature that had leaped into its yard with it.

Brand whirled this way and that, mechanically seeking a way out. There was none. The walls of the great enclosure were not like the wall of the tower. Here were no rough hewn stones, with protruding ridges of mortar set between. These walls were as smooth as glass, and just as smooth was the curved wall of the dome building behind him.

The monstrous beast stalked nearer, almost on its belly now. As it advanced, the great tail stirred up a cloud of reddish dust, and left behind it a round deep depression in a surface already crisscrossed with a multitude of similar depressions. A bellowing hiss came from its gaping mouth, and it increased its pace to a thunderous, waddling rush.

CHAPTER NINE
Into the Enclosure

In the torture chamber Dex wavered slowly back to consciousness to get the growing impression that he was being immersed in a bath of liquid fire. Burning, intolerable pain assailed him with increasing intensity as his senses clarified.

At last he groaned and opened his eyes, for the moment not knowing where he was nor how he had come to be there. He saw strange torture instruments and tall monstrosities with pumpkin-shaped heads surrounding him closely in a semicircle, and staring at him out of great, dull eyes.

Remembrance came back with a rush, and he gathered his muscles to spring at the hateful figures. But he could not move. At waist and throat, at wrists and ankles, were hoops of metal. He closed his eyes again while the burning waves of invisible fire shot through him recurrently from head to foot.

Dully he wondered that he was still alive. His last recollection had been of the Rogan leader pointing his shock-tube full at him, his shapeless countenance working with murderous fury. However, alive he was; and most unenviably so!

His hands, circumscribed to a few inches of movement by the bonds on his wrists, felt the smooth substance at his back. And with a thrill of horror he realized his position: he was crucified against the metal slab on which the slave had writhed in agony a short half hour ago.

Again he strained and tugged, vainly, to get free. Off to one side, pressed back against a huge glass experimental tank, he saw the beautiful Greca, her eyes wide with horror; and caught her frantic pleading message to her "Great White One."

The Rogan leader, squealing and grimacing, advanced toward the victim on the metal plate. One of the long arms went out and a sucker-disk was pressed to Dex's cheek. Dex quivered at the loathsome contact of that soft and slimy substance; then set his jaws to keep from groaning as the disk was jerked away, to carry with it a fragment of skin and flesh.

Gingerly, the tall leader felt the twitching, blackened stump of his blasted arm. Dex grinned mirthlessly at that: he'd struck one or two blows in his own defense, anyhow!

At sight of the Earthman's grin, an expression of defiance and grim joy that needed no interpreting to be understandable, the Rogan leader fairly danced with rage.

His long arm went out to the switch beside the plate, and pulled it down another notch—just a little, not nearly to the current that had torn at the slave.

At the increased torment resulting from that slight movement of the regulating lever, Dex yelled aloud in spite of all his will power. It seemed as though his whole body were about to burst into self-generated flame. Every cell and fiber of him seemed on the verge of flying apart. He could feel his eyes start from his head, could feel every hair on his scalp stand up as though discharging electric sparks.

A minute or two of that and he would go mad! He cried out again, and twisted helplessly in his bonds. And then the terrible torture stopped.

The Rogan had not touched the switch—yet whatever sort of current it was that charged the plate was abruptly clicked off, as though someone at a distance had cut a wire or thrown a master-switch.

Simultaneously with its ceasing, an invisible, crushing sea seemed to envelope everything. Dex felt his body sag against his metal bonds as if it had been changed to lead.

Before him the Rogans, who had been crowding closer to watch gloatingly each grimace he made, shot doorward as though their pipe-stem legs had been swept from under them. The leader fell on the stump of his seared arm and, a deafening squeal of rage and pain came from his little mouth. His tube fell from his grasp and rolled over the floor half a dozen yards away from him.

Amazed, observing the stricken creatures only dimly through a haze of pain, Dex saw them struggle vainly to get up again, and heard them chattering excitedly to themselves. For the moment, in the face of this queer phenomenon, the prisoner seemed to be forgotten. And Dex was quick to seize the momentary advantage.

"Greca!" he called. "The tube! There—on the floor!"

The girl raised her head quickly, and followed his imploring gaze. Laboriously she started for the tube. At the same instant the Rogan leader began to feel around him for his lost weapon. Not finding it, he raised his head and glanced about for it. He saw the girl making her way toward it and, with a squeak of terror, began to crawl toward it himself.

He was not quick enough. The girl, though not nearly as active under the increased pull of gravity as a person of Earth might be, was yet more agile than the Rogans. And she was the faster mover in this tortuous, snail-like race. While the Rogan leader was still several feet away, she retrieved the shock-tube.

"Kill him!" begged Dex. "And all the rest of the filthy creatures!"

With feminine horror of the thing that faced her, Greca hesitated an instant—a hesitation almost long enough to be fatal. Then, just as the Rogan leader was reaching savagely out for her, she leveled the tube at him and turned it to its full power.

One last thin squeal came from the Rogan's mouth, a squeal that cracked abruptly at its height. What had been its gangling body drifted up in inky smoke.

"The others!" called Dex. "Quick! Before they get their weapons—"

Greca swept the death-tube in a short arc in front of her, over the bodies of the remaining Rogans, as if spraying plants with a hose. One after another, toppling in swift succession like grotesque falling dominoes, the creatures sagged to the floor and melted away. That one small part of Jupiter's red spot, at least, was cleared of Rogan population.

Long shudders racked Greca's body, and her lips were a bloodless line in her pallid face. But she did not go into womanly hysterics or swoon at the slaughter it had been her lot to inflict. Moving as quickly as she could, she went to the metal slab and began, with shaking fingers, to undo the fastenings that held Dex prisoner.

"Good girl," said Dex, patting her satiny bare shoulder as he stood free again. "You're a sport and a gentleman. You don't understand the terms? They're Earth words, Greca, that carry the highest praise a man can give a woman. But let's get out of here before another gang comes and takes us again. Where can we hide?"

"I don't know any hiding places," confessed Greca despairingly. "The Rogans swarm everywhere. We will be seen the moment we try to leave here."

"Well, we'll hunt for a hole, anyway," said Dex. He essayed to walk. What with the tendency of his muscles to jerk and collapse with the aftermath of the torture he had endured, and the sudden and inexplicable increase in gravity that bore him down, he made heavy going of it. "First we'll go up and get Brand."

"Yes, yes," said Greca, a soft glow in her clear blue eyes. "Let us go quickly."

She started toward the door, panting with the effort of moving. But Dex halted an instant, to stoop and pick up another of the tubes.

"We might as well have one of these apiece," he said. "You've proved you have the grit to use one; and maybe the dirty rats will think twice about rushing us if we each have a load of death in our hands."

They made their way out of the torture laboratory, and up the incline to the street level. And it was just as they reached this that the burden of gravity under which they staggered was lifted from their shoulders as quickly as it had descended on them.

Dex raised his arms just in time to fend his body from a collision with the wall in front of him. "Now what!" he exclaimed.

Greca lifted her hand for silence, inclined her head, and listened intently. As she did so, Dex heard the same noise her quick ears had caught an instant before his: a distant pandemonium of ringing gongs and siren shrieks, and squealing cries of a multitude of agitated Rogans.

"What the devil—" began Dex. But again Greca raised her hand to silence him, and listened once more. As she listened, her sea-blue eyes grew wider and wider with horror. Then, frantically, she began to race down a long corridor away from the street door.

Dex hastened to follow her. "What is it?" he demanded, when he had caught up to her flying little feet. "This is not the way up to the room where Brand—"

"Your friend is not there," she interrupted. She explained swiftly, distractedly: "From the shouts of the Rogans I learn that he got into the great dome building, somehow, and then was driven into the pen of the…"

Dex could not get the next term she used. But her telepathic message of the peril she mentioned formed in his mind clearly enough.

He got a flashing brain picture of a great, high-walled yard with a monster in it of the kind he had caught a close-range glimpse a short while before. Also, he saw a blurred, tiny figure, running from wall to wall, that was Greca's imagining of Brand and his efforts to escape the enormous beast.

"Good heavens!" groaned Dex. "Penned in with one of the things they showed me while I was stretched on the rack! Are you sure, Greca?"

She nodded, and tried to run faster. "This way," she gasped, turning down a passage to the left that ended in a massive metal door. "This leads to the enclosure. Oh, if only we can be in time!"

Her slim fingers tore at a massive bolt that secured the door. "Here," said Dex, wrenching it open for her. And they stepped out into thin sunlight, onto a hard surface of reddish ground that was crisscrossed with innumerable rounded furrows like the tracks old-fashioned, fifty-passenger airplane wheels used to make on soft landing fields.

Greca shrieked, and pointed to the far end of the enclosure. Down there, flattened against the wall of the dome building, was Brand. And waddling toward him with a tread that caused the ground to quiver, was a mate to the hideous creature the Rogans had used to terrify Dex in the torture chamber.

Dex leveled the tube he was carrying, swore, hit it frenziedly against his hand. "How do you work this damned thing, Greca—Oh! Like that! There—see if *that* puts a sting in your hide!"

The distant monster stopped its advance toward Brand. A raw white spot as big as a dinner plate leaped into being on one of its enormous hind legs. It whirled with an ear-splitting hiss, to see what thing was causing such pain in its rear. The frightful head whipped back at the end of the long neck, to nuzzle at the seared spot. Then the giant lizard turned toward Brand again.

A second time Dex pressed the central coil that formed the handle of the tube, as Greca had showed him how to do. A second time the ray shot down the field to flick a chunk of flesh weighing many pounds from the monster's flank. And this time it definitely abandoned the quarry behind it. With a scream like the keening of a dozen steam whistles, it charged back over its tracks toward the distant pigmies that were inflicting such exasperating punishment on it.

Dex swept the tube before him in a short half-circle. A smoking gash appeared suddenly in the vast fore-quarters of the monster. It stopped abruptly, its clawed feet plowing along the ground with the force of its momentum. An instant it stood there. Then, with its head swinging from side to side and lowered so that its looped neck dragged on the reddish, dusty ground, it began to back away from the source of its hurt, bellowing and hissing its rage and bewilderment.

"Brand!" shouted Dex. "This end! Run, while I hold the thing off!"

Brand began to race down the long enclosure, ten feet to a leap. The great lizard darted after him, like a cat after an escaping mouse; but a flick of the tube sent it bellowing and screaming back to its corner.

"Dex!" gasped Brand. "Thank God!"

For a moment he leaned, white and shaken, against the wall. Then Greca caught his hand in both of hers, and Dex put his arm supportingly around his shoulder. They retreated back through the doorway behind them, and slid the bolt across the metal door.

CHAPTER TEN
The "Tank Scheme"

Thank God you came when you did," repeated Brand. Then, with a moment in which, figuratively, to get his feet back on earth, the wonder of Dex's appearance struck him.

"How did you manage to get away?" he asked. "I was sure—I thought—when they dragged you out of the tower room I wouldn't see you again—"

Rapidly Dex gave an account of his ordeal in the torture chamber, telling Brand in a few words how he had attempted to win free of the Rogans, how he had almost succeeded, only to be caught again and clamped to the death-plate on the wall.

"But just as the big fellow was about to cook me for good and all," he concluded, "something happened to the current, and to the gravity at the same time—"

"That was when I pulled the lever in the dome building!" exclaimed Brand.

He told of what had befallen him in the Rogan power-house. "That lever, Dex!" he said swiftly. "It's the keynote of the whole business. It absolutely controls the pull of gravity, and Lord knows what else besides. If we could only get at it again! Perhaps we could not only shut it off so that Jupiter's pull would function again, but also reverse the process so its gravity would be *increased*! Think what that would mean! Every Rogan in the red empire stretched out and immovable, possibly crushed in by his own weight!"

"It's a wonderful thought," sighed Dex; while Greca's eyes glowed with a sudden hope for her enslaved race, "but I don't see how we could ever—"

He stopped; and glanced in alarm down the passage behind them. Greca and Brand, hearing the same soft noise, whirled to look, too.

Far down the passage, just sneaking around the bend, was a group of Rogan guards, each armed with a death-tube.

"Back to the pen!" cried Brand.

He slid the bolt, and jerked the door open. They rushed into the walled enclosure again, the slamming of the door behind them cutting off the enraged squeals of the Rogans.

"This isn't going to mean anything but a short delay, I'm afraid," said Brand, clenching his fists in an agony of futility. "They'll be in here in a minute, and get us like trapped rats."

"Not before we get a lot of them," said Dex grimly.

"But that isn't enough, man! We don't want to die, no matter how decently we do it. We've won free, and stayed free this long; now, somehow, we've got to reach our ship and get back to Earth to warn them of the danger that hides here for our planet!"

He strode tensely up and down, smacking his fist into his palm. "The lever!" he exclaimed. "That lever! It's our only answer! If we could get to it… But how can we? We couldn't break into the dome, now the Rogans are on the watch for us, with anything less than a charge of explosives. Or a tank. God, how I'd like to have an old-fashioned, fifty-ton army tank here now!"

Greca exclaimed aloud as Brand's fleeting mental picture of one of Earth's unwieldy, long-discarded war tanks registered on her brain.

"There is the great beast there," she said hesitantly, pointing a slim forefinger at the huge lizard that had backed into a far corner and was regarding them out of dull, savage eyes. Then she shook her head. "But that is impossible. Impossible!"

The men stared at her, with dawning realization in their minds. Then they gazed at each other.

"Of course," said Brand. "Of course! Greca, you're marvelous! Wish we had a tank? Why, we've got one! A four-legged mountain of meat that ought to be able to plow through the side of that dome like a battering ram through cardboard!"

"But it's not possible," replied Greca, her head dropping dejectedly. "My people, as driven slaves, till the fields with great animals that were trapped in the surrounding jungles. They harness other great animals to haul burdens. But none of the beasts are like *this* one. This kind cannot be tamed or harnessed. It is too ferocious. It is used only as a scourge of fear, to crush us into complete submission."

"Can't be tamed?" Brand said. "We'll see about that! Come on, Dex."

"Just a minute," said Dex. He flattened against the wall, motioning them to do the same. Then he leveled his tube at the door.

Slowly, cautiously, the door began to swing back; and the Rogan that Dex had heard fumbling with the bolt stuck his huge head out to locate the escaped prisoners.

Dex pressed the release coil of his tube. Without a sound, the Rogan slumped to the ground, a smoking cavity in its shoulders at the spot where its head had been set. In an instant the body, too, disappeared; an upward coiling wisp of black smoke marking its vanishing.

Another Rogan, tiptoeing out, met the same fate; and another. And then the door was banged shut again, and the bolt ground into place on the inside.

"That'll teach 'em to be careful how they try to rush us from *that* door," said Dex, through set teeth. "Now let's see if that tank scheme of ours can be worked."

He picked up a tube dropped by one of the Rogans, and handed it to Brand; showing him which coil to press to get full force, as Greca had in turn informed him.

"Down the field," commanded Brand. "We'll go about thirty yards apart, and try to herd this brute back through the walls of the dome building. Once it's inside, we'll try to rush to the lever before the Rogans can down us, and jam the thing past its terminal peg and into reverse action. I don't know that there *is* a reverse to it—but we can try.

"Greca dear,"—the girl started at the warmth of his thought, and a faint pink rose to her pale cheeks—"you'd better stay by my side. Your place as hostage-priestess of your people wouldn't save you if those devils catch you now. Besides, you can keep your tube leveled at the doorway as we go, and discourage any Rogans who might pluck up courage to try coming out again."

They started down the field toward the nightmare thing that snarled and hissed in its corner. On one side of the big enclosure walked Brand, with Greca close beside him, glancing continuously over her shoulder at the rear door, and holding her tube in readiness to check any charge the Rogans might attempt to make from the tower building. On the other side, keeping an equal pace, advanced Dex.

With tubes of death as whips, and with death for themselves set as the stake for which they gambled, they went about their attempt to drive the brainless monster before them through the solid wall of the dome building. And there followed what was probably the strangest animal act the universe has ever witnessed.

The first thing to do was to rout the enormous lizard out of the corner where sullen fear had sent it squatting. Dex contrived to do that by standing next to the wall at its side, and sending a searing ray that just touched the scaly, tremendously thick hide. The monster bellowed deafeningly, and, with a spot smoking on its flank, waddled sideways to the center of the field. Its head and swaying long neck faced the Earthmen and its back was against the wall of the dome building. To that extent, at least, they had the creature placed; but they soon found that the struggle had only just begun.

Brand got far enough around to focus his tube on the tip of the huge tail, in an effort to swing the gigantic thing about. There was an unearthly shriek from the colossal beast, and a foot and a half of its tail disappeared.

"Careful," called Dex, his jaw set and grim as the monster lashed out in its wrath. "If you bore in too long with that tube there'll be nothing left of our tank but a cloud of smoke."

Brand nodded, wordlessly, walking on the balls of his feet like a boxer, holding himself ready to swerve the thing should it charge them. Which—next instant—it did!

With a whistling bellow it gathered its tons of weight and thundered with incredible quickness at the gnats that were stinging its flanks and tail.

Desperately Brand played the tube across the vast chest, scoring a smouldering gash in the scale-covered flesh just above the gash Dex had seared a few moments before.

"Sorry, old fellow," Brand muttered to the screaming beast. "We hate to bait you like this, but it has to be done. Come on, now, through that wall behind you, and give us a chance at the lever."

But through the wall behind it the vast creature, not unnaturally, refused to go! It darted from side to side. Backward and forward. Up to the wall, only to back bewilderedly away from it. And constantly the tubes flicked their blistering, maddening rays along its monstrous sides and tail, as the Earthmen tried to guide it into the wall.

"Hope there's enough left of it to do the trick," said Brand, white-lipped. The monster was smoking in a dozen spots now, and several of the hump-like scales on its back had been burned away till the vast spine looked like a giant saw that was missing a third of its teeth. "God, I'm thinking we'll kill it before we can drive it through that wall!"

Greca nodded soberly, keeping her eyes on the distant door to their rear. Twice that door had been opened, and twice she had directed the death rays into its opening to mow down the gangling figures behind it. But she had said nothing of this to her man. He was busy enough with his own task!

"The door to the dome—" Dex shouted suddenly.

But Brand merely nodded, even as a discharge from his tube annihilated the Rogan that had appeared in the doorway before them. He had seen that door stealthily opening even before Dex had.

"It had better be soon, Dex!" he called. "Rogans in front of us—Rogans behind us—and—look out! On your side of the fence, there!"

Dex whirled in time to pick off a grotesque, pipe-like figure that had suddenly appeared on the broad wall of the enclosure. Then he turned to the frenzied problem of driving the monster through the building wall.

"The thing's going mad, Brand!" he cried, his voice high-pitched and brittle. "Watch out!"

It was only too evident that his statement was true. The baited monster, harried blindly this way and that, hounded against the blank wall behind it by something that bit chunks of living flesh out of its legs and sides, was losing whatever instinctive mental balance it had ever had. Its dimly functioning brain, probably no larger than a walnut in that gigantic skull, ceased more and more to guide it.

With a rasping scream that set the Earthmen's teeth on edge, it charged for the wall on Dex's side. Dex just managed to swerve it with a blast from the tube so prolonged that half its great lower jaw fell away.

At this the titanic thing went wholly, colossally mad! It whirled toward Brand, jerking around again as a searing on that side jarred its dull sensory nerves, then headed at last straight toward the stone wall of the dome building.

With the rays from both tubes flicking it like monstrous spurs, it charged insanely toward the bulge of the circular wall. With all its tons and tons of weight it crashed against the stonework. There was a thunderous crackling noise, and the wall sagged in perceptibly, while the metal roof bent to accommodate the new curvature of its supporting beams.

The monstrous lizard, jerked off its huge legs by the impact, staggered up and retreated toward the two men. But again the maddening pain in its hindquarters sent it careening toward the building wall. This time it raised high up on its hind legs in a blind effort to climb over it. "It must be five stories tall!" Brand nearly shouted. Thunderingly its forelegs came down on the edge of the roof.

There was another deafening crash of stone and shrieking of torn metal. Just under the cornice, the wall sagged away from the roof and the top rows of heavy stone blocks slithered inward.

"Again!" shouted Brand.

His tube was pointing almost continuously now at the metal door leading from the dome building. The Rogans inside, at the shocks that were battering down a section of their great building, were all trying to get out to the yard at once. In a stream they rushed for the doorway. And in loathsome heaps they fell at the impact of the ray and shriveled to nothingness on the bombarded threshold.

"Once more—" Brand repeated, his voice hoarse and tense.

And as though the monster heard and understood, it rushed again with all its vast weight and force against the wall in a mad effort to escape the things that were blasting the living flesh from its colossal framework.

This charge was the last. With a roaring crash a section of the building thirty yards across went back and down, leaving the massive roof to sag threateningly on its battered truss-work.

It was as though the side of an ant-heap had been ripped away. Inside the domed building hundreds of Rogans ran this way and that on their elongated legs, squealing in their staccato, high-pitched tongue.

With blind fury the mad monster charged in through the gaping hole it had battered for itself. In all directions the Rogans scattered. Then an authoritative tall figure with a tube in each of its four sucker-disks, whipped out a command and pointed to the great coils which lay immediately in the berserk monster's path.

The command restored some sort of order. Losing their fear of the beast in their greater fear of the damage it might do, the Rogans massed to stop it before it could demolish the Rogan heart of power.

At this point Brand saw an opening of the kind he had been praying for. The Rogans had retreated before the terrific charge of the monster in such a way that the space between its vast bulk and the control board was clear.

"After me!" he shouted to Dex. "One of us has got to reach that lever while the creature's still there to shield us!"

The two Earthmen dashed through the jagged hole in the wall and raced to the control board just as the huge lizard, a smoking mass, sank to the floor. Brand gazed almost fearfully at the lever-slot.

Was there a reverse to the gravity-control action? There was room in the slot for the lever to be pulled down below the neutral point, if that meant anything...

Behind them the great bulk of the dead lizard was disappearing with incredible quickness under the rays of the tubes directed on it. Now the pumpkin-shaped heads on the opposite side were visible through a fleeting glimpse of a skeleton that was like the framework of a skyscraper. And now the colossal bones themselves were melting, while over everything hung a pall of greasy black smoke.

"Hurry, for God's sake!" gasped Dex.

Brand threw down the lever till it stuck. At once that invisible ocean poured crushingly over them, throwing them to their knees and sweeping the Rogans flat on their hideous faces just as half a hundred tubes were flashing down to point at the Earthmen.

"More—if you can!" grated Dex, whirling this way and that and spraying the massed Rogans with his death-dealing tube. Dozens went up in smoke under that discharge; but other dozens remained to raise themselves laboriously and slowly level their suddenly ponderous weapons at the Earthmen.

Brand set his jaw and threw all his weight on the lever. It bent a little, caught at the neutral point—and then jammed down an appreciable distance beyond it.

Instantly the blue streamers, that had stopped their humming progress from coil to coil with the movement of the switch to neutral, started again in reversed direction. And instantly the invisible ocean pressed down with appalling, devastating force.

Greca and Brand and Dex were flattened to the floor as if by blankets of lead. And the scattered Rogans about them ceased all movement whatever.

"Oh," sobbed Greca, fighting for breath. "Oh!"

"We can't stand this," panted Dex. "We've fixed the Rogans, all right. But we've fixed ourselves, too! That lever has to go up a bit."

Brand nodded, finding his head almost too heavy for his neck to move. Sweat beaded his forehead—sweat that trickled heavily off his face like drops of liquid metal.

With a tremendous struggle he got to his knees beneath the master-switch. There he found it impossible to raise his arms; but, leaning back against the control board and so getting a little support, he contrived to lift his body up enough to touch the down-slanting lever with his head and move it back along its slot a fraction of an inch. The giant coils hummed a note lower; and some of the smashing weight was relieved.

"That does it, I think," Brand panted, his voice husky with exhaustion and triumph.

He began to crawl laboriously toward the nearest street exit. "On our way!" he said vibrantly. "To the space ship! We leave for Earth at once!"

Slowly, fighting the sagging weight of their bodies, the two Earthmen inched their way to the street, helping Greca as they went. Among the sprawled forms of the Rogans they crept, with great dull eyes rolling helplessly to observe their progress, and with feeble squeals of rage and fear and malediction following their slow path.

On the street a strange and terrible sight met their eyes.

Strewn over the metal paving like wheat stalks crushed flat by a hurricane, were thousands of Rogans. Not a muscle of their pipe-like arms or legs could they move. But the gravity that crushed them rigidly to the ground did not quite hold motionless the shorter and more sturdily built slaves.

Among the thousands of squealing, panting Rogans that lay as though paralyzed on the metal paving, crawled equal thousands of Greca's enslaved people. Their eyes flamed with fanatic hate. And methodically—not knowing what had caused their loathed masters to be stricken helpless, and not caring as long as they *were* helpless—the slaves were seeking out the shock-tubes that here and there had fallen from the clutch of Rogan guards. Already many had found them; and everywhere gangling, slimy bodies were melting in oily black smoke that almost instantly vanished in thin air.

As it was in these streets and in the great square in the center of which rested the Earthmen's ship, just so, they knew, was it being repeated all over the red empire. Slowly crawling, fiercely exulting slaves were exterminating the tyrannous things that had held them so long in dreadful bondage! Before the sun should set on another flashing Jovian day there would be no Rogan left in the red spot.

"And so it ends," said Brand with a great sigh. He moved over beside Greca, and touched her lovely bare shoulders. They were shaking convulsively, those shoulders; and she had buried her face in her hands to keep from gazing at the ghastly carnage.

Brand pressed her to him. "It's terrible—yes. But think what it means! The knell of all the Rogans been sounded today. As soon as the secret of these death-tubes has been analyzed by our science and provided against, my friend and I will return from Earth with a force that shall clear the universe of the slimy devils. Meanwhile, your people are safe here; with the gravity what it is, no Rogan attacking hordes can land."

They crawled tortuously over the square to the space ship. Brand turned again to Greca; and now in his eyes was a look that needed no language of mind or tongue for its complete expression.

"Will you come to Earth with me, Greca, and stay by my side till we return to set your people in power again?"

Greca shook her head, slowly, reluctantly. "My people need leaders now. I must stay and help direct them in their new freedom. But you—you'll come back with the others from Earth?"

"Try and stop him!" grinned Dex. "And try and stop me, too! From what I know now of the way they grow 'em on your satellite"—his eyes rested on Greca's beauty with an admiration that turned her to rosy confusion—"I'd say I'd found the ideal spot to settle down in!"

Brand laughed. "He's answered for me too. And now, a salute that is used on Earth to express a promise..." He kissed her—to her utter astonishment and perplexity, but to her dawning pleasure. "Good-by for a little while."

The two Earthmen hoisted themselves heavily over the sill of the control room of their ship, and crawled inside.

They secured the trap-door, and turned on the air-rectifiers. Brand moved to the controls, waved to Greca, who was smiling at him through the glass panel, and pointed the ship on its triumphant, four hundred million mile journey home.

THE END